Once I started reading Lisa Lickel's Requiem for the Innocents, *I truly could not put it down. And after I'd finished reading, I couldn't quit thinking about the book. Each narrating character has a distinctive voice, resulting in a powerful story, most intriguingly told. I loved the subtle interplay of good and evil, along with the author's insightful exploration of relationships and loss. Brava!*
~**Carlene Havel**, award-winning author of biblical and contemporary fiction

Every now and then you run across a book that affects you to your very core. It was that way with me when I read Lisa Lickel's book, Requiem for the Innocents.
~**Shelley Wilburn,** author of *Walking Healed*

A complex group of protagonists, a sinister plot, and a curvy road of twists and turns. Lickel knows how to bring to life an issue from today's world, and an illness that perhaps most men-kind dread. Add to that the choices being made, and you will have a book that will open your eyes and keep you thinking long after you finish it.

Deeply researched, interesting, and intense: Well worth your time to read this excellent book. Great job, Ms. Lickel.

~**Carole Brown**, author of the award-winning *The Redemption of Caralynne Hayman*, and several mystery/suspense series

Lisa Lickel consistently delivers Christian fiction that goes beyond the surface to deal with real life issues, yet she does it in a sensitive and tasteful way. I look forward to each of her new releases – not even kidding!
~**Tracy Krauss**, award-winning and best-selling author

Fox Ridge Publications

Requiem for the Innocents

Stories from Paradise House
Inspirational Fiction

Other Books by Lisa J. Lickel

The Buried Treasure Mystery Series
> *The Last Bequest*
> *The Map Quilt*
> *The Newspaper Code*

Healing Grace

Meander Scar

Centrifugal Force, available in 2017

A Summer in Oakville, with Shellie Neumeier

The Last Detail

"Three Rings for Alice" in *Brave New Century*

First Children of Farming for early readers
> *The Potawatomi Boy*
> *The German Girl*
> *The Saxon Boy*
> *The French Girl*
> *The Yankee Boy*
> *The Irish Girl*

"Gangster's Ghostcapade," a radio play in
> *A Wisconsin Harvest,* vol II

Everything About You, novella

UnderStory

Requiem for the Innocents
Copyright 2016 by Lisa J. Lickel
Originally published as Innocents Pray

ALL RIGHTS RESERVED

Cover art by Lisa J. Lickel & Rodney Schroeter

This book is a work of fiction and any resemblance to persons, living or dead, or places, events or locales is purely coincidental. The characters and scenarios are the product of the author's imagination and used fictitiously.

The unauthorized reproduction or distribution of this copyrighted work is illegal. No part of this book may be scanned, uploaded or distributed via the Internet or any other means without the permission of the author.

Scripture quotations are from the English Standard Version.
The ESV® Bible (The Holy Bible, English Standard Version®) copyright © 2001 by Crossway, is published by the ministry of Good News Publishers. All rights reserved.

Fox Ridge Publications
Hillsboro, Wisconsin
Print ISBN 978-0-9904281-0-7 First Edition, 2016
E-book ISBN 978-0-9904281-1-4
Library of Congress Control Number: 2016908998

Published in the United States of America

www.lisalickel.com

Remember: who that was innocent ever perished?
Job 4:7

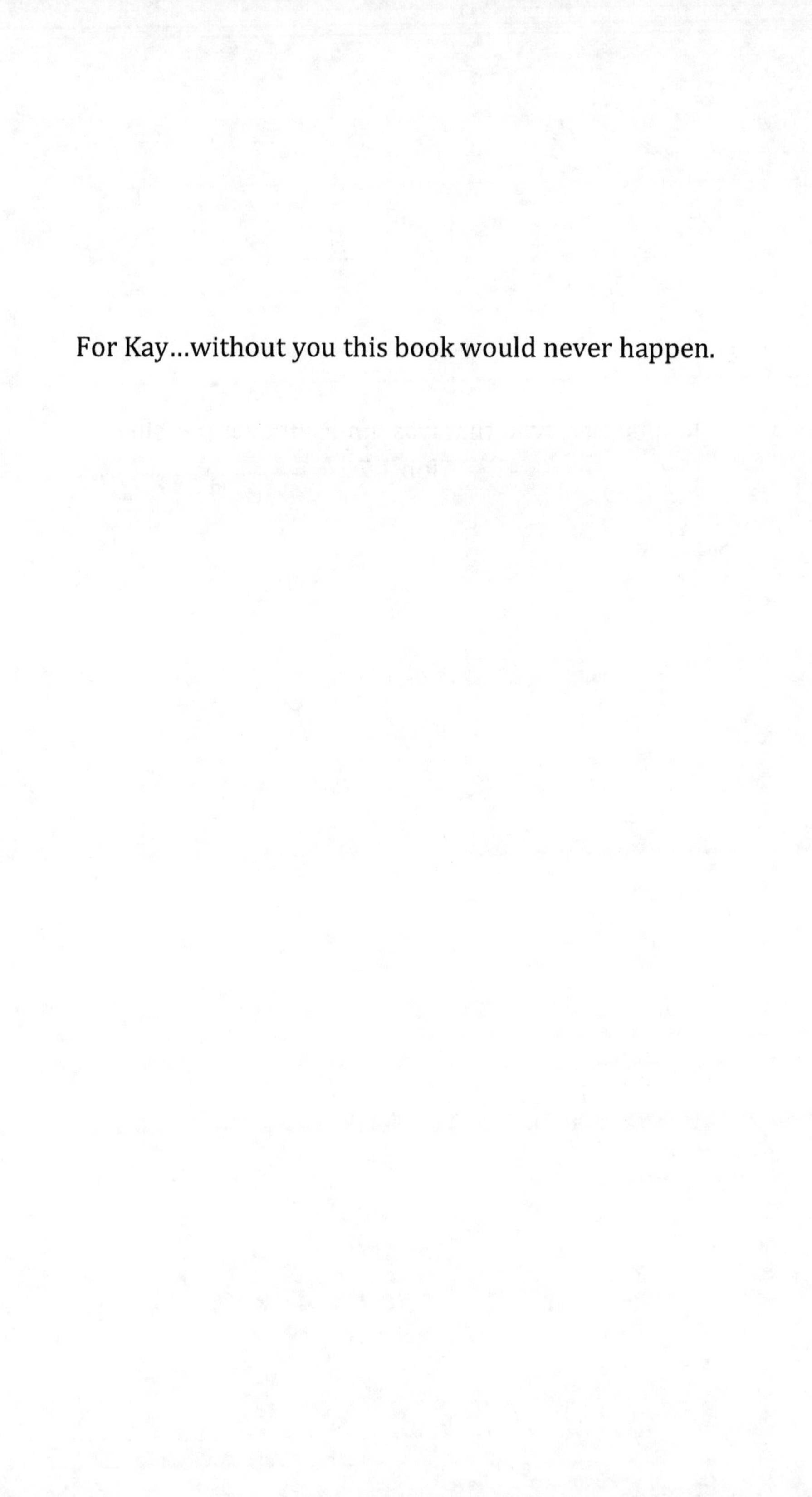

For Kay...without you this book would never happen.

Scripture in Chapter Descriptions

I Corinthians 13

7 Love bears all things, believes all things, hopes all things, endures all things. 8 Love never ends. As for prophecies, they will pass away; as for tongues, they will cease; as for knowledge, it will pass away. 9 For we know in part and we prophesy in part, 10 but when the perfect comes, the partial will pass away. 11 When I was a child, I spoke like a child, I thought like a child, I reasoned like a child. When I became a man, I gave up childish ways. 12 For now we see in a mirror dimly, but then face to face. Now I know in part; then I shall know fully, even as I have been fully known.
13 So now faith, hope, and love abide, these three; but the greatest of these is love.

Micah 6

Hear what the Lord says:
Arise, plead your case before the mountains,
and let the hills hear your voice.
2Hear, you mountains, the indictment of the Lord,
and you enduring foundations of the earth,
for the Lord has an indictment against his people,
and he will contend with Israel.
3 "O my people, what have I done to you?
How have I wearied you? Answer me!
4 For I brought you up from the land of Egypt
And redeemed you from the house of slavery...
6 "With what shall I come before the Lord,
and bow myself before God on high?
Shall I come before him with burnt offerings,
with calves a year old?
7 Will the Lord be pleased with thousands of rams,
with ten thousands of rivers of oil?
Shall I give my firstborn for my transgression,
the fruit of my body for the sin of my soul?"
8 He has told you, O man, what is good;
and what does the Lord require of you
but to do justice, and to love kindness,
and to walk humbly with your God?

9 The voice of the Lord cries to the city—
and it is sound wisdom to fear your name:
"Hear of the rod and of him who appointed it!
10 Can I forget any longer the treasures of wickedness—in the
house of the wicked,
and the scant measure that is accursed?
11 Shall I acquit the man with wicked scales
and with a bag of deceitful weights?
12 Your rich men are full of violence;
your inhabitants speak lies,
And their tongue is deceitful in their mouth.
13 Therefore I strike you with a grievous blow,
making you desolate because of your sins.
14 You shall eat, but not be satisfied,
and there shall be hunger within you;
you shall put away, but not preserve,
and what you preserve I will give to the sword.
15 You shall sow, but not reap;
you shall tread olives, but not anoint yourselves with oil;
you shall tread grapes, but not drink wine.

CB

1 - ABLE

Now we see in a mirror dimly...

The same expression burned into his heart hundreds of times over the course of a year. Husbands were easy to read. When they felt despair, it leaked from their very souls. When they had given up, they were so stoic it was a mask as universal as a three-piece business suit. Wives or lovers melted or bucked up and took it. This silver-haired but powerful man's grief was old but still oozed.

Able sensed a fresh wound, too. He made his way over to the man's table in the Beijing Capital International Airport private lounge—to do what, he was not certain. The Lord never nudged him without purpose. Just doing his part to keep harmony in this airport. He kept in a grin at his pun about the Chinese name of the airport.

The man closed his computer and signaled a waitress.

She leaned in. "Mr. Davis?"

"A club soda, please."

Able set his hand on the back of a nearby chair. "May I join you?"

Davis twitched and swiveled. He opened his mouth, but apparently thought of something different to say before speaking as his eyes settled on Able's throat. He inhaled and quickly composed himself. "Certainly. Can I get you something, Father?"

Able inclined his head and pulled out the chair. "Thank you, but no. I merely wanted to introduce myself, since it seems we're on the same flight back to the States."

"Oh? I don't recognize you, Father."

"Hayden International was kind enough to pick up the tab for my return trip. At least, I assume you have something to do with Hayden. I have been in Beijing to speak at a hospice conference." Able smiled. "I'm grateful for the ride. And it's Brother, not Father."

"Victor Davis. And, yes, I do work for Hayden."

"Brother Able. Able Fenwick."

"Brother?"

"I'm an Alexian Brother, not a priest."

"I didn't know there was a difference."

"Most people wouldn't. My order works to spread Christ's healing love and concern to the sick and dying." Able's suspicion was confirmed by Davis's fleeting jaw clench.

"You're a hospice chaplain, I take it," Davis said a heartbeat later. "I've heard of the Alexians. In Wisconsin. Is that the same?"

"Yes, that's where I'm from. But I live in California now."

Davis took a drink from the glass the young woman had placed in front of him. "You're sure I can't get you anything?"

"No. Thank you." When Able was certain Davis would not ask about California, he posed another question of his own. Eventually he would get around to Wisconsin. "And may I ask about your work with Hayden?"

"I'm the International Team Leader. We're currently overseeing the fitting of the new hospital in Longkuo."

"I'm delighted with the amount of charity work that the company does around the world. I looked it up on the Internet." Able folded his hands.

"The Internet, Father? I mean, Brother?"

Able laughed. "Yes, even members of religious orders must keep up with the times, to discover where best to be of service."

"Of course. Hayden has an active grant program. It is our

honor to participate in humanitarian aid as much as we can. But we can't do it alone."

"True. Too true these days. There's so much need."

Davis's mouth pinched. He took a drink, as if to wipe away a sour taste.

Able prodded. "Your work is going well, I hope?"

"Everything's going well so far." Davis whirled his glass between large hands and looked out at the rainy twilight. Able decided not to press. They had hours and hours on the way back. If the man needed an outlet for his grief, Able would listen. He liked to exercise his PhD in family counseling on others beside the patients and staff at the hospice.

Able woke with a snort.

"Just some turbulence," Davis said, without looking up.

"Ah." Able took a breath. "Thank you, Victor. I hope I didn't disturb you."

"No." Davis went back to his computer.

The men sat in the company plane outfitted with comfortable loungers and wide work spaces. Able had relaxed and put himself to sleep after prayers, knowing from past experience it would help him recover from jetlag more quickly. His dreams had disturbed him more than the turbulence, however, which he welcomed as a wake-up call. He rubbed his eyes, hoping to erase the images from the back of his retinas.

Rich, again. Dr. Richard Bernard, laughing with Joanie after her recovery. Weeping later. Cursing God. Always, the cursing came last when Able had the dream. No matter what he did, what he said to Rich, the doctor cursed God. It had been five years since Joanie died. Rich laughed again, but not with joy. His sole purpose in life was to find and beat the monster that had destroyed his happiness.

* * *

Able got up to use the restroom. Davis didn't move from his position in front of the computer screen. Able splashed water on his face, enjoying the moisture after the dry air of the pressurized cabin. He wiped drops from his mustache and decided he could use a trim. On this private plane, the bathroom was much larger than the usual tiny compartments on commercial flights. He worked his knees up and down and twisted his back and torso to get the blood moving. At fifty-five, he needed to keep active, ward off blood clots. The success of the hospice program kept him traveling. He was glad to share with others the relatively simple recipe of their award-winning methods of offering compassion. He had often been invited to speak many places around the world. Part of the popularity, Able guessed, was the lack of a requested fee. *Poverty.* And when someone else could be prevailed upon to pick up the cost of travel, like Hayden International, his speeches and workshops were that much more attractive. Able squelched the little flare of anger at the price of his vow of poverty. Twenty-seven years. One would think he'd conquered it by now. *The Lord always makes a way.*

Beijing had been beautiful, despite the dirt and smells. Now he had more stories to share with residents at the big hospice complex. His Chinese guide and translator, a monkey-faced little man, had told tales of seemingly endless relatives stretching back to their first steps on the alien continent. Able smiled at his reflection. *We are all aliens in this world, are we not? Especially those afflicted with terrible diseases. Even so, come, Lord Jesus.*

But not too soon. Maybe he would go on to Milwaukee after all.

No—get thee behind me, Satan.

This man, Victor Davis, could still speak with you.

Chastity. Able checked his watch. Six more hours, at least. Plenty of time to talk, before heading on to California. Home, now. *Remember your vows. Obedience.*

The smell of braised beef greeted Able's return. His mouth watered. Conversation always seemed easier with food. Perhaps this would be a good time to ease into a talk. "I'd forgotten about dinner, Victor. May I offer thanks?"

"Please."

Able blessed the food. He opened his eyes to see Davis finishing the sign of the cross. "You're Catholic?"

"Yes." Davis speared a chunk of beef. "My wife is Protestant. I attend worship with her when I'm home."

"You travel a lot."

"Yes."

Able concentrated on the food. He felt the man's mood in the clipped answers. How could he encourage Davis to talk without turning into an interrogator? Davis seemed like a private man. "What part of the country do you call home?"

"Wisconsin."

"Ah. So that is why you had heard of my order." Davis's unhappiness hummed around them. He obviously was not going to be drawn out by small talk. Their steward brought more coffee. When they finished eating, he reappeared and took their empty plates. "Captain says we're on time, sir. We'll stop in Los Angeles for refueling and for Brother Able to disembark, then head directly to Milwaukee."

Able's heart lurched at the sound of the place even though he had made peace with that desire hours earlier. It no longer clawed; merely caressed him like an echo. He would not go to Milwaukee now. California had been his assignment, his earthly home for the last twenty-five years, compelled by the love of Christ.

"You look far away, Brother Able."

"Oh?" Able realized he'd been staring out of the window,

black with night that reflected the interior of the cabin as much as his thoughts. "I was just thinking about some of the people under our care. What changes might have occurred in my absence."

"How large of a place is it?"

"We have room for two hundred souls, but that's including families who come to share their loved one's last days."

"So many." Davis got up and walked to the other side of the cabin, bent and stared out the window, as darkly blank as the one on Able's right.

"Forgive me, Victor, but you seem burdened."

Able could barely hear Davis's reply. "My wife was ill. Not long ago." The man straightened as far as he could, though he was too tall to stand completely upright. He turned to face Able, but kept his distance. "I had a call from her companion, who thinks she might have relapsed." Davis gripped the arms of the seat nearest him and bent over it. "Pray with me," he whispered. "Pray that she'll live."

 Cʒ

2 - LIBBY

...But then, face to face

When I think back on my death and life, I recall Jordan's eyes in perfect detail. I realized that, as his mother, I should have known, should have understood him. But if I had, I wouldn't have lived.

Events were changing too fast for me to control that morning, I realized, as I lay trapped in the nether moments between sleep and wakefulness. Jordan's eyes were black holes threatening to pull me in. I knew that if I let that happen, I'd be lost forever.

He wanted me gone. I've known that for the last three years. This time he might get his wish.

Shaking, I came fully awake. When I saw the clock, I knew I would have to pull myself together in a hurry so I could say good-bye before Nona took my son to school. At fourteen, it was easier for him to be seen with anyone but his mother. The tingle in my left thigh that bothered me on and off for the past six weeks turned into a throb as I made my way down the stairs. In the kitchen, I heard Nona quiz him about homework and the contents of his backpack. Good, she would cut him no slack.

She thrust a cup of coffee into my hands as I shuffled in. I greeted her and Jordan, who looked at me with a smile that went no further than his father's dimples. Could he see my fear? Smell it or feel it?

"Morning, Libby," Nona said. "I took a message off the machine earlier. Mrs. Rodgers asked you to make matching napkin rings for the coasters she ordered last year." Nona shrugged into her jacket and jingled the car keys. "I left the note at your table.

"Thank you. Have a great day, Jordan. I love you," I said to my son's back. I'd been lobbing "I love you" at him for eighteen months. So far, he hadn't cracked and sent one back.

Jordan turned and flashed those storm-at-sea eyes at me, assessing, probing. I watched his mouth move and noted the hairs darkening his upper lip.

"Later." The word struggled to escape his throat. His voice had changed last summer. Soon he'd start shaving. Vic should teach him about that. Next time he came home.

Nona smiled and shook her head. I adored Nona Roland. Vic brought her home three years ago when I had been diagnosed. We decided that she could not leave after that horrible year that robbed me of my womb. She was indispensable, not just as a great nurse practitioner, but as the glue that kept everything about this family from ripping apart. I would have given her my first-born child in order to keep her.

In fact, I think I did.

"I'll be back in a little bit," Nona said. "Did you need anything from the store?"

"Thanks, but I'll probably have to pick up some supplies once I check my orders." Jordan stood in another dimension during our exchange. "How about you?" I asked him. "Need anything? Or did you want to go shopping with me this weekend?"

If he'd been younger, he might have faked gagging. "Nah. Project due. With Tony."

"Right." I made one more desperate attempt to engage my only child in conversation. "The one about the effects of trying to drain the marsh?"

He'd already headed toward the door. "Yeah. We'll be late."

Nona let out a noisy breath but said nothing as she was sucked along in his wake.

After the two of them left, I rinsed Jordan's breakfast plate and put it in the dishwasher. I insisted Nona not act like our housekeeper, and we shared duties as if we were both mistresses of this home. She had worn her brown cords and a yellow blouse today. I'd have to decide on something else so we wouldn't look like twins.

Bending and rising in front of the dishwasher increased the pain in my leg. I poured another cup of Nona's dark roast and sat to think about the order of my day. I decided to call the pain a cramp and ignore it. It was only a pulled muscle. I walked yesterday. I walked too far on our strip of Lake Michigan beach.

Vic wasn't due home for four more days. The pain would be better by then. I could always hope that he had a good trip and would be happy to be home for a whole week. Maybe he would forget to worry about me and not notice the hitch in my step.

I pushed up from the kitchen table and went to look at the message Nona left. Our work room filled the space between the breakfast nook and the back of the four-car garage. Sunlight threw long shafts on the polished oak floor. Shellac and linseed oil and the sweet smell of sawdust tickled my nostrils. Nona kept a small corner table for her jewelry-making. She occasionally cut and soldered pieces of malleable metals into custom designed necklaces and earrings. Mostly she enjoyed beadwork, and we often spent a companionable afternoon together when she didn't work a shift at the facility where her mother lived.

I stared at the heading on my invoice forms. Liberty Taylor Davis, Designer.

My mother named me Liberty in some sort of seventies protest backwash. A misnomer, to say the least, but I loved the distinction. It brought me Vic Davis. Sometimes I wonder what would have happened to my career if Vic hadn't stopped in London where I had gone that fall after graduation to study at the Tate. He'd remembered my name when he heard it in a deli order call. Life wasn't the same afterward...for either of us.

I clicked my computer screen to life to see that Nona had

already updated the Liberty Creations website this week and highlighted more orders. With the holidays approaching, I would stay busy designing and painting window scenes and creating unique table decorations for my customers.

I wandered up to my room to wash, thinking about the supplies I needed to complete my waiting projects. While I dressed in black jeans and red beaded sweatshirt, I heard Nona return. According to her schedule, she would visit her mother for the afternoon and then pick up Jordan from school. In the evening she would go out to her car, as she did every Tuesday, to talk on the phone.

I popped a couple of painkillers and hustled down the steps to the kitchen. "How was traffic this morning?"

Nona's serene expression washed me in peace. Her reddish-blond hair in the smooth chin-length cut she wore never looked out of place.

"No worse or better than usual. I can't wait until they finish resurfacing the by-pass."

Milwaukee constantly upgraded or rearranged its highway system. Fifteen minutes to traverse downtown? It should never take that long! Vic laughed whenever we ever discussed it. Milwaukee had nothing in traffic snarl-ups compared to Chicago, LA, or Rome. I yawned, and tried to cover it.

"You slept in," she accused me. "Up late, reading again?" Her gentle smile held no criticism. I had long ago given her the unspoken privilege of bossing me around. She earned it during the year of surgery, radiation, and the worst treatment, hormone therapy.

"You know me," I replied. It was easier than complaining about the waves of hot flashes that kept me from sleeping a full night.

"Remember, Jordan will be home Thursday and Friday,"

Nona said. "There's no school. And I'll be working away this weekend."

Once in a while she could irritate me. Of course I remembered my own child's schedule. I acknowledged her reminder with a curt nod. "Thanks. I think I'll make a list, head downtown soon. Let me know what you need."

"Sure. I want to do a couple loads of laundry. One last gasp at the clothesline before it gets too cold to hang wet clothes outside."

I went into my workroom, thanking God for the fence that kept our yard private. It looked like tenement wash day at our house whenever Nona had to get her fix of air-dried clothing. I sat at my high draft table, rubbing my thigh.

Had she noticed my shuffle? Nona honed in on even a simple fever before any of us suspected we had one. What would she think if I told her about the pain?

And Vic...would he do more than get that hard, determined glint in his eyes? The one that vowed he would find the latest, best treatments, then stand off and watch? Where was he now, anyway?

I checked his itinerary stored on my phone. Yes, China. Longkuo, where Hayden International was outfitting the new hospital. Vic would come home for a while, then go back for a month. I used to travel with him before my mother died when Jordan was two. My passport boasted pages of colorful marks. It expired next year.

I banked this new pain, not afraid this time. I would be the one to decide if and when and what I would say if the cancer had, indeed, metastasized. One thing I knew. I would not stand in front of the congregation at Northbay Christian and be anointed with healing oil again.

The analgesics were not working. I rested my forehead on

my wrists. *If I beg for release from the pain, from another round of useless treatment, Lord, but my husband prays to lengthen my life, who receives the mercy? How do you decide to answer prayer?*

3 - WEB CHAT: SHAREMYDISEASE

Surviving11 says: Is this fair? In the big picture of life, is anything fair? I know, I know, I know, I KNOW! Why should I have to go through this whole mess again? Did I not learn enough the first time? Now what? What's supposed to happen to me now? The last time I barely made it through. They told me it was gone, we were all better and things would be fine. Operations, visiting the hospital, going to the hospital, the clinic, seeing all those people who had no hair, their gross cheeks puffed, who smiled and spit and whose mouths were red with blood and vomit smiling, smiling, smiling as if they were glad just to be here. How can anyone be happy just to breathe and puke and cry and watch them poke you one more time? Watch your skin turn red and peel away and another vein collapse from the needles and the poison.

I won't do it again. They can't make me. Please don't make me go to him.

Just one. Just a little one, I'll just do one little one.

I crank up the volume, I ignore the symptoms. Pain, pain, pain. Feel the pain. I'm so numb, I can hardly feel anything anymore. They don't want to know. What does it matter—how will it end—that's what I care about—that's all i want to know—when will it end—when willit allbeover

Mary says: I'm praying for you. Jesus loves you. Please, let us know how you are. We love you. Jesus loves you. Don't give up.

Tyler says: You should get some help. Seriously. Call me. 555-3019.

Anonymous says: I hear you. I feel your pain. You are not alone.

Tin man says: Don't let them take you. Fight.

 ॐ

4 - LIBBY

Now I know in part...

When the garage door rumbled an hour before I expected Jordan home from school, I knew.

So Nona had picked up on my discomfort yesterday morning when it hurt to walk. She called him. But when? Vic needed at least twenty-four hours to get here, traveling across the breadth of the planet. Air moved when he paused in the doorway.

I continued to daub teal onto a sketched feather. I would carefully outline the peacock "eye" in gold when the paint dried. Acrylic did not take long. Then I would shellac. I repeated the teal once, twice, on three of the twenty rings, before his hands touched my shoulders. He must have stood there, waiting, until I was ready to move on to the next piece. He wouldn't startle me and ruin my work. Thoughtful of my husband.

I decided to play innocent.

I stuck my brush in water, knowing he'd wait. I couldn't. I jumped up but tangled my long, narrow foot in a rung under the stool and tumbled into his arms. "Vic!" Laughing, I grabbed his shoulders to hug him and save myself from a fall. "What a surprise!"

He trembled. He did not laugh.

We ate in the dining room that night. Nona said she'd made other plans. I was outraged at her underhanded tattling, but had no place to loose my fury. Under no circumstances would Jordan be told why Nona thought to ask his father to come home early.

Besides, we knew nothing at this point. Nothing at all. Why make so much out of a strained muscle? How could she justify recalling Vic all the way from China just because I'd exercised too hard?

"Everything was going well," he told Jordan and me over my pork and kraut that night. "I was ready to come home. I may need to stay longer when I return."

Jordan acted more animated than I'd seen him since school started last month. "Now that you're home and I have the next four days off, we can go hunting up at the marsh. Maybe even just us once, without Tony and his dad."

Before Vic could say no, I stepped in. "That will be super, Vic. I have to finish this order and start on window designs for the Griegs. It'll give you some time with Jordan. That's one reason you came home early, isn't it?" I smiled, challenged him to deny it in front of his son. "Please pass the rolls. Would anyone like something from the kitchen?" I shoved my chair back and steeled myself to rise in a smooth motion, pushing off with my right foot.

"The turkey tags came, too, Dad. I want to go with you, try out the new Benelli you got me for my birthday. Not just target practice. I've been waiting to take it out and sight it in since you got here. I went twice with Tony and used the Remington, but we didn't get one."

Vic was a spring, coiled so tightly he could speak only in croaks after clearing his throat. He blamed it on the long journey and nodded at our son. "Let's put our heads together after supper and plan it out."

Jordan's return chatter followed me to the kitchen. I put our dessert plates on a tray and stood still for a moment, savoring the bonding on the other side of the door. I picked up the tray but my left leg would not obey me and I lurched.

For ten months I had stuck to my New Year's resolution to stop cursing. I should have been proud.

◦ ◦ ◦

The resulting crash brought them both running.

"Stop! There's glass." They peeked through the door, the tall distinguished man who wore my ring and our child who had passed my height last spring. I held up my hand. "Just an unexpected load shift. Stay where you are. I'll clean it up."

"You're all right?" Vic asked.

Jordan moaned. "That was caramel sauce, wasn't it?"

I grinned, happy to see his playful side. "Don't worry. There's more. I'm fine. I picked up the tray and moved too fast, that's all. Go back to the table, now. I'll bring more."

"Carefully."

"Yes, Jordan. Carefully." Jordan squirreled out from under his father's hand across his shoulders. Vic studied me. I felt his eyes even after I turned away and went for the broom. When the door whooshed behind me, I skirted the mess to set out new plates. A brownie, a scoop of ice cream, sauce, nuts. A cherry for Jordan. I would never be able to eat all of mine. This time I picked up a plate in each hand and delivered dessert without the tray.

Jordan's pale cheeks burned with red patches as he listened to his father's quiet talk. "...Not the whole weekend, son. But we'll work it out. I promise."

Dark, deep-set eyes fixed on me as I handed over his brownie. "Here you go, kiddo. Better than the first."

Vic touched my hand as I put his plate in front of him. "Where's yours?"

"I'll go back and get it." I returned to the kitchen to hear the rumble of the garage door and shivered at a draft of cold air.

Nona stood there, looking at the mess. "You could have just said the brownies were awful. You didn't have to throw them on the floor."

My hands trembled and the heat of Jordan's anger burned through me. I grabbed the edge of the counter and shifted goals.

• • •

"I fixed you a plate, too, Nona. Why don't you go out there and sit with them, eat? I'll clean up."

She set her purse on the built-in desk. "Thank you. Perhaps we can have coffee together later." She took the plate with the melting ice cream and sidestepped my broken dishes.

I heard Vic and Jordan greet her as the door swung shut. I plugged in the coffeepot before I bent to pick up the biggest shards. Vic's phone chimed loud enough for me to hear. A few moments later, he stuck his head around the door. "Rafe says the company seats to the final preseason Bucks home game are open tonight. I'm taking Jordan."

"Good."

"We'll talk later."

I agreed, but wouldn't look at him. Not yet ready to show my hand, I needed to deal with Nona first.

She must have sensed that I was prepared to fight, for she was not at the empty dining room table. I poured myself a cup of coffee and sat across her from place to wait, refusing to seek her out.

The ice cream on her plate I'd prepared for her had puddled around the brownie. I bet the coffee in her cup was cold. Fifteen minutes later she came back, having changed into a lavender and white-striped wind suit. Little white slippers cuddled her feet. Her pinched mouth probably mirrored mine.

I sipped my coffee, watching her spoon up a dribble of ice cream and put it in her mouth. When she finally looked at me, I was in control enough to talk. "I thought we were friends."

She got up to warm her coffee from the carafe I'd placed on the sideboard and spoke with her back still turned. "That's what makes my job so hard."

"Your *job*? You think of being here, being my friend, as *work*?"

She whirled and leaned against the buffet, holding her cup like a tiny shield. "Libby, I *work* for Vic. I *am* your friend, but we both know that if I worked for you, I wouldn't be your friend. In fact, I wouldn't even be here now."

I unclenched my teeth. "What are you talking about?"

She measured her steps back to the table as if to give herself time. When she sat next to me, she reached toward my hand. I couldn't help it. I pulled away.

"Look, honey," she said. "I love you. I consider you one of my dearest friends. Like a sister, even, and you know I have nothing to compare that to."

I stared at her, hurt starting to override anger. In this we were surely sisters at heart, as both of us claimed a parent near the end of life and no siblings.

"Vic hired me to take care of you. You and Jordan, when you were so sick you couldn't do that yourself." She swallowed and cleared her throat. "I'm sorry." I watched her dab at her eyes with a cloth napkin Vic left at his place.

"Nona—"

"Wait. More than likely we wouldn't have met if you hadn't been sick, right?"

My lips twisted, though not to smile. "You stayed." My voice came out as a whisper. I hated begging.

"I stayed." Her voice wasn't any stronger than mine. "Because both you and Vic asked me to. I work for Vic. He pays me to stay here and help you. Not just around the house, but *you*. If I worked for you, and you got well, I'd be gone. You know that's true."

"So you were both waiting for me to get sick again?"

Nona's cup clattered in the saucer. "I stayed because I am your friend." She lowered her voice. "But I have to report to Vic."

I let her put her hand over mine this time, and didn't stop the tears when she said, "Let me help you. Don't hide from me." She got up, hunkered near and put her arms around me. "This is why I'm here. Oh, Libby, you are loved. God holds you in the palm of his hand."

"No God would allow my child to endure such turmoil a second time," I mumbled against her shoulder.

"I'll talk to him, help him understand."

I lifted my head and pushed away from her. She fell back. "No. I am not sick. It's just a pulled muscle. That's all. You can work for my husband, but when it comes to Jordan, I am his mother. I decide what he needs to know and when. I'll take him away if I have to."

Nona stared up at me from her awkward squat. Her sympathy sliced me deeper than any surgeon's cut.

A cold hand touched my cheek. I blinked. "Vic. What time is it?"

"About eleven thirty." He came and sat on the edge of the sofa where I'd fallen asleep waiting for him and Jordan to come home from the game.

"Where's Jordan?"

"Upstairs."

I moved to sit up. Vic took my arm and pulled.

"How was the game?"

He held me while I righted myself on the carpet. "Okay. Jordan had Mason sign a jersey for him, so he was happy." My husband raised his brows. "Libby."

"It's late, Vic. Let's just go to bed, okay?"

He did not reply. I held my breath, hoping he wouldn't insist on having this discussion when we were both tired. He turned out the light on the end table and we walked up the stairs together. When we got to my room, we both stopped. I wondered if he would ask to stay with me tonight, but didn't have time to

* * *

think of an excuse before he kissed my mouth and went across the hall.

I crawled into bed thinking about us. I'd met him the summer before I graduated from college. We'd been introduced at my father's Door County retreat, and I had thought him too distinguished and mature to notice me. The next year when I went abroad to study and work, I remember the look on his face when he turned around at the sound of my unusual name being called at the lunch counter in London. He happened to be eating there, too. Seeing a familiar face in a foreign country was always a relief, like opening a dresser drawer in any hotel and finding that the Gideons had been there.

I had not gone on to Rome as I'd planned, though I've visited many times since. Vic brought me home and married me for Christmas that year.

What would Vic do if I really was sick again? Would he stay home more for Jordan's sake? I held no illusions that Jordan would get both of his wishes. It would be nice if Vic wanted to stay home for his son.

I hoped Nona wouldn't tell him what I had said about Jordan. My deep breath came like a whimper as I tried to summon empathy for my angry son. He would never go anywhere with me willingly. How foolish I'd become.

I welcomed the brightening sky. For the past month I tried to slow my slide into the emotionless valley where I lived for a year when I'd been sick before. Turning my feelings off had been the only way I could cope, even though I knew my family suffered as if they shared my disease. The elephant of a question I attempted to hold back with all my strength threatened to roll back over us, and I didn't want to consider the implications, even to myself. I had nothing left to turn off if it was happening again. My back itched. I turned over in bed, twisting my nightgown around my knees. When Vic came into my room, I switched on the lamp. Six thirty.

I cleared my throat and struggled to right the blankets. "Did you sleep?"

He lifted the covers and slid in bed next to me. "Libby, we have to talk."

I shifted out of the warm huddle my body had made, irritated yet glad of the coolness on the far side of the bed that soothed my skin. I swiped my forehead.

Vic touched my face. "Are you feverish?"

"No. Stop it. I'm not sick. What did Nona say? She had no business calling you without talking to me first."

"She said you were favoring your left leg."

I snorted. "And for that you come halfway across the planet. Honestly." I sat up and made to toss the blanket. "I went for a walk the other day. On the beach. I was out longer than I should have been. I'm out of shape."

Vic touched my arm. "Come back, Libby. I miss you."

I lay back down beside him. I put my finger on the crease between his brows. "Don't worry."

"You can't give a husband a directive like that."

He turned his face so his breath was warm on my palm. I pulled my hand away. He opened his eyes and stared at me. Flecks of steel mixed with blue. His lashes were stubby and lines fanned into his temples. "How long has it hurt?"

"Not that long. It would have been over if you'd come home when you were supposed to."

"Libby. We should visit Anna."

"Doctor Marbrey is too busy to deal with muscle strain."

Vic put his hand on my shoulder. "Your oncologist wants to know what's going on in your life."

"I have a checkup in two months."

"Promise me you'll make an earlier appointment."

I ground my teeth. "When you are finished at Longkuo."

"Libby—"

"Anyway, Jordan's happy to have you home." I closed my eyes.

He turned onto his back. "I know. I've been thinking about cutting down travel time."

"How would that work?" I was intrigued. We might not be able to reclaim the passion we'd once shared, but it wasn't too late for Jordan to get to know his father better. Vic played his role well when he was home. He simply wasn't here often enough to be closely involved in the life of a teenaged boy who had outgrown his mother. I'd done what I could; now I needed to pass him on to his father.

"I could consult."

"After Longkuo?"

"Libby, if you need me—"

"No. I'm getting up." I pulled myself upright again, even as his hand tightened on my shoulder.

"It's been over a year," I heard him say. "Libby, maybe we could—"

"I can't. I can't stand it. And you don't...seeing how you react, or don't react...Vic, I just can't. I told you." I rushed into the bathroom, praying he would be gone by the time I returned.

● ● ●

5 - WEBPOST: THEPLEASUREOFTHEHUNT

Let's get this straight: fall is God's gift. The ritual of the hunt outshines any other activity, as far as I'm concerned.

Every year, you get your license, just waiting, dreaming of putting shotgun to shoulder, lining those birds up in the crosshairs, squeezing the trigger. Fetch!

Today we'll focus on geese, as in: Geese are so prevalent, they're just target practice any more.

The laws of nature are changing. Any fool can see the migratory season is messed up for generations of birds that no longer fly north in the summer or south in the winter. They breed all over, pollute the parks and make a nuisance of themselves. Forget about shaking eggs or hiring dogs to control the population. Let's change the bag limits, donate the extra to food pantries, like venison. Tell us what you think.

If you have a recipe, go ahead and post it.

But, back to the ritual.

You hold that permit in your hands when it comes. You sort out the carcass tags and their ties.

You re-read the regulations. You set your watch.

Clothes. You cannot wash the vest. Ever. You pull it out from storage. You inhale last year's hunt—the odor of adrenaline and sweat mixed with oil and blood. Maybe you'll find a bit of down in the sling and roll it in your fingers. Close your eyes. Sniff.

The hat must only be used for this purpose. You must not break down and get it out for anything else—not fishing, not any other kind of hunting—only for pheasant or grouse or turkey. Preferably a different one for each. And c'mon—no flaps.

Sticker on the license. Stuff in wallet and zip in place.

The blind is ready to go. A portable one in the back of the truck, or use the boat.

Which do you prefer?

You get the coffeepot and thermos ready. Set the alarm, if you need it.

Next week—decoys.

46 comments

deerstalker43 says: Hey dude, did you ever get it right. I can smell the grass. You got a point about the enviro. Maybe we should get the pols to stop gassing and do something.

themanandhisgun says: Boat all the way. You cannot do any good without one. Put your camo cloth on it, get some cattails, reeds, junk like that. But the main thing is get there early enough. Too many yokels come out from the city, don't know what they're doing, shooting at everything. Then there's the idiots with a hundred decoys. You gotta be kidding me.

SharraT says:

Recipe—hey, I liked the one you had on here last spring.

I thought I'd share mine. You make it in a crock pot.

2 fully dressed duck breasts

3 cans fully loaded cream of celery soup – not the fat-free crud, or the low-sodium stuff. It doesn't taste as good

1 of those bags of wild rice—you know, not the stuff that's real rice, but the Indian stuff. You can use half a bag if you don't like it so much

1/3 bag of dried cranberries

I start my crock pot before I go to work, kind of on a lower setting. I put the duck and soup into it. When I come home for lunch, I stir it up and add the rice. When I get home, I stir it up and add the cranberries. It's really good. I suppose if you can't get home at lunch, you could put the rice in right away, too. Some people like onions. You can add one, if you like it.

Well, anyway, I hope you like it. Let me know. E-mail me.

● ● ●

pleasureofthehunt replies: Well, thank you, SharraT. Anybody else have a good one to try?

adman21 says: Where do you hunt? Pardon me, manandhisgun, but it's a free country, and I for one want to stay out of your way. Me and my nineteen decoys.

BobbyJ says: What kind of dog do you have?

Hunterman says: He had a picture of it up last year. Man, you gotta post that again. She sure is a sweet hunter.

pleasureofthehunt says: Rondo's a golden lab. Four and a half years old and knows what to do. Trained her myself.

◌◌

6 - ABLE

…Then I shall know fully…

Able continued to pray in the Los Angeles airport lounge after the airplane carrying Victor Davis left for Milwaukee.

"Can I do anything for you, Father?"

Able raised his head at the young woman's question. He had long ago stopped correcting everyone who breezed in and out of his presence. Wearing a habit, which in his case was a black suit and white clerical collar, in public was a useful statement of faith. The Alexians were one of the few orders who used the term "Brother" for all. "No, thank you. I'm on the connecting flight to San Diego."

"Ah, yes. You've another thirty-minute wait, then. Let me know if you need anything."

He nodded, serene on the outside after his commune. Inside, the Spirit still groaned for Davis, who apparently must go through a second time of doubt and anguish with the other half of his mortal flesh. Able allowed himself a touch of that forbidden knowledge, the love of another he'd once shared, as a measure of self-flagellation. His order didn't practice such extreme measures of punishment, or adulation, of course. Sometimes to understand and appreciate the pain of those he counseled, Able felt the need to recall the depth of loss. Empathy for loved ones, as well as those who were dying, could not always be taught.

He needed to check in with the hospice office to be prepared for the current status of patients and staff. Able sought an open seat at a wireless café and powered up his mobile unit. His personal link included patient data as well as staff updates, the weekly menus and weather forecasts. All these things, along with a daily program log, helped in his ministry. A staff note indicated that Dr. O'Brien left on her planned maternity leave. She'd wanted to stay longer, but Able assigned one of his Brothers, Michael, to fill her schedule. He came a month ago to begin learning the background of her caseload of families.

Two of the housekeepers had been replaced. Good. In the hospice atmosphere, trust was tantamount. Those two had been less than kind, openly complaining to the patients about their schedules and assigned duties and begrudgingly filling family requests.

Moving to the patient site, Able noted with regret the passing of little Gina Maitland. Expected, but still, Able had hoped. Miracles occurred, but apparently not for the Maitlands, whose daughter dealt bravely with a genetic disorder. The rest of the family had asked for and received genetic counseling. Able's staff spent more time with members of families going through the terrible guilt of surviving than with the patients who accepted the outcome of their condition. He had not expected a child so young to comprehend death, but Gina had surprised and pleased him, even comforting her father, who had proved to carry the dominant deficient marker in his DNA. Sometimes Rich Bernard's news hurt worse than death.

Able scrolled down to see that Mr. Kestwick clung to the sinew of life. Not everyone was brave or complacent about their illness. Daniel Kestwick was one of the angry ones. The hospice never turned anyone away. One of Able's duties was to profile incoming patients and create a buffer between those who suffered in spirit as much as body. Kestwick became nearly demonic in his anger as the weeks passed and he lost control of his body. Able thought the man would be difficult, but not to that degree.

● ● ●

Scrolling down more, Able pinched the bridge of his nose when he didn't find another name he sought. He backed up carefully. No, Helen Harding was not there. She'd come a month ago, alone, so close to death that she could barely gasp enough air to keep her lungs inflated. Rich's pain-relieving treatments made her more comfortable. She even improved her breathing enough to hang on longer than she hoped. Or wanted.

Rich must have spoken to her. She must have agreed. Able closed his eyes and prayed until he heard the announcement for his flight.

ℭℬ

7 - LIBBY

...even as I have been fully known

We attended family night at church on Wednesday, Nona and Jordan and I. Northbay Christian Family Center held a mid-week prayer service, with an occasional speaker for the adults, while the kids had their education program. Jordan was in confirmation class, preparing to make a profession of faith in the spring if he felt ready. I was grateful Vic worshiped with me on Sunday mornings, but he wouldn't come on Wednesdays.

Jordan trotted downstairs to the Retreat, the hangout for young people. The kids in his class met Pastor Dean, the youth minister, there instead of in one of the upstairs classrooms. Jordan had asked, just once, to skip tonight since his father was home. Vic had said no first. At least I didn't look like the bad guy this time.

I greeted people I knew. Greer was my closest friend and we hugged for just a second in passing. "Hi, Cynthia." I waved to Pastor Alan Grant's wife. She was nice. She'd brought a casserole over to the house last summer when Nona was on vacation. Tuna.

Nona and I settled into our padded seats, ready to listen to the opening music. Northbay's sanctuary had a regular stage with blue velvet curtains and all the accoutrements, including a podium and requisite potted silk ferns. We had a thriving theater group and put on three community plays a year.

They were singing now. Most everyone stood. I was tired. Nona was up for a couple of songs, "My Cup Overflows," and "Lord of the Harvest." She sat down by me afterward.

"Surely goodness and loving-kindness will follow me all the days of my life," sang a young girl on stage, probably not much older than Jordan. Eighty-year-old Maude Sotheby raised her trembling hands and swayed. She was one of the most faithful persons I'd ever met. I loved to listen to her pray at the ladies Bible study meetings. Maybe if she'd been a deacon three years ago, things might have turned out differently for me.

"Hallelujah! Hallelujah!" I didn't know what song they were singing now. Nona clapped her hands in time to the beat.

Before confirmation class, Jordan and I hadn't been faithful to family night. I knew Vic went to Mass wherever he was around the world. In our early years, we'd even made a game of going to church. Sometimes we raced to find either Mass or a Protestant service. If I found the time and directions first, that would be the one we would visit, and vice versa. I became ashamed of my careless attitude about church on the Easter after my mother died when I saw Vic's tears and the number of candles he lit at the cemetery's chapel. I stayed home with Jordan more often. Vic and I never resumed our foolish contest.

Pastor Grant, wearing jeans and a sweater vest, stood behind the podium. The Bible verse from the gospel of John flashed on a screen. "In this world..." I closed my eyes.

"Tonight's message is a hard one. Loving God involves risks," Pastor Grant said. He came around to the end of the stage and looked out at the congregation, engaging us with his whole being, gesturing, looking us over.

Was I religious? Probably not in some people's eyes. I let them anoint me with oil when I had cancer. Greer Wendell told Pastor Grant about my illness after I broke down crying at Bible study. Being sick had been so new, so overwhelming. I'd been surprised at the number of women who shared my experience. Even Greer had tumors in her breast. Benign, she said, but scary until she knew for sure. I don't think any of them had it twice. Recurring cancer was a death sentence, wasn't it? Anyway, back then for the ceremony they dressed me in some kind of rough cloth and scarf for my hair. The pastor and some of the deacons got in a circle around me and touched my back, shoulders, and head. Pastor Grant dribbled oil in my brow and temples. They prayed. I'd felt cold and shivered.

Then I had radiation.

The tide seemed to be turning on the issues of saving life no matter what. There were stories in the news all the time about removing feeding tubes, disconnecting hoses, palliative care. What if God wanted me to have cancer? What if I was supposed to be sick? Pastor Grant was always talking about how God's ways were higher than our ways, and who could know the mind of God?

"So, my friends," Pastor Grant said from the stage. "Jesus is the God of love, yes, but also Lord over everything in our lives. Hatred, greed, envy. Let him take it. Let him bear it."

Even tonight, the message was about dealing with the hard things in life. One of those things was Jordan's coldness toward me. Was he mad at me, or at what was in me? What was harder than having cancer? Except that I didn't have cancer. Again. Not now.

We prayed, then we sang another song, then Nona and I waited for Jordan as people slowly filed out, chatting in companionable groups. Being friendly exhausted me.

On the way home, Nona asked Jordan about confirmation class. Jordan sat in the front passenger side so I could stretch my legs along the back seat. I listened while he talked about the catechism book they looked at. "In the old days kids used to have to memorize the whole thing," Jordan reported. "We don't have to do that."

Nona was not impressed, I could tell by the way she clenched the steering wheel. "What part did you look at?"

"The Apostle's Creed."

"What did you think about it?"

"I remember we say it in church sometimes."

"What else?" Nona was patient. She had the gift of being able to pick until the truth lay exposed, like a gleaming white nerve bundle.

"Did you know that once there was only one church, and it was Catholic? That's what catholic means. Universal. Why don't we go to Mass, instead of making Dad come here, when he hates it?"

I suppose the question had been directed at me. I shifted, put my leg down and leaned forward to stick my chin over the seat. "What makes you think Dad hates coming to church with us?"

"He never comes on Wednesdays."

"A lot of people don't come on Wednesdays."

"I just don't understand why we have to go twice a week. Once is hard enough."

"We come for confirmation."

"It's not my fault. I'd rather not go to confirmation."

I regretted my hasty comeback even as my son spoke. I counted to five. "Dad said he doesn't want you to miss confirmation."

"It's not fair. He's not home that much. We could have done something fun together tonight."

He had a point, although Jordan's idea of fun mostly involved outdoor activities that required sunlight. I didn't point out that his father had taken him to a basketball game and spent all of the past Saturday with him at Horicon Marsh.

Nona stopped the car at the gate of our home. "Sorry, I forgot the remote." Her car window glided down and she leaned out to stab at the buzzer. We lived on the north side of Milwaukee, where our yard met Lake Michigan and you could not see the road from the house. In our neighborhood, people put high iron fences with fancy locked gates around their property. Privacy. Elegance. I imagined Vic, dressed in cardigan and slippers, with the paper in one hand, absently getting up from his overstuffed chair in the family room when he heard the buzzer, walking to the corresponding keypad, and punching the button.

The gate slid open and Nona drove in.

Vic was home for one more weekend. His flight back to China left early Monday morning. Maybe I would drive him to the airport. He met us in the kitchen after, I was certain, he had stacked the newspapers neatly in the basket beside his chair. "Hiya, Jordan."

Jordan hung his jacket on a hook near the back door. Vic looked gravely at Nona and me. I took my time putting my coat away, waiting until their backs were turned so they could not see how my arms trembled. Eventually I made my way to the family room, where flames flickered in the fireplace. My husband and my son sat on either side, talking quietly. I stopped in the doorway to soak up the scene.

"Libby." Vic got up and took my hand. He guided me to the sofa where we sat together. "Jordan was telling me about the universal church," he said. I held my smile at Jordan's scowl.

"I'm not making it up, Dad."

"Do you guys want a snack?" I asked to break up the tension.

"Sure," Vic said. "What do we have?"

"C'mon, Dad. Nona bought some bear claw ice cream. Let's go get some."

"I'll be right there, son. Go ahead." Vic hadn't let go of my hand. I let my head fall against the back of the sofa and stared at the flames. If I gazed hard enough, would I see the past when Vic and I were crazy in love? Newlyweds who couldn't stand to be out of each other's sight?

"Libby, you look tired."

"I am."

"You worked hard this week."

"It's only Wednesday, Vic. I have a lot of orders, and you know the holidays are always busy for me."

"I just don't want you to wear yourself out." He examined my hand, turning it over to stroke the sensitive fingertips. "How is your leg tonight? Better?"

"Yes, better." I smiled at him. "I told you. It was just a muscle strain. I'll have to use the treadmill more regularly over the winter." I pulled my hand from his to push hair behind my ear. "Jordan's waiting for you."

"Yes. I mean it, Libby. I plan to cut back at Hayden."

"Good."

"Can I bring you something?"

"No, thank you."

I studied him as he left the room. My husband came from old money and was ten years older than I. Vic was old-fashioned debonair. I used to love it when other women watched him, thrilled that he never looked back, or even seemed to notice. When had I stopped wanting him? I stared at the flames in the fireplace.

We'd been together nine years before we had Jordan. I found out I was pregnant one afternoon in Israel. I had suspected for a while. At the hospital where we were working, I asked if I could use the lab for a test. They sent the results to Vic first, who was overseeing the installation of X-ray equipment. He thought there'd been a mistake.

Did we have the strangest marriage? In Europe, no one asked us when we planned to produce heirs, or questioned our reproductive status or mental health. Vic and I married, bought a house in Wisconsin, and traveled for a living. I photographed and sketched the installations for the brochures Hayden used in marketing. Vic and I enjoyed each other. Did we talk about a baby? Maybe, but in sleepy bedtime conversations on the shores of the Mediterranean or under canvas in Africa. Someday, we'd said.

Jordan was not an interruption.

My men returned to the room, bearing bowls of ice cream. I watched them set up the chessboard, eyeball each other, contemplate their strategy as if they were strangers with reputations. I had never stopped loving Vic. My soul shattered at the horror in his eyes the first time the big machine shot its killing beam at my pelvis. The instruments he occasionally designed, but mostly sold and installed for everyone else, suddenly became real. I don't think he ever understood before that, with them, he controlled both death and hope. I wanted the old Vic back. The one who controlled both life and fate.

But in the same way a clear glass plate can't be seamlessly repaired, our relationship could never be the same.

8 - CONFIRMATION JOURNAL

I'm calling this **NOTMYGRANDMASGOD**, like a blog, you know. They said I could write anything and no one would look. I don't believe it, but if somebody really wants a look inside my head, I have nothing to hide. They told us to write down all our questions, and if we wanted, we could ask them in class.

So, this is the garbage they tried to make me swallow tonight.

"I believe in the holy spirit, the holy catholic church, the communion of saints, the forgiveness of sins, the resurrection of the body, and the life everlasting."

I can memorize the apostles creed, but why would anyone want to? All this stuff about spirits. Yeah, yeah, I know they mean god, not ghosts. But if you're not supposed to believe in even holy ghosts, where did the idea of an unholy one come from?

And that catholic thing. I mean, my dad's catholic. Some people say it's bad. What's so bad about it if my dad believes in it? Anybody I know who's catholic goes to catholic church, no matter what the other parent does. They have to go on certain days. Sometimes you go on Saturday. But some of the guys have to go on Wednesdays, too, like this. Catholic school, or whatever. They don't talk about it. I could never ask what it's like for them. All I know is, it's like, you go to hell automatically if you don't go to catholic church. Mass. Whatever.

Maybe because you think mass, like a tumor. Maybe that's why it's bad.

I ask again, what kind of god would let another person suffer? I could accept the forgiveness thing if you really mean it, but do you have to do it in order to go to heaven? What do you do if you didn't do anything wrong, but everyone thinks you did? They make you confess, say you're sorry, but you didn't do it in the first place. Isn't that a sin, too? How can you be forgiven for something you didn't do?

What about bad people who don't know they're bad? Or bad people who can't help it? What if they're not sorry? Can you be forgiven for someone else? But what if you think you're right and someone else says you're wrong and you need to be forgiven.

And anyway, what does it matter? Who wants to live forever. Especially if you're stuck the same way as when you were alive. Like if you were sick, suffering. Is that the resurrection of the body. What if it's bad. Does your body get resurrected if there's something wrong with it? I wouldn't think god would want something bad in heaven.

I could love my mom, if I wanted to.

I can't look at her. All I see is sick.

Life everlasting sounds like a long time. So what do you do up there?

☙

9 - ABLE

As for prophecies...

Able squinted in the bright light of southern California through glass at the airport. "Ah, Brother Michael. Good of you to be so prompt."

"Welcome back, Brother Able. Let me help you."

Able had checked the large case that held his heavy workshop supplies. His personal items were easily managed with a carry-on, even for a week's stay in China, but the other bag had to go to the baggage compartment. Even though it was on wheels, he was happy to let the spare, bespectacled Brother Michael heave it off the carousel at the airport before towing it behind them along the concourse. They walked to the parking area where the younger man led the way to the Hospice-owned vehicle he brought. Habilus was only a short drive north along Torrey Pines. Able loved that road. Water and seagulls were the same in Milwaukee, but the snap of salt and brilliance of sun and year-round heat were a happy contrast with Wisconsin's inland lake water and cold weather.

Habilus managed to retain a small-town milieu, even with the encroaching monstrous beach houses, golf courses, and drive-happy tourists. The world-renowned hospice complex was set back from the beach; close enough to see the soothing waves, but too far for the very ill, if they were bent on hurrying the process of dying, to hike. Enough things were fished from the sea as it was.

After a respectful silence, Brother Michael asked about

Able's journey.

"I'm confident the Lord will bring blessing upon blessing as we spread Christ's healing mission to those who need it most. Our brothers and sisters in China were eager to learn new ways to care for the sick of their communities." Able shared a few stories and answered Michael's questions about the people.

"They were curious about our order. One day it may even be the Lord's will to establish an Alexian mission in China."

"A blessing indeed, Brother Able. Many pray for the salvation of our Chinese brothers and a new opening to minister to their spiritual needs as well as their bodies. China has a long-respected, but sometimes impractical, view of healthcare."

"Yes, I agree. I was glad to know people who didn't rely solely on folk remedies."

"Herbal medicines have their place."

"As do all things under God," Able replied.

Brother Michael drove into the hospice complex, past the main administration entrance and around by the kitchen where the Brothers kept a few rooms. The back entry served as an easy egress to their short corridor. Brother Michael wheeled the heavy case into one of the empty cells. Able followed with his own case and tossed it on the single bed in his room.

"I'll join you for dinner and prayer, if I may, Brother Michael. Thank you again for coming to pick me up today."

"I look forward to seeing you later. Dr. Bernard may come, as well as Mrs. Carrelton."

"Thank you for the warning."

Brother Michael paused before taking his leave. "I have some questions I wish to ask."

"Oh?" Able studied the man while he unpacked.

"When I have completed my analysis. And prayed."

"I'll be here, Brother Michael. You know you're always

. . .

welcome."

After Able spent some time in contemplative prayer at the kneeling bench he'd had to install after arthroscopic surgery, he felt refreshed enough to perform his daily amble around the main building. He began in the kitchen.

"Ah, Manuelo, it's good to have you back. Your son's surgery went well, I hear."

"*Si.* Constantino will soon be back to school."

Able looked into Manuelo's fine Havana cigar-colored eyes, touched his round shoulder and moved on to the desk of the head cook. "Marion, I see you had your hair cut after all."

The square-faced genius swiveled from her computer screen. "Brother Able. Welcome back. Yes, Joe didn't want me to, but it gets so hot back here."

"He'll understand."

Able whisked through the doors. Along the well-lit children's wing, decorated with framed splashes of primary colors, he introduced himself to two new families and offered commiseration to Gloria, Gina Maitland's caregiver.

"Brother Able, I die a little inside every time it happens, you know? But with that little girl's attitude, I think I gained more than I've ever lost."

"That's good to hear. I'm grateful for your dedication."

Able reached the elaborate silver and maroon-themed front of the building and ventured into the outer office of hospice director Liz Carrelton. Her assistant, Mary, a comfortably familiar sight in one of her big-flowered dresses, shook her head at him, indicating the absence of her boss. Able waved and backed out. He wouldn't disrupt Mary's phone conversation. He had hoped, but not expected, the redoubtable Mrs. Carrelton to be in her office. Now he might bump into the wandering director anywhere.

• • •

By the time he stood outside of chief oncologist Rich Bernard's office suite, the fatigue buzz of international travel touched him. Laura Reeves, Rich's chief executive assistant, motioned him in.

"You're looking well, Brother Able, for a man who just spent the last twenty-four hours traveling."

"I'll take that to mean I could use a cup of coffee."

Laura was already pouring it and stirring in a dash of sugar. She indicated the door to Rich's office with a head jerk. "He's just finishing up a teleconference." Rich's assistant smoothed the skirt under her thighs as she sat next to Able. "In the meantime, tell me about your journey."

Able reached into his coat pocket and presented Laura with a tiny paper box. "Here. I brought you something." Laura Reeves reminded Able of an exotic white tiger, regal, and without pretense. Her smooth white-blond hair was usually held tightly to her head and her pinstriped suits emphasized the length of her waist and legs. Not that he noticed such things.

Laura sighed with pleasure at the sight of the miniature lacquered bottle decorated with hand-painted bamboo. "It's marvelous, Brother. And, I mean a thing to marvel at. How do they do such exquisite work?"

"As with all things done well, patience."

"Thank you. Have you come back with more quotations for your talks?"

"Of course." His habit of sharing famous quotes from any field of study at his required seminars inspired friendly competition among the staff. Only one person had ever bested him at citing a source, and that had been Joanie Bernard.

"Was it as dirty as they say?"

Able blinked. "I apologize. My mind was wandering."

"I asked if you found cities in China polluted."

"Ah. Yes, the manufacturing areas had some horrific problems. Fixable, of course, if they applied a few regulations. One of the problems is the pace of growth, which is currently unchecked. Rich, there you are."

Laura unfolded herself and returned to her desk.

Rich Bernard reached down to first shake, then tug on Able's hand to raise him. "Welcome back, Able. Come on in, tell me all about it so I can live vicariously through you."

"Good to be back, Rich." Rich fooled few, as he traveled a couple of times a year and had been in China more than once. Able followed the doctor into the inner office.

Rich flipped the switch under his desk that controlled the sound system. A faint whoosh of waves accompanied their conversation. Even if Rich's office was too far from the ocean to pick up the sound, Rich kept the sea bottled for his personal use. After years of tuning in to each other, Able learned that the volume of Rich's background noise measured the depth of his inner struggle. Able had to listen hard for the sound today. He carried his coffee to a small round table near the corner windows.

When Rich joined him with a glass of iced tea poured from the jug in his personal refrigerator, Able covertly examined the doctor. Successes and failures carved their passage across the man's tanned face. Fine lines etched fans away from his intense indigo eyes. When a course of treatment did not alleviate the suffering of a patient, Rich's cheekbones stood in bas-relief, like the Sierra Nevada, which meant he'd lost a few pounds he could ill afford. Able used to run with him for an hour in the desert or on the seashore at five in the morning. After knee surgery, Able was slow coming back and missed that extra time they spent together.

If Laura was a white tiger, Rich was the perfect ringmaster, the enigmatic man in the center light who knew how all the tricks worked and brought the audience under his spell.

After Able shared his impression of the hospice workshop, he allowed Rich to reminisce about his own last venture to Asia. They returned to the present.

"Liz will want a report to show potential donors the success of your program," Rich said. "She's coming to dinner."

"So Brother Michael informed me earlier."

Rich's mouth puckered. He leaned forward to set his empty iced tea glass on the table. "Able, I'm not sure Brother Michael is the best choice to take over O'Brien's caseload."

Able steepled his fingers under his mustache, soothing the hairs with his forefinger. "What makes you think that?"

"He has wandered outside the parameters of patient counseling."

"Brother Michael was a medical missionary to the Philippines before being called to counsel souls. He has a substantial talent in surgery."

"Why didn't he stay in the field? Oh, that's right. God told him to stop."

The weariness threatening Able was only partly to blame for his mental exhaustion. He slipped into the comfort of an inward prayer, "Blessed are those who mourn," before responding to Rich's outburst. "What exactly about Brother Michael makes you believe he is unsuitable to care for patients in this facility?"

"Just direct him to occupy himself with his current patient files. I've always been able to work with your people before—"

"They're not my people."

"—so I continue to expect the same high-caliber personnel you have recommended in the past. I do not need a medical doctor at this time. This facility needs another counselor."

"I'll talk to him. Was there a particular—"

"Just tell him to focus on counseling. You know that's the key ingredient to making this place function."

"Yes. I read the patient manifest before I got here."

"I trust *you* to stay on top of things." Rich checked his watch. "I have an appointment." He got up, forcing Able to follow suit. Rich stopped at his desk to check his calendar.

"How is Helen?" Able asked quietly, before the doctor could wiggle away.

Rich's lips clamped tight. One hand reached for the hidden switch. Seagulls shrieked and waves crashed.

When Able stopped back at his office, Gert Berry, queen of admin, took one look at his face and ordered him to bed.

Able laughed. "After you hand over my messages."

Gert put a hefty black-skinned hand with shocking pink flamingos stenciled on the long nails over the stack of yellow and white paper and jiggled her tightly-wound glossy black curls. "Nothing that can't wait till tomorrow. That's why we're a community, Brother Able. You can't serve if you're asleep on your feet."

"You'll call—"

"You know I will."

"Brother Michael, Dr. Bernard and—"

"I'll tell 'em for you."

"Gert, what would we do without you?"

"Find another Alexian Associate."

Able's fatigue crossed into the spiritual, he admitted to God from his kneeling position in his room. He had gone through his usual routine, apologizing for the yawns which intruded now and then. He decided he could address the Savior from under the beckoning sheets before his eyes closed.

"Father, love that man, Davis, and his family." Able had

prayed with Vic Davis on the plane—when was that? It felt like days ago, not just hours. "Keep his fears from overwhelming him. Keep him strong in his faith, Lord."

What about Rich? Able squeezed out prayers for Rich Bernard's soul, the one the doctor refused to acknowledge.

"Helen Harding." Able was falling, falling. "Bless her, Lord, and keep her…"

Brother Michael met him at the bottom of the shaft. Michael stood in a beam of light. Able watched the man's mouth make words, but he couldn't hear what his colleague said. Able cupped a hand behind his ear. It didn't help. "I'm sorry, Brother. It will have to wait," he told Michael. "Just a few more hours, and I'll be with you."

In the morning, Able discovered that one of the messages Gert held back from him last night had been the recall of Brother Michael to Wisconsin.

He contemplated the issue with part of his mind briefly as a distraction to his conscience later that morning, knowing the only answer was to confront Rich. Able grimaced while he clutched Helen's knuckles during her procedure. She was alone in the world, and being with her now was the least he could do. Already her skin felt like old parchment, the ink faded. Who would remember the story of her life when she was gone?

Her eyelids closed over pale irises Able watched dull with pain. Blue veins along her temple made a map of nowhere. Her shoulders moved once while she lay on her side in the narrow bed.

"Please, try to stay still," Rich commanded. "This won't take long."

Able squeezed her dry fingers, hoping he wouldn't hurt her any more than Rich had. The rooms for the dying were

• • •

beautifully appointed in quiet mauves and old blues, with soothing abstract paintings and wood-like vinyl on the floor. "Helen, you were telling me about your students."

Helen's voice crackled like dry leaves as she told of a kindergartener's up-close and personal encounter with a pet gerbil kept in the room. Able had heard the story twice already, of how the animal latched onto the child's lip in a love bite and had to have its jaws pried loose.

Helen had shriveled to a few memories by the time Rich let him visit after his return from China. She had been officially released from hospice care and moved to the separate lab wing of the hospice that Rich built for those who chose to work with him.

Helen had taught school for many years. Some would have called her a spinster, for by sixty-four she had not married. By the time ovarian cancer had been diagnosed, the woman had little hope of survival. With no parents or children or other close family, she told Able that she finished the school year last spring, then spent the summer sorting through her belongings and settling her small estate.

"Mmm," Helen moaned through bitten lips.

"All done." Rich set something on the tray behind him and soothed ointment over the wound he had opened in Helen's spine.

"Is it...help...ing you?" Helen asked, still lying on her side with her eyes closed.

Rich settled the pale blue gown across the woman's back and pulled a thin thermal blanket to her shoulders. "Yes, you're helping me, Helen. I learn more from every test."

"Good." Helen's mouth stayed open as she succumbed to the repose of the unconscious.

Able soothed a lock of silky gray hair behind her ear while

Rich capped the vials and wrote on them. He put the samples in a red plastic container to take to the lab. When Rich left, Able followed. "Are you really learning more, Rich?"

The doctor didn't slow his pace.

"Or are you still hoping to recreate the miracle that saved Joanie?"

Able followed as Rich dove through the door of the lab. "Not now."

Able made himself at home on a round metal stool in his usual corner, set where he could watch Rich work the complex microscope. There were no questions Able could ask that would speak for Rich now. From past experience Able knew Rich would become so immersed in his task that outside stimuli could not penetrate his focused concentration.

Wormlike structures inside of Helen's cells appeared on a screen in front of Rich. Dark spots clustered along the chromosomes. Able's medical background was limited, but he instinctively disliked the dark clusters. Rich made notes and fiddled with the instruments, mixing his sample with other liquids, smearing slides or filling test tubes, cutting blocks of something that looked like wax, and doing other strange things Able did not want to know about.

"You see?" Rich said, as he waved his hand at the magic screen. "You see this repair in the very structure of the cell? I can do this, where your god cannot."

"Cannot? Or will not? It's not your place to corrupt what God has done, Rich."

"Corrupt? I? Nature corrupts. I'm the one who can return the design to its original parameters."

"How do you know that God didn't intend for this design to change in just this fashion?"

Rich looked at him. "You? Joining the mutant crowd now? I

never would have guessed you would change sides, especially since you have so much at stake."

Able wished this man with his piercing blue eyes, who had once been the closest of friends, the most loving of husbands, could hear how he sounded. He ignored the unusual threat.

"Are you helping Helen now?" Able asked.

Rich's lips narrowed. Able felt the darts like lightning bolts from the other man's eyes before Rich turned away. "Too late for her. But maybe not for the next. The more I learn the sooner there will be a permanent fail-safe cure. For everyone. I will find out what it takes to coerce normal alleles of any defective genes into somatic cells to reconstruct their proper condition. No matter what the defect is."

When Mary Schumacher, Rich's pale, silent lab assistant, glided in, took things out of cryostorage and seated herself before another computer screen, Able closed his eyes to pray.

❧

10 - LIBBY

Prophecies...they will pass away

"**I** promise," Vic said to Jordan Monday morning. "I'll be back before the end of the season."

I tossed my usual farewell. "Bye, Jordan. I love you."

Nona hustled Jordan out to the car, mumbling about being late for school. Vic frowned. He obviously didn't understand that we had a contest going to see how long Jordan could hold out telling us he loved us. I played with my coffee mug, feeling the bitty smile teasing my lips. A smirk.

Vic studied me. "We need to leave for the airport in about twenty minutes, if you're taking me."

I held up and jingled my keychain. "I've got the keys right here."

"I could take a cab."

I should have let him. I don't know why, but this time I wanted the thrill of driving into the airport complex, to feel the big engines revving, to pretend I was going somewhere. I could stand being a captive audience to Vic for half an hour. "Traffic should be cleared up, not a problem. It's been good for Jordan to have you home. He misses you."

"Sometimes I wonder if he would like me if I were here all the time."

Once, my husband would never have said anything like that out loud. "Oh, Vic." I got up from my chair and went behind him to wrap my arms around his neck and lean over to touch his cheek with mine. "I'm sorry you think that."

His grin was half-hearted as he pulled me around to face him. "Sometimes I'm not fit for human ears."

"If you can't express yourself in your own home, where else can you?"

We stared at each other. I knew he would say it. "In the confessional."

I slipped my loafers on and grabbed my purse. We headed for the garage where Vic shoved his bag in the trunk of my car as I got behind the wheel.

He tugged his seatbelt while I backed out. "How long has he been this way?"

I cruised to a stop at a four-way and waited for two elderly women ambling along in the sunny crisp day to cross in front of us. "You mean Jordan? What way?"

"Sometimes it feels like he's looking right through me."

"He's a teenager. He's got a lot on his mind."

"School's been okay?" Vic asked. "He has friends, right, besides the Chandlers?"

"His grade reports have been fine, more B's than I want, but still good. Friends?" I signaled to enter the freeway ramp, I-94 eastbound, which in Milwaukee runs south. "Well, he sees kids at church. Who else? Oh, Glen Beecher's boy, you know, um—"

"Ryan."

"You remembered."

"Nona's taking Jordan to school now?"

"Every day. Since the start. He's a typical teenaged boy, Vic. He doesn't want to be seen with his mother."

We were passing through the cement loops of the downtown interchange with a lot of merging and lane-changing. Vic waited until we were on the other side, with the former Allen Bradley clock tower in sight to speak again. "How much time does he spend with her?"

"Time? Oh, not that much. I don't think."

"They do that often, like yesterday?"

"What? You mean, cooking?" I signaled and moved into the correct lane when the sign for the airport loomed. "It was good, wasn't it? And boys should learn to cook. You know how."

"They spent a long time on the Internet, looking for a recipe."

"Yeah, so? It was your goose. You guys cleaned it first."

"Just drop me off, Libby, don't go into the parking ramp." Vic directed me to the International passenger drop off loop. Vehicles were not supposed to idle long. Our time was shortened when a porter met him with an empty luggage cart.

I got out of the car to say good-bye, staring at his profile, trying to draw strength and patience to last until he returned.

"I'll call you," he said.

Vic was good about calling home, if not actually being there.

"I hope the rest of the install goes as well as the first," I told him, instead of "I love you."

He kissed my forehead, then my lips, as if I would break. I knew he wanted to tell me one more time to go and see Anna. We both knew what I would say and didn't want to leave each other on a sour note. He touched my hair instead. "Bye, Lib."

There was so much traffic that I didn't dare linger at the curb and drove away, under a plane already climbing. Detroit, maybe. Or Florida. I shivered and turned on the car heater, even though it was a nice day.

When I pushed open the door to the kitchen from the garage, I heard the phone ringing. "Nona!" Her car was in the garage. Where was she? I snatched the handset without looking at caller ID. "Hello?"

"Libby, Anna Marbrey here."

I kept my voice even. "Anna, how are you?"

"I'm supposed to ask that first, aren't I?" She had a throaty laugh that made me want to cough. "I'm doing well. In fact, that's why I called. I'm going on vacation next month and wanted to move our appointment up."

"I thought you had help for this sort of thing."

"Well, you know I like the personal approach. So, how about it? Got your calendar handy? And, by the way, my mother loved your New Year's centerpiece last year. She wants another. And I may ask you to do something for Christmas if you're not booked solid."

"My calendar is pretty tight, Anna. But for you, let's see, how about if I work in your Christmas project and do your mother's centerpiece, we hold off on appointments until, maybe March?"

That laugh again. "I don't think so. Okay, no Christmas project. It was going to be a couple of wooden apples for my aunt, by the way." Anna had never married and pampered her oodles of relatives. "How about next Thursday, say, five fifteen?"

"For what, the centerpiece? You can fax over the directions."

She was quiet. I smelled a setup. "Who was it?" I asked. "Nona or Vic? Or both?"

"What are you afraid of, Libby?"

"You know, Anna, I ask myself that question almost every morning. I'm sorry. I'm pretty busy until after New Year's. How about I call and make an appointment then? It's only a couple of months away. I hope you have a great vacation, somewhere hot so you come back with tan lines. I'll come see your pictures, okay? I have to go now." I didn't give her time to answer. I broke out in a sweat as I hung up on her.

"Nona!"

The shower ran in her suite on the other side of the kitchen.

I put my jacket and purse away, then booted up the computer in my workroom. A little while later, I heard Nona open a cupboard door. I took a quick cleansing breath and went out to meet her.

She spoke first. "You're back. How was the trip?"

As if we'd been gone days. "Good travel time. Nona, I had a call from Anna while you were in the shower."

"Oh?" Nona poured herself orange juice and held up the container in invitation.

"No thanks. Nona, who called her?"

She turned her back to me while she stowed the juice in the refrigerator. "I don't know."

"What do you mean?"

"I don't know if Vic called her." She sat down on one of the tall stools at the island and buttered a roll, adjusting the towel around her head before taking a bite.

"But you did? Why?"

"Look, Libby, at the place where my mother is staying, I heard she was going on vacation. I wanted to make sure you could have a different appointment. Why are you so upset about this?"

"I'm not ready to be sick again."

"No one is."

"I have to be in control this time. I have to be the one to say what's going to happen to me."

"Libby, we just want what's best for you."

"But we don't even know that I am sick again."

"That's why you should keep your appointment. One step at a time."

"More like one shove at a time."

Nona pulled the towel from her head and draped it across a chair. She stared out at the patio, where goldfinches fluttered between feeders and ground. I felt my unreasonable anger dissipate. "I'm sorry, Nona. I just don't want this to happen again."

"I believe that you love us, Libby. Please, will you see Anna for Vic? For Jordan, or me?"

"I know you love Jordan, even when he's at his most difficult. You're more of a mother to him than I am."

She got off the stool to grip my elbows. "That's not true. You gave birth to him, loved him, took care of him. I only filled in some of the empty places when you got sick."

"I let my mother have him at first, you know." I sighed and pulled away from her. I checked the coffeepot and poured myself a cup. "He can't really remember her, but I think her death hurt him more than I understood at the time. There's been something so sad, so deep in him, since before I had cancer. Maybe I'm afraid of him—of his pain, or what will happen to us. But, Nona, you love him. I know you do. Promise me you won't abandon him."

"Of course not."

"If anything happens to me, you... you and Vic. You could."

I had never seen Nona flabbergasted. She opened and closed her mouth twice, shook her head, folded her arms. She acted like she couldn't have been more surprised if I'd put a straightjacket on her. Then she laughed.

I was serious. "I've never begrudged you anything. You know that."

"Libby. Don't talk like this. You'll fight. You beat it before."

"What if I didn't?"

"I'm not going to take your husband."

"It wouldn't have to be—"

"Stop it!"

"Nona." I set my mug down. She backed away from me, eyes wide. "I know there's someone. I've always thought that. I assumed he was unavailable. Nona, I'm sorry. I don't mean to pry, but if you can't be with this man, maybe...maybe—"

"You have no idea, Libby. Don't judge me, or try to second

guess my situation."

"I've never judged you. I've never asked you a thing. You have your secrets. I've never even asked about your mother."

Nona's mouth pinched. "You don't know anything about it."

I wanted to show her how trustworthy I was. "I'm not asking even now. Of course not. That's what I'm trying to say. I've never pried. Maybe I should have, to show that I cared. I never want you to think I don't care. Of course you don't have to…stay with Vic, if you can't…"

Nona turned the tension around like she always did, as if dousing me with a cold blast from the garden hose. "Listen to us! Like Rachel and Leah fighting over Jacob."

Once she put it like that, I had to laugh. She joined me. "Only he doesn't know it," I said.

I wanted to put her in my box with me, to make her see my life. Maybe even live some of it. Was I selfish? I only wanted to give her something to remember me by, even if it was my family. "I do love you, Nona. You're the sister I would have wanted if I could have chosen. I'm never as grateful as I should be. I wish we'd met under different circumstances."

Her hair had started to dry in fluffy waves around her face. I liked to see her pretty like that. She fixed me with a stern stare. "So, you'll let me be the sister who nags you to make that appointment?"

I told her yes, I'd make an appointment.

• • •

11 - WEB CHAT: SHAREMYDISEASE

Surviving11 says: Okay, so I want to have an honest discussion on metastasized cancer. That's when it spreads through the lymph system. I looked it up.

Current symptoms: pain, fatigue, limp. I looked them up, too. Classic. I don't know about the other stuff, maybe a fever. The pain's in the leg. Is that skeleton, or muscles, or veins, or tissues, or what?

When you get another cancer besides the first one, that's bad, isn't it?

It's a whole separate thing, or is it the same thing?

So, one kind of cancer can spread through your lymphatic system, and it can latch onto something else when you don't kill it all the first time. That must be a bad doctor who doesn't kill it all. I mean, first they say it's bad, then they say they cut it out and stitch you up, then they burn you and light you up with poison, then they say you're cured. Then you can't walk.

You wouldn't seriously go back to the same doctor, would you? How could you let somebody screw with your life like that? He might as well kill you rather than do all that stuff to you again.

What about the family? The little kids who have to watch their moms and dads get chopped and sewed and burned and still be sick.

You might just as well kill them all and be done with it.

12 - LIBBY

As for tongues...

During the first week of November, after I returned from delivering Arla's peacock napkin rings, I stopped at church where I drew the preliminary outlines for a decorated window in the front entry. The wide, tiled area was chilly from the door opening and closing so often. Northbay Christian Family Center was busy with people who met with the large staff or picked up their children from the preschool program.

Occasionally a youngster held back her mother's hand and stopped to watch, solemn with curiosity. I greeted those I knew, but continued to work. I made, of course, a Thanksgiving theme, a faux stained-glass cornucopia with fruit of the spirit I had designed with my computer's art program. Once the steel colored borders were puttied in a three-dimensional outline, I daubed some of the light-filtering gel colors inside just to see what they would look like at eleven in the morning. An unappealing kaleidoscope flashed into the sanctuary, causing me to change my mind about the placement of the decorations and colors. I chose instead a muted blue in varying shades for a Renaissance feel. I loved painting, the act of creating something lovely for others. I would miss that part of my life, if it was possible to have such feelings in the afterlife.

I'd been hiding my increasing pain, even going to the free clinic to get a prescription painkiller. No one could trace me there, as I used old health records and paid cash. The effects wore off quickly, though they allowed me to work uninterrupted for a couple of hours. Anna had called again. Nona was out, and I didn't answer the phone. Anna left a pointed, wounded-sounding message, as if I'd been a best chum who stood her up.

When Nona found the pills in my desk drawer during one of her cleaning frenzies, she made an appointment for me and drove me there herself. I pouted. In my secret heart, though, I was glad to have the decision taken out of my hands. At least Nona hadn't summoned Vic again.

Anna Marbrey was a coarse-faced woman with thick, curly ebony and silver hair. She made me wonder how she would look, dressed in ragged silks, stepping out of a colorful painted wagon to search the depths of a crystal ball or read palms. Sometimes I wondered, indeed, if such a ball would help her discern life and death.

She had squeezed me into her exam schedule, which I knew meant that if she wanted to eat that day, it was a sandwich on the run in the hall between rooms. During one of her past visits to me on hospital rounds, she'd told me that surgery days were almost more relaxed for her. Today, Anna wore her clinical face. She felt along my hip and thigh with her firm, cool fingers. The bump on the top of my thigh bone was obvious. I hissed at the pain. She looked deeply into my eyes and told me she would order blood work and an X-ray and talk to me later. I knew then my days of walking on the beach were numbered.

If I'd stared at her across a scarred wooden table in the woods, a fire crackling behind me, other weathered faces circled around us and balalaika music in the background, her crystal ball would have been clouded with death. The shut-down part of me absorbed the chill sentence into my brain, where I would rationalize the steps I should take while not spiking terror in my heart. I was not afraid, not this time, but disappointed in my inability to conquer the disease. I could try to blame Anna and her failed attempt to make it go away, but that was not fair.

I waved to Nona who sat in the waiting area on the way downstairs to the lab and X-ray department at the clinic. Anna had offices in one of the squat concrete cubes just off the interstate, hulking in the bilious shadow of Memorial Teaching Hospital. What the hospital had once memorialized, no one recalled now. For me, it was the place I lost the part of myself that belonged to Vic.

Anna didn't call for three days. Jordan and I spoke to Vic nightly, which for him was in the middle of the morning. We decided not to tell Jordan of my visit to the clinic. There was nothing to say at this point, I made sure Nona wouldn't let anything slip. Vic would come home from China at Thanksgiving for certain, he said. He'd stay here at least through January. While I knew Nona told him that I'd gone to see Anna, even she wouldn't dare break patient-doctor confidentiality.

By the time Anna called at eight thirty on Thursday evening, I had almost convinced myself that I'd troubled her for nothing.

"Libby, I need to see you and Vic right away. Can you come in tomorrow?"

"What about?" I stalled, feeling powerful for stealing a minute of Anna's precious time.

"Libby, it's serious."

"If it was that serious, you'd have called me yesterday. Anyway, Vic's not home until Thanksgiving. Can it wait until then?"

"How fast can he get here?"

"Two weeks. Am I gonna die before then?" I knew I was being facetious in light of her gravity, which in the past had meant she couldn't promise this round of radiation would satisfy her.

"Libby, cut it out. I'd rather tell you face to face, but I think you know. Your enzyme and calcium levels are too high. I saw two suspicious areas—the thigh, and another on your pelvis— we need to biopsy. Now. I'm scheduling you tomorrow afternoon—"

"No. I'm busy tomorrow. I have to—"

"Libby, do you want to live or not? Because if you don't, I have plenty of other people who at least want to try, and there's only so much of me to go around. I'm willing to do everything I can for you, but you have to want it."

I was on the extension in the front hall, next to the stairs, when Jordan came thundering down. He looked right through me as he passed, probably on his way to the kitchen for a snack.

"Help someone else," I whispered, and hung up.

I made myself busy the day after Anna's call. Nona took Jordan to school as usual, saying she had a hair appointment and wouldn't be back all day. I closed the door to my studio and went to work on the Internet.

Anna had not spoken about metastatic disease to me before for a very good reason. As I checked a few government, and later, quack treatment, sites, I developed a mantra. The repeated phrase was based on a bit of song called "In Christ Alone" that had stuck with me. I almost hypnotized myself with "no fear in life, no fear in death" when I read through those statistics. The carcinosarcoma, a pretty word, wasn't it?, I realized I hadn't beaten, tended to be quite lethal. A joke, get it?

I shut down the computer screen at lunchtime. I made a pitcher of raspberry lemonade and took a glass of it out to the brick patio. Wearing a sweater made the weak northern climate sunshine bearable. If I closed my eyes, it was spring, not the dying time of late fall. Smoke and mold drifted on the breeze. A dog barked far away and the rustle of brittle leaves on the driveway settled the case for winter's onset.

Should I have the biopsy? Did it matter? The phone rang for the third time that day. When the answering machine did not pick up, I went inside to the kitchen extension.

"Hello?"

"Look, Libby," Anna's voice, exhausted, said on the other side. Fridays were surgery days, so I knew she was in between procedures. "I'm sorry. I was harsh with you last night. I was...afraid for you. Libby, will you at least let us biopsy? Or do you want a referral to someone else?"

I looked at Jordan's school schedule on the refrigerator. He had Open House next week. "No referral. Biopsy. Do I have to go the hospital for that?"

"No, I can do it in the procedure room here."

"Okay. What should I do next?"

"Did you call Vic?"

"This is my life, Anna. I have to be the one to decide what to do this time. Let's wait until we're sure. There's still a chance we caught it early, right?"

"Libby, every study shows that you need your family and all of your friends behind you, supporting you, if this is going to work, no matter what stage."

My brain refused to let me think in straight lines. Easily distracted, I saw Jordan's school pictures that had come in on Monday. They were still on my desk in their envelope. Nona had taken one for her room to replace last year's; it was the only one removed from the packet. "I know," I told Anna. "I need to be sure, first. You can't tell anybody. That's the law. You can't breathe a word to anyone, or I'll know it was you."

Her gusty sigh practically raised the tendrils of hair that curled by my ear. "Libby, you should try to stop bullets with that stubbornness. But it got you through the first time. I have to go. Call Jenny at the office and say you're scheduling the biopsy."

● ● ●

I wasn't hungry after the call to Anna's office. I went back to my computer and looked up hospices. I had watched my mother die from colon cancer over five long months, bald from chemotherapy, puking blood at the end. I touched my own shoulder-length, dark blond hair, reflecting on the shape of my skull underneath. No fear in life...not of hair loss. Certainly not. I recalled the look on Vic's face the last day he had been there with me in my mother's room as I supported her head over the basin, before she begged them to let her die. Maybe some fear in death... Dad had run weeks earlier, taking the sailboat who knew where. He hadn't returned until long after the funeral.

I would never let them treat me like that. No chemotherapy. That had been the only blessing in my cancer. Chemotherapy had not been recommended then. Only later had I wondered if hormone therapy might have been worse. I scheduled the biopsy for Tuesday, when I knew Nona was busy.

Over the weekend, I told Jordan that I was having a check-up and would he fix dinner for himself on Tuesday. My son stared at me. I wondered what I'd forgotten. Open House was Monday.

"I'll be at Open House, Jordan. I know you have a sculpture on display. Your teacher e-mailed about it."

"Will you be able to go to church on Wednesday?"

"I'm not sick, Jordan. I'm just having a little procedure."

"What for?"

"Just to check on something from an X ray."

"When did you have an X ray?"

"Last week. I didn't want to worry you. Nona took me. It's nothing to be concerned about. I think I just strained something last time I walked on the beach."

The gleam of potential interest in my medical condition in Jordan's eyes went dull. "Oh. I'm going to Ryan's house, then. After school. We've got a science assignment we're doing

* * *

together. I'll tell Nona, so she won't have to pick me up."

I smiled at him. "What's your assignment about?"

"Stem cell research."

"That's pretty cutting-edge for ninth grade."

He shrugged. "Call us over-achievers." Jordan pulled a mug of steaming milk from the microwave and added hot cocoa mix.

He didn't leave the room. Cluing in on his possible desire to keep the conversation going, I asked, "So, what have you found out so far?"

"A lot of people are mad about it because in order to get good research to study real early cells, you have to abort babies."

"Jordan! I—I don't think that's true. Any more. And no one aborted babies just to study stem cells. Where did you do your research?"

"From the newspaper clip service Ryan's dad has."

"Did you look on line? I know the University of Wisconsin is doing some studies just with skin cells. We could see if we could hook you up to interview someone over there."

"Yeah." He seemed to lose interest.

I remembered something from years ago—fourteen years. "Jordan, a long time ago, when you were born, as a matter of fact, some of the newest technology to be developed—partly by Hayden—was for saving umbilical cord blood."

Jordan picked up his mug, took a swig and started to back away from me.

"Your dad was testing the new cryo tanks at City Memorial when you were born. Yours is the first cord blood ever saved there. Wouldn't that make an interesting angle to your assignment? They use cord blood to get stem cells, too."

"Dad? He saved my stem cells? Can I see them?"

Anything to get him away from topics like abortion I knew would cause problems in school. "Why not? When Dad gets home, I'm sure he can arrange that."

"Our assignment has to be in before then." Jordan tromped out of the kitchen, leaving me staring at the swinging doors.

"What's got him so punked up now?" Nona asked a moment later. She had been to the library that rainy Saturday and came in with a stack of mysteries and travel magazines.

"Missing his dad, I guess. We were talking about his science assignment. When Vic's name came up, he got a little grumpy. Oh, and he said next Tuesday he'll be at Ryan's house after school, working on a project, so you don't have to pick him up."

"Sure. I'll make a note. Vic said he would be home through Christmas, right?" Nona helped herself to a glass of ice water from the fridge door. "Maybe I'll take off for a while. You know, get in a break from winter." She leaned against the counter and gave me one of her everything's-right-with-the-world stares. "If you don't need me. Go visit my cousin in South Carolina."

I snorted. "It's not like I don't need you, but I do envy you. Some place warm in December sounds great. Vic said he was staying stateside into January. We'll miss you, of course."

"Of course."

I could still use the "we" for a while, at least until I decided what I should do for sure about my current situation. More research would help.

13 - INTERNET SEARCH ENGINE

Query   cancer treatment options
Answers   Definition of cancer

Find *cancer treatment options* in our on-line bookroom!

Shop for *cancer treatment options* in our on-line store!

Recommendations

Dr. Tresbykowski, the cancer man. Latest laser treatment options. Affordable prices. Will work with your insurance company.

Cancer Care Treatment Centers of the United States

Research treatment study available. Have you recently been diagnosed with cancer? Call us.

Government Institutes of Health Treatment Guidelines and Standards

Search for *Options*

Cancer care options - Hospice

Query   Hospice

Find *hospice* in our on-line bookroom!

Shop for *hospice* in our on-line store!

Definition of Hospice – see our online encyclopedia

Hospice jobs

Hospice photos

Search for Hospice in Wisconsin

Testimonies of Hospice care families

• • •

CB

14 - ABLE

Tongues...will cease

Able halted on the threshold of the activity room in the children's wing at the hospice, blinking and laughing inwardly in the sight. Director Liz Carrelton was on her knees. Carrelton's pleated navy skirt brushed the carpet. The heels of her pumps stuck out from under the poofed fabric. Chains on her glasses swung in arcs above her shoulders as she leaned forward to point at something on the table.

Despite the director's brusqueness with the adult staff, she could not be more kind to the patients. Able knew that Carrelton had her share of disappointment. Her husband had deserted her upon her own diagnosis of breast cancer twenty years earlier. Able watched as she showed a child how to scrunch a colored square of tissue paper. She applied white glue to the piece without concern for her expensive manicure.

Able moved into the room, greeting the other two families who were in various stages of Thanksgiving Day projects. Carrelton looked at him over the glasses perched on her nose. Her narrow lips, decorated in a swath of red lipstick, were pursed in concentration.

"There, Tyler," she told her art partner, a seven-year-old leukemia patient. Carrelton wiggled her fingers, then rubbed away the glue. She rose with an audible creak in her knee and touched the child's bowed bald head. Tyler had responded to a treatment Dr. Havern tried. If the boy went into remission he could be released. Tyler sat at a table, filling in the outline he had drawn of their outstretched hands with orange and brown and yellow tissue paper to make the feathers and body of a turkey.

Able pressed Tyler's mother's trembling hand and said, "You both look wonderful today."

"Look, Brother Able, here's Mom and here's me. I have the beard," Tyler said.

"A beard? You're not old enough to shave."

The child gazed at him. "A turkey beard. Turkeys have beards."

"Ah. Well, I can see the resemblance."

"I'll stop in later," Carrelton told the family. She turned her attention to him. "Brother Able?"

Able walked with Carrelton to the front lobby, where the sound of falling water along the marble wall was supposed to be soothing. The sculptured stone was beautiful. It had a name, which Able could never recall.

If Laura Reeves was an exotic animal and Rich the ringmaster, Liz Carrelton would be the barker. She was the public face for the big-name sponsors, the first stop for fund-raising, and the go-getter. She was gruff, but sturdy, efficient and steadfastly dedicated to her work at the hospice.

"Sit, please, Brother Able." Carrelton walked around her desk. She picked up some files and thrust them across to him. "Here are the names of several individuals who could come in place of Dr. Hernandez."

"So, he decided not to stay?" Able had signed Hernandez, a clinical psychology professor finishing a sabbatical, after Brother Michael had been recalled. Able hoped Hernandez would find their work intriguing enough to give up his teaching and stay with the hospice. "All of this personnel shifting is unsettling to the patients."

"Tell me something I don't know." Carrelton plopped into

her oversized maroon leather chair, rolled back from the desk, and rubbed her knee. "We have to be prepared in the event that Dr. O'Brien either wants more time off or chooses not to return."

"This was her third child?"

Carrelton sat up. She fluffed a scrap of stray brassy curl back into place behind her ear. "We don't consider her personal situations. Nonetheless, that's right. Another boy. That's two boys and a girl. We could also use more counselors in any event, couldn't we?"

Able found the director fair-minded. She did not directly interfere with her department heads unless she had a good reason. In her supervised weekly meetings department supervisors gave general reports on personnel, and any incidents between staff and patients and patient accounts were supposed to be turned in immediately. Able matched his counselors with patients, but like every other aspect of the great complex, much depended on the ever-changing patient census. Able loved to work with patients and their families, too, but administration was where the Lord called him this past decade; he was content.

Able brought his hands together over his lap. "Perhaps. I had a candidate here earlier. You remember Brother Michael?" The director nodded. "It would be beneficial to know that I had control over my staff."

"It was my understanding that the man had been recalled." Carrelton crossed her legs and tapped on the arm of her chair.

"The request to transfer came from our side."

"I was put in a difficult position."

"By whom? Were there complaints?"

"Yes, there were complaints," Carrelton said. She uncrossed her legs and leaned her elbows on the desk. "You know I'm not at liberty to discuss personnel issues like that." She shuffled some envelopes on her desktop. "If there were complaints from patients, of course I would let you know. There was no impropriety between staff or patients," Carrelton said when Able opened his mouth. She held up her hand. "Dr. Bernard felt Brother Michael's talents as a surgeon would interfere with the emotional needs of our people."

"Michael is a fully trained psychologist."

"I understand. But he wanted information that didn't seem pertinent to the emotional needs of the patient. In that respect, he interfered with how patient information is disseminated." The intercom sounded. Carrelton pushed a button. "Yes, Mary."

"Director Loomis on line one."

"Thank you." Carrelton raised her brows at Able. "Excuse me, please. If you could look through those files today I would be most grateful, Brother Able."

CB

15 - LIBBY

...as for knowledge...

My list of hospices was growing. I took pains to hide them in a file marked "hospitality" deep in the folder I kept for church, under one of the sub-committees I had served on last year for the annual women's tea. I even erased the history and cookies and temp files carefully after each visit, so my curious geeks wouldn't trace my paths on our home computer network. Maybe I should have checked to find out if paranoia was a symptom of cancer.

How far could I get before I couldn't run anymore? My fantasy hideouts were mostly in the warm dry west, like El Paso or Phoenix. I liked mountains, though. I should look there too. Colorado, maybe. I could die at peace in the mountains. How about an island? Did Hawaii have hospices? Probably. There were ten places on my list. I'd have to narrow them down. My constant fatigue made me need to close my eyes for little disorienting naps more than I wanted. I wondered about insurance. Inane stuff like that to keep myself distracted.

Anna had asked me if I wanted to live. Could I be truthful with her? I was exhausted from thinking about it. Vic couldn't be allowed to go through any more despair on my account. It just wasn't fair. He had to keep faith that his machines would work, at least for those whose time had not yet come. He could go on living, maybe marry again. He was a wonderful provider and a good husband. The last time we dealt with my health, I had selfishly sucked up everything Vic was, leaving Jordan in a vacuum. Without worrying about me this time, Vic could spend more time with his son, help Jordan with that frightening blankness behind his eyes. No, I didn't need to live any more.

Our son. Jordan had been so beautiful as a baby. Long and dark, like a little roasted peanut. My mother cooed and said that was just how I had looked at that age. Now, he stood straight like his father, with sleek brown hair and deep eyes. I had always held him at arm's length, I realized, like some Victorian parent who only spent time with her child when the nanny brought him for an hour each afternoon. I was at fault for not bonding as other mothers did. I loved him, but I let go of him too early, afraid of the pain of losing him if anything bad happened, as I had lost my mother. Vic was older than I. With his work, I routinely expected the worst to happen: the phone call saying his plane went down, or that terrorists kidnapped him, or that a freak accident during installation killed him. Emotionally, I'd always been prepared to lose him. If I didn't cling too tightly to anything, it wouldn't hurt too much when I wasn't necessary anymore.

Had I always held everyone on the fringes like that? I loved Nona, but I purposefully gave her privacy. I had to, since we lived so intimately in other ways. Greer Wendell and I were the most alike of all the ladies who attended Bible study. Our children were the same age. Her daughter, Abby, was in Jordan's class at the exclusive Northbay Academy, and we had known each other for ten years. I could tell her anything, if I wanted to. I'd patted her shoulder through a miscarriage and her favorite aunt's death. She called me more often than I called her. We prayed together and shopped together for birthday and Christmas gifts. Sometimes Nona came along, but I knew Greer wasn't sure what to think of this woman who lived in my house, who was not a servant, less than a sibling, but more than a friend.

I took a cab to the clinic the next Tuesday. The biopsy was over before I worked up much dread. Anna used her procedure room in her suite, draping me so I couldn't see the size of the needle she said she was using, then let me lay there while she prepped the sample.

"I'm sending this over to Gellefson. He's the best specialist around here, and I know his path guy."

I was a little woozy from the mild narcotic she'd let me have on top of the local anesthetic. I had a vague notion of what she said, but I didn't really care.

Anna stood over me, touching my arm. "Where's Nona? You'll be able to go home in a little bit."

"Cab. I took a cab. Jenny knows to call."

Anna's eyes narrowed, but she didn't say much.

"Nona will be home before she picks up Jordan."

"I don't like it, but okay. Roberta will check on you in a minute. Then you can get dressed. Remember, you'll be sore when the anesthesia wears off. Take it easy. I'll call you when the results are back, but I've put a rush on it."

A couple of hours later, I was glad to have the house to myself when Nona and Jordan were both gone. My whole hip was sore even with the painkillers Roberta, Anna's nurse, gave me. On the sofa I snuggled under an afghan my mother had crocheted, tea and the remote for company. During commercials, I let my thoughts wander, sometimes not even making it back to watch the program. I turned the television off when I realized I had no idea what was going on.

Would knowing how deeply the cancer soaked into me make a difference? I thought about what I had accomplished so far in my life. Had I done everything I needed? What about my family? Would my father understand? What would anyone say for a eulogy?

I reached into my soul to pray, and had a crazy urge to hold Vic's rosary in my hands, wanting something tangible and comforting to touch.

During a Wednesday afternoon phone conversation with my husband, my call waiting signal interrupted Vic's story about an intern at the Chinese hospital who brought his whole family to see the new MRI unit. I ignored the repeating buzz until Vic stopped and asked me to take it. He'd wait.

I reluctantly pressed the button to answer the other call.

"Libby?"

"Yes, it's me." I did not trust call waiting and wish we had never installed it. I hoped Vic couldn't hear Anna on his side.

"Libby, I made room for you to see me tomorrow at eleven fifteen. We have some decisions to make."

"Okay." I thought I should say something else, even be curious, but I couldn't make any more questions come out of my mouth. "I'll be there. Thank you." I clicked back to Vic. I hoped. Why did people say thank you even in such odd situations as being told terrible news or after undergoing a painful medical procedure?

"Vic? Hi, I'm back."

Vic asked about the call. "One of your friends?"

"Yes. So, tell me more. How many people ended up watching the install?" By the time Vic got through telling me about the picnic lunch spread out on the floor, I was laughing.

"Your turn," he said. "What did you do today?"

"I finished the painting on the church window. It turned out pretty well, I think. A cornucopia."

"Take a picture for me, won't you?"

"You'll be back in time to see it."

"Yes, but all those children go by and touch it. It won't be the same as when it's fresh."

"I'll take the picture." Jordan was going to Ryan's house again

* * *

after school. I told Vic about the science project. "Too bad they couldn't bring you in for show and tell," I teased my husband. He grunted the way he did when he was embarrassed by a compliment.

"And how's Nona?"

"The same. She said she'd probably go visit her cousin Laurie in South Carolina for Christmas."

"That will be good for her. We don't let her out much, do we?"

"It's not for lack of trying."

"How about you? Would you like to go somewhere for the holiday?"

My side hurt. I rubbed the area gingerly, avoiding the place where Anna had stuck me. "I don't want to make you travel again. I know how you like to relax."

"I wouldn't mind," Vic's voice said, the end crackling with static. "I think I'm losing the link up. I love…"

My ear rang with the tickle and pop of the lost call and I hung up. Christmas seemed like forever away, and yet too close. What would I find out tomorrow?

❧

16 - LIBBY

...knowledge will pass away

I sat flat-footed and vulnerable in one of Anna's office chairs, gripping the armrests with sweaty palms. Crossing my legs would hurt. Anna sat next to me instead of behind her desk. She'd tossed the large file folder with its telling X-rays and lab results on the low table between us. "Dr. Gellefson wants to do a CT scan to help us see how far this has spread. CTs are clearer," Anna said, in her sympathetic tone.

"How necessary is another test? We know it's there."

"The scan will help us decide the best treatment."

"What are my options?"

Anna touched my wrist in order to make me look at her. "We want to try pinpoint radiation first. If we can kill enough of the bad cells, bone could start to restore itself."

"Radiation again? Isn't that what got me in this place?"

She shook her head, battle lines drawn tight around her mouth. Her silver earrings tinkled. "No, Libby. Radiation didn't cause the cancer to spread to your bones. Your case was already in stage two when we did the surgery. Lymph nodes were involved then. We talked about how stray cancer cells could possibly be carried throughout your body, even after we took the affected glands and treated you."

I wondered how many times a day she repeated herself. I didn't ask her this time if I would die.

"There's also another option we discussed," Anna said. "I looked at the research studies going on around the country. I think you should also talk to Vic about it, and consider participating. I've picked out four." She got up and went to her desk. From a file drawer, she pulled out an envelope and brought it to me. "Between Dr. Gellefson and myself, we would refer you to one of these. I put a brief description of the study criteria in here."

"Are these taking place here in Milwaukee?"

"No. Only one is in Wisconsin, at University Hospital. The others are scattered around the U.S."

"So I'd have to leave home? What, for how long? And where would I stay?"

Anna put a hand on my shoulder and another under my elbow to help me up. "The information is in the file. These studies are sponsored by drug companies or foundations. They also cover your living expenses—meals and room—while you're enrolled." We walked to her door. "Think about it, Libby, for a few days. Not much longer. Let's get the CT set up in the meantime, okay?"

We stopped at Jennifer's desk, where Anna left me to pick up another patient's chart. Jennifer had worked in the office long enough to keep her emotions in check. I stared at the picture of her son she kept on her desk. Two years ago, he'd been a toddler.

"Your little boy is growing up," I said, to cover the awkward silence while she clicked at her keyboard. "Enjoy these years. The time passes so quickly."

Jennifer smiled and handed me a slip of paper. "Everything changes. That's what I keep telling myself."

I took the paper, noting that the appointment was scheduled for Friday, and nodded to her. I went home to think about what to tell my son. My husband would return next Tuesday. Some things never changed, no matter what you did.

17 - CONFIRMATION JOURNAL: NOTMYGRANDMASGOD

Our stupid assignment is to write down what we're thankful for. It's Thanksgiving, and we have to be thankful for something.

I'm thankful my dad is back. And that he's staying around for a while, so mom can go away. They didn't have to make a big deal of what's going on. I may not remember everything from the last time, but I have a clue now. She's sick again. Bad. She planned a trip for Dad and me. I saw Dad with his rosary. Stupid, saying the same thing over and over. If there was a god, it would get awful tired of hearing the same thing from a million people all the time. Someday he'll see it.

I'm thankful my mom is going away, if it means my dad can stay.

I'm thankful for the Benelli.

I'm thankful Nona is here. I wish she were here now.

I'm thankful for good eyesight, so I can hunt.

I'm thankful I'm good in science.

There, am I a good enough boy now?

Soccer is over.

$\text{\reflectbox{G}}\mathcal{B}$

18 - LIBBY

For now we know in part...

Vic came home on Tuesday—another eventful Tuesday in my life. I was beginning to not look forward to Mondays, since Tuesday followed right on. I never understood how he seemed to adjust himself to overcome the effects of jetlag so quickly. That ability was a gift. I think I ran mostly on caffeine for the first dozen years of our life together. Nona, who usually sat in her car for her weekly telephone call, had gone away, not to return until Sunday afternoon. I was surprised, because she usually enjoyed worship with us on the Wednesday before Thanksgiving Day. Of course she wasn't expected to keep the holidays with us. I would have thought that she wanted to see Vic and spend the day with her mother.

I got Jordan from school just after lunch, which he didn't protest, and we went to pick up Vic from the airport. We only had to wait forty-five minutes in the bustling, echoing concourse, during which I plied him with a mochaccino and asked if he'd like to spend Christmas somewhere tropical.

"It's not even Thanksgiving, Mom. Why are you thinking so far ahead?" He gave me one of those teen-aged looks that made me feel like I'd asked the dumbest question in the world.

I used my best grandmother imitation voice. "Ach, you young people, never thinking far enough ahead." He couldn't remember my mother, but I did. She'd been so practical it hurt. "Christmas will come soon enough. We have to make reservations for anywhere exciting. Already it might be too late."

"Would I miss school?"

Ah, the catch. "Perhaps." If my plan were to succeed, he would miss a week or two. "If your grades at quarter reports would allow it." Two could play that game. The thoughtful look on his face was answer enough. "Check the screen," I told him for the third time since we arrived.

Jordan dutifully got up and wove through scurrying people hauling wheeled luggage behind them to look at the arrivals and departures. They were posted on television-sized screens throughout the public waiting areas. He came back to me. "His flight's on time. Can I go look through the gift shop?"

"Sure." I tossed a ten in his direction. "Knock yourself out. I'll be out in the big square." He pouted at the size of the bill, but went. I moved from the enticing smells of the coffee bar to the large square of hard seats near the information booth. I smiled at the elderly uniformed man behind the desk, but didn't approach him. Vic usually came from the direction of the airline terminal where Hayden rented space.

If Jordan agreed in advance, Vic's plan to spend the holiday somewhere other than winter in Wisconsin would work fine. For them. If I got my way, I'd be somewhere warm, too; just not with my family.

Since I refused to consider chemotherapy, which had begun to be used more often in treatment, the study therapy opportunities had been reduced to one: a treatment development program in Dallas, supposedly to go on for three months, half of it treatment, half of it rest. I could jump on board in December. They would cover the cost of my stay, at least for the two weeks of therapy.

"It's not exactly a drug trial, Libby," Anna said. "They're still studying effects of the therapy."

Fine with me.

Vic and Jordan broke my reverie. I lifted my face slowly to smile at them. Jordan had his father's garment bag slung across his chest. Vic plopped his other carry-on at my feet and slid into the hard plastic seat next to me. "Hi, Lib." He kissed me.

"Hi, yourself. How was the trip?"

"Long as always. My bags are coming. You're in your usual parking spot?"

"Yes." I glanced back at Jordan who stared at us as if we were specimens under a scope. I cocked my head, pretending to study him back, until he noticed and scowled.

A porter driving a wheeled luggage rack came toward us with Vic's trunk. "Let's go."

Jordan led the way down the ramp into the parking garage. In the car on the way home, I brought up the idea of a Christmas getaway. Jordan needed to understand that I wanted them to have this time together, and if Vic changed his mind about a holiday vacation, I was not the wet blanket.

"Vic, I've been thinking about your idea for a trip," I said from the back seat, when a lull in conversation let me in.

Vic's eyes met mine briefly in the rearview mirror. "Oh?"

Jordan piped up from his place on the passenger side. "Yeah, Mom said I could get out of school and everything. She said we could go somewhere exciting."

My son's eyes challenged mine in the mirror. I watched as we got on the freeway.

"What do you think, Jordan?" Vic asked. "Where would you like to go? Surfing? Skiing?"

I would not be able to do either of those activities, that's for sure. That put a new spin on the plan. Did Vic have this thought out? I listened to them toss ideas back and forth until we pulled into our garage. Vic's glance flicked at the empty parking space where Nona's car would have been. He didn't say anything, just hesitated before popping the back gate to unload his luggage.

Tantalizing beef stew aroma met us when we entered the house. I had set the slow cooker on low this morning before starting my last holiday centerpiece, which I delivered on the way to pick up Jordan. I could relax for a few days. I thought about what I needed to say to Vic, then about the orders waiting for me. Where would I find the courage and strength to do what was needed?

After supper, while Jordan showed his father the science papers and other work he had been doing, I checked my inbox. A message from Greer, wishing me happy holidays and where were we meeting for our annual Friday after Thanksgiving shopalooza? Some things could stay the same, after all.

I sorted through a few ads, then stopped before hitting the delete button on one of them, intrigued by the name. I supposed that my Internet searches for hospice information had prompted advertisers to send me more of the same. The place was called by a truly heavenly name.

Everyone could use a bit of Paradise now and then.

❧

19 - ABLE

Forgive me, forgive me, forgive me. Never will I be able to stand in your presence in Paradise, Almighty God, Lord of all. Never can I be worthy, never can you look upon this sorry, sin-sickened soul. I am but a creature without conscience, without the ability to give love or to receive it. Forgive me, forgive me, forgive, I pray.

My transgressions are ever before you, but your cup of forgiveness runneth over.

Hail, Mary, full of grace. Again, and again. Pray for me. All the saints, pray for me.

If not for the love of your son, Jesus, his great sacrifice, the gift of which I am unworthy to receive, would I even be able to kneel here, would I willingly dare to think your name in my polluted mind, would I know that I may call upon you. Thank you, thank you, thank you.

You have called me to this place, called me to show comfort, to make known the glory that is you. I fail. I am not worthy to the task. It is you who stands in the breach, who completes the task, who fights the good fight and wins the race. I am but a poor vessel. Use me, use me, use me. Despite my impurity, work in the lives of those around me.

I cannot comfort your son, Rich Bernard. I have tried, I have tried. Forgive me. How long must I wallow in my own evilness? Take this thorn from my side, I beg you. Take this thorn, take this thorn.

If I confess, will you abandon me? Must I give up the life to which you have called me and I have answered? What will you have me do? In your great mercy, do not cause those I love to suffer because of my despair. If I abandon the only means I have to support them, where shall I go? What shall I do? Show me what I must do. Show me what I must be. Show me the way to go.

Yes, Lord, this is your will. I give myself to you, as I did those long years ago when I first heard your voice and obeyed. You ask me to love you here, in this place. Teach me to be obedient. Help me to use the vow of chastity to overcome temptations around me. Use the poverty of my vow not for me, but for your children. Lord, care for them in your great mercy. Do not let them suffer because of me.

I am yours, Lord, I am yours. Your reasons are too lofty for me. Your ways are beyond my comprehension. You taught me to serve you through guiding the souls of those in pain. Thank you for these gifts. Keep me ever in your presence. Show me how to serve those around me. Help me, help me, help, Lord Jesus. Remove the scales from my eyes. From my heart.

How can I be the balm to one so determined to thwart you? For I, too, have stood in your way. I have abandoned my first love. How can I show him that you have called some to suffer? You have called some to be martyrs, some to be poor and sick to teach us how to love each other. How can we love each other here on earth if we cannot love you first? You have called me to show them the way to love you. Teach me to be patient and kind. Grant me, your poor slave, grace in time of need.

Bless the soul of Helen, your servant, who loved you, who desired unselfishly to help others even though it cost her life. Make her sacrifice worthy, oh Lord. Make Rich's eyes open to you, most high. Help him to find what he needs to see. Help him to heal his broken heart before it is too late.

20 - WEB CHAT: SHAREMYDISEASE

Surviving11 says: I've heard a lot about people who think religion can heal you.

Truman says: You can't discount meditation. It's a proven fact.

Faithhealer1 says: Everyone is full of disease. Since the fall, that's how our bodies were left to decay. When you have an emotional problem, your immune system takes a hit and some disease leaks out. You have to learn to listen to your body. You can counteract the factors that led to your disease. All sickness is caused directly by emotional upset. Listen! I can help. Free introductory stress relief lesson. Long distance rates apply. See my website. I can help you prevent the manifestation of the disease that lurks in your cells.

MaryJoKalen says: Anyone who charges for healing is a fake. Don't be fooled. Prayer is powerful. Mother Mary will pray for you. Resist the devil and he will flee from you. I'm praying for you. I can feel your pain from here. I release you.

EchoEcho says: Everyone has the power within us to effect true healing. I don't care if you call it the force, man, or the farce. Fact is, energy is everywhere. Just get out a compass or something, a Geiger counter. You can see how nature has its own power. They were right, man. You just have to learn to harness it.

whether.trs says: There has never been any scientific evidence of organic healing. Every one of those quacks who claim they have healed someone just with their thoughts are dangerous freaks. All those television and stage show frauds prey upon the most vulnerable. See a real doctor. Don't be taken in by these charlatans. I repeat, no studies have ever proven the benefit of prayer or mind over matter or channeling or anything like that. Ten percent is nothing but explainable or even skewed stats. National journals even published articles that don't give credence to such garbage. Hospital studies are a hoax. It's not that hard. Don't waste your time or money.

prayerwarrior says: The power of prayer cannot be disputed. Patients whose surgeons and nurses are true Christians pray with them before and after surgery are proven to have better experiences and quicker healing after their procedure. There have even been several studies done on using prayer to ease pain that cannot be controlled by drugs. Ten percent is a big number, whether.trs.

Jen_Wu says: There are more reports of death by neglect or fake religion than real miracles. Diet is the way. The food we eat today is full of chemicals and pesticides and unnatural hormones. You have to eat the way nature made it.

Believer says: No one needs to boast if you experience a real miracle. All I know is that I had a heart attack and died. No, I did not have the floating experience or the tunnel of light. I was ding-dong dead. Nothing. Flat line. Then I came back, after the doc called me out. Twenty minutes after. They were all ready to toe-tag me. My granddaughter had called our prayer chain as soon as I went in the ambulance. The only thing I know is that my people begged God for my life. And here I am. It's true, money can't buy life. But true faith can. Only believe.

miraclesRreal says: You're all forgetting that God allows suffering and illness for a purpose. Think to the future, to the resurrection and the celestial city where there will be no more suffering, tears or death. If you feel a need for healing, pray to be spiritually healed.

Surviving11 says: before organized religion kicks in, I'll sign off. Didn't realize I was causing such a big whoop.

• • •

⌇

21 - LIBBY

...and we prophecy in part...

"Yes, this is what I should do," I told Vic. "It's early, we got it right away. I need to do what she advised. You have to let me take care of myself this time, Vic. Jordan needs you."

Vic's face looked like a misshapen glob of cement. I would rather not have told him anything to hurt him, but he knew I went to see Anna. Once Jordan had gone to bed, Vic took me up to his room and shut the door so we could talk privately. My husband had taken the room across the hall from mine after my surgery so that we could both rest. As the separation turned into years, he hung mementoes from his many travels abroad on his walls, imprinting the bedroom as his own. A photo album hung off the edge of his bureau. I picked it up before sitting in a leather chair and hoisting my good leg onto the low stool. I knew Vic often read here, under the lamp. Sometimes he sat, working, late at night at the desk under the window. The album contained pictures of Hayden's latest project—pictures I once would have taken. I leafed through it. The memories it invoked brought both nostalgia and anger at what disease did to our lives.

"Our son needs both of us. How bad is it this time?" Vic leaned against the desk with arms folded in front of him, cupping his elbows. He looked like he could use a break from anything stressful. I'd never seen him so spent. The wings of gray had spread, so that his whole head now looked steely. I tried to summon a pinch of heartache for us both, but quickly shut it down again. If I allowed myself to hurt at all, nothing would stop the flood of emotion and I would drown, pulling them all after me in my panic. I had to be strong to keep my resolve. In the end, Vic would thank me.

"She did a biopsy."

Vic closed his eyes and bowed his head. His lips moved, and I knew he had begun to pray.

"This study I signed up for is a new kind of treatment for this kind of disease. I want you to take Jordan away for Christmas."

"You're not coming."

"I'll go down to Dallas, to the hospital there, for the study. It involves IV treatment." I did not say that it asked for two weeks of each of the next three months of our lives. "I have to stay there, but I'll be all right. It's early," I repeated. "No surgery this time, Vic."

His lips moved, even as he turned away from me.

"What are you praying about?"

"For the strength to do as you ask."

We were silent for a while, quiet in each other's company. Vic prayed his rosary, telling me not to leave when I started to rise. I looked through the album, lingering at the photographs that included Vic, sometimes in coveralls or a hard hat, in charge, competent and strong.

When Vic looked up at me, I knew he had finished. "Where's Nona?"

"She said she would be back on Sunday. I think she just needed to get away for a while."

"She didn't say where she was going?"

"No. Vic, I think I'll go to bed."

He rose from the desk chair to come help me up. He did not let go once I was on my feet, but folded me against his chest. He still smelled of alien places, overseas airplanes and the recycled breath of a thousand strangers. I squeezed my eyes against the dampness threatening to spill from the corners. I would not cry in front of him. He had to stay strong, but for Jordan, not for me. I had no more use for courage in the face of death. Vic would want me to fight, but my battle was already done. Vic would slow down at Hayden, stop traveling so much and stay home. He needed to be prepared to be a father to Jordan when I was gone.

He trembled. "Tell me, Libby, when you pray, what do you pray for?"

22 - CONFIRMATION JOURNAL: NOTMYGRANDMASGOD

So we get to the part with the lords prayer.

Teach us to pray

You're supposed to have a goal. Pray for something specific and believe it will happen. Then be thankful that it will happen. Sounds pretty techno new age to me. What would mother say if she knew this is what they're teaching kids today?

Seems backward. Before I was supposed to find things to be thankful for. Now I'm supposed to learn how to pray, then be thankful I'll get what I pray for. Of course, there's strings attached, just like everything else. Can't pray for a million bucks, can't pray for bad things to happen to other people, can't pray for an A and not study.

What about three aces in a row? Or a twelve-point buck? Or a five-curl mallard?

Teach us. Who's supposed to teach us. I mean, if jesus did live, he's been dead a long time. Beecher doesn't believe that garbage. me either.

There's some guru who says you just have to wish really hard and you get whatever you want. That seems more real to me. Wishing is so much better than praying. I mean, nobody has to teach you to wish, right? You just close your eyes, click your heels...sorry, wrong show. Haha

But I do think you gotta close your eyes. Then you can see what you want, inside your mind. It's your mind that makes things happen. Not some invisible presence. Oo—ooh. Boo.

I close my eyes. I see Dad, home for good. I see him, in our own boat with our dog. I see Nona cooking our ducks. I see Dad at the state tennis meet. I see gramps choking blood, begging me to help him. But I won't. I just watch the old.... he's so old, anyway. gaga in the head, rolling eyes, drooling. Disgusting. Why should he still be alive? If you call that alive. gross. Can I pray for god to take someone away? Especially if they're sick?

• • •

☙

23 - ABLE

...but when the perfect comes...

After morning Mass at Our Lady of Sorrows, an echoing adobe chapel perched on the edge of Habilus proper and surrounded by date palms, Able returned to his room at the hospice. He had run a mile earlier, and his knee ached. Able flexed it a dozen times before setting out for a difficult patient visit.

Daniel Kestwick's wide door was ajar. Able paused on the threshold after he received a desultory summons to his knock. Kestwick had fought his prostate cancer with every weapon his insurance carrier would cover. When an experimental treatment had been denied after a prolonged argument between the carrier and his employer, he ran out of options. When would insurance realize that everyone was different? Each case was unique? No one's body reacted to the same treatment, just as no one's mind processed knowledge exactly the same way.

Able pushed the door wider and went in. He pulled up and straddled a chair. Since their previous discussion three days ago, the once furious man now reminded Able of a Mylar balloon that had begun to deflate. Kestwick sat, slumped, on the sleeper sofa in his room.

Kestwick said the same thing every day for a week. "I should have gone in earlier. I ignored the symptoms too long, afraid and proud."

Able stroked his mustache and composed himself to listen. Gentle music piped through the speaker on the nearby desk. Kestwick had chosen the soft violin.

"Did I tell you that I hadn't been to a doctor in fifty years?" Kestwick said.

Able nodded when Kestwick raised his grizzled head to look at him. Kestwick's pupils were huge from the IV-administered narcotics which were meant to keep the worst of his pain at bay.

"I was proud of that."

"Many people have the same feeling. Good health is easy to take for granted. Quite often, the scourge of disease strikes us unaware. Not even those who keep regular medical check-ups are immune."

Kestwick shifted on the sofa, grimacing. He gripped the IV pole with a thin, mottled hand. Able knew the patient was sixty-three years old, but could have passed for eighty.

Kestwick shifted again. "Tell me, truly. What will happen to me in hell? For I'm surely not bound for heaven." Able leaned forward to offer assistance. Kestwick held up a shaky hand. "No. Don't fuss. Can't stand any more fussing."

Able took a deep breath, willing the Spirit to speak for him. "What makes you think you're not bound for heaven?"

"Never been religious, never had much use for church. I been divorced twice and not sorry—my fault both times."

Able waited through Kestwick's long pause, sure there was more to hear. As an Alexian Brother, Able had never been put in the position of Father Confessor, but his role as hospice chaplain and counselor gave him access to those holy moments of life and death; times when people naturally felt the need to rectify themselves.

"And I killed someone."

Able gripped the olivewood cross he wore around his neck and prayed for the right response. "Do you want to tell me about it?"

Of course he did. A few beers, a rainy night, flashing yellow and red lights and a collision. One dead co-ed in the passenger seat of the other car. "Kid told me later, after the hearing, they'd just picked out her ring. He put his last two hundred dollars down on it. You know what I'd been doing? Do you?"

"What, Daniel, my friend? What had you been doing?"

Kestwick leaned forward, gripping the IV pole with both hands. "Celebrating my first divorce." Kestwick gasped and choked a little, but waved Able off. "Every night," Kestwick said, "always, every night, the last thing I see before I close my eyes is blond curls stuck in the smashed window of that Honda."

"You said there'd been a hearing."

"Yeah, got six months' probation. Fine. Lost my license for a year. Then I married the probation officer. She had red hair that came from a box. After I got my license back, I left her. Lots of women, lots of booze. No booze in heaven, so what do I care if I go there or not?"

Able felt the mood shift. The false bravado signaled terror of more than death. Able sniffed it, like heated copper jewelry made by someone he knew decades ago. "I sense, my friend, that you wish things were different."

Kestwick quirked his lips. "Maybe."

"How do you feel about the things you have told me today?"

"How I feel? What does that matter?"

"Do you rejoice in the accident that took that young woman's life? Does it give you a feeling of victory?"

"No, no," Kestwick's head swung from side to side. "Of course not. I'd give...anything to take it back."

"Remorse is often a first step on the path to forgiveness."

"How can she forgive me?" he whispered. "She's dead."

"In a case like that, you can ask forgiveness of others you have wronged. The most important part, though, is that you accept the forgiveness of our Lord and Savior, Jesus Christ."

● ● ●

"He wasn't there."

Able uncrossed his legs and leaned forward. He put his hands on Kestwick's. "He was, Daniel. He was there as much as he's here with us, now."

"No, no. You're not going to get me with that gibberish. Kid was in the intersection on a flashing red. It was his fault, not mine. But I had to pay the penalty because of a few beers. That's not fair."

"What are you afraid of?"

"I don't want to die."

"When this poor imitation of life is all you have, it's hard to let go. Daniel, there's so much more. If you believe in hell, you must believe in heaven."

"I told you, I'm not good enough."

"No one is. But there is another way. May I tell you about it?"

Able watched as Daniel Kestwick released his death grip on his silver IV pole and collapsed against the sofa. With his lips tight, Kestwick gave the briefest of chin bobs before he turned his face to stare out of the wide window. Able looked out, too, at a crimson bougainvillea twined about a redwood trellis. Spent petals spilled like drops of blood on the mulch underneath. Relentless blue sky pushed everything down on the ground.

Able kept several parables stored in his mind, to pull out and paraphrase for those who might not be comforted by his reading directly from the Holy Scriptures. He decided on Matthew 20, the parable of the laborers in the vineyard. Before he began to speak, Able repeated internally some of his favorite phrases from a manifesto of the Alexians: "I am a radiating power, an influence—sometimes in obvious ways, sometimes in hidden ways. Here and now, I influence people, institutions, and the world around me. Through faithfulness to my call, my presence reflects Christ's Words and Deeds either knowingly or unknowingly."

"Daniel, you asked me about what you can expect. May I tell you a story?"

"I'm not a kid."

Able laughed. "Well, that's another message altogether. Perhaps sometime we can talk about the appropriate time to think like a child. Anyway, the story goes like this. In a time when a lot of people were out of work, men would gather in the center of town and wait for farmers to hire them to help with the harvest. When his olives were ready to be picked, a landowner went out early in the morning to hire workers for the day. The landowner and the workers agreed to wages. In this case, we'll call it, oh, fifty dollars."

"For a day."

"It's a story."

"Sort of like migrant workers following the crops."

"Yes. So, the harvest was going well, but it was a hot day, and by noon, the landowner knew he'd need more help. He went back to the center and hired three more workers. He agreed to pay them fifty dollars, too."

"Wait—"

"And so on. As the day wore on, the landowner remembered how many workers were standing around, and he felt sorry for them, so he went back at two and again at four in the afternoon, agreeing to pay the workers each fifty dollars if they would work hard."

"You gotta be kidding me. Where do I sign up?"

Compassion for Kestwick encouraged Able to tell him the truth. "Daniel, that's the point. You could have signed on any time. The offer was always there."

"No one ever told me anything. Anyway, why would I want to go with a lousy outfit like that? No one in his right mind would hire a man just because he felt sorry for him. Those first workers must have raked in a bundle, though, come end of the day, if the others were coming in at fifty bucks for a couple of hours work."

"That's where you're wrong. Each worker received what they were offered. It was the best deal made."

"The others must have complained. That's not fair."

"Only in your mind."

"You said that's from the Bible? No wonder religion is so hokey. Who'd want to have anything to do with such a stupid way of doing business. You can't tell me that story has anything to do with church."

"It has everything to do with the perfect church, where everyone is invited and treated the same, no matter when they come."

Kestwick bent his head over his knees again as if in pain and reached to grasp something solid. Able watched his knuckles turn white where he gripped the IV pole. "No matter when they come, you said?"

"Even if you go to work for the landowner at the last minute of your life, Daniel Kestwick, you will be welcomed and receive the same reward as those who began work when their lives were just beginning."

"Now? How could I do that? How could he want me? All the others will hate me."

"What others?"

Kestwick looked at him. "Like you. Religious folks who have been good all their lives. You can't want someone like me polluting your heaven."

Able leaned across and placed his hands on Kestwick's head, weeping inside at the thought of deceiving anyone by allowing him to think that he, Able, deserved anything but hell. Able gathered the frail body close. If only... "The best part of the story is that the landowner is compassionate. He wants only for you to come. He is fair in that he keeps his promises and you can know that he'll do what he says he will do, even to the point of giving up his own life."

"Christ."

Able hoped Kestwick breathed the word in prayer, and gave him the benefit of the doubt. "The best part of being fair, or compassionate, is that he doesn't keep track of when you came. That's why everyone gets the same wages. It doesn't matter to him. He kept his promise to everyone he invited to join him. And in the end, it doesn't matter to the workers, either, for it will seem as if we've always been there."

"I didn't get an invitation."

"You are now. And I know that I would be sad in heaven if I couldn't continue to meet with you there."

Kestwick's shoulders heaved as he gasped. Tears formed in the corners of his eyes. "I can't cry. Don't make me cry. Only the weak...and then you get punished."

"No one here will punish you, my friend."

"I'm not Catholic. Will it still count?"

"I'll tell you something I believe if you promise not to tell anyone but God. Catholics do not have the market cornered on grace and mercy." Able patted Kestwick's head as the man unburdened himself.

When the storm of weeping passed, a prayer of contrition said, the words of forgiveness planted in Kestwick's heart, Able looked with compassion upon the man in his arms. Kestwick had fallen asleep. At least, Able, hoped it was sleep. He buzzed for the nursing staff to help the man to his bed. As he helped lift, Able marveled. Kestwick could not have weighed even a hundred pounds. How had he managed to linger in such a disease-ridden frail body?

* * *

The answer came as Able stared down at him in repose. Able had seen Kestwick only when the muscles of his face were scrunched in anger or pain, never when his lips relaxed in the semblance of a smile, as they did now. Able breathed in deeply before he thumbed the sign of the cross on Kestwick's forehead. "Be at peace, my friend. If I find the same consolation, we will have many a good talk in eternity."

24 - WEBPOST: THEPLEASUREOFTHEHUNT

Fall gun-deer season in Wisconsin. I know there are plenty of you boys and girls out there with a passion for bow or muzzle loader, but give me a rifle at sunrise, a tree stand above the morning mist and clear bead on a monster buck, unaware that you're sitting right above him, watching your breath steam, taking aim.

Never mind the early season. After the corn is harvested, the last round hay bales covered, the heavy equipment put away, this is our time. A family ritual in the woods. The day after Thanksgiving, the men get up in the dark, head down to the kitchen, still bulging with the smell of turkey and dressing and pumpkin pie. You cook up a skillet of eggs and bacon, fill the thermoses and start in on the mountain of blaze orange clothes.

Those of you lucky enough to be in the eradication zones sort out your extra tags. You decide on strategy: trophy or food. What time you're going to meet for a drive. You grab a last slurp of coffee and head for the truck or directly to the woods. You don't have to decide who's going to sit where to wait for a deer. Those are traditional spots, handed down from father to son, occasionally shared, but never given up.

The morning is cold. The perfect season has a dusting of snow to make it easier to track. You climb and wedge yourself into your spot, maybe it's a stand, or a cleft in a rock face, or near an old piece of farm machinery, left where it died decades ago. The white ball of sun touches the horizon before it crests. There he is—the one you let go last year so it would have a more impressive rack this year. You hold your breath. Aim for the easy kill, drop him, don't make him run. Squeeze.

Next week—field dressing for safety.

56 comments

rifleman says: You have to adapt to no snow with the world wide climate change. When was the last time you had snow for the November hunt?

themanandhisgun says: That's taking a huge chance, waiting a year for your trophy to grow. What if someone else comes in and takes it? You gotta take it when you see it. There's so many out of staters coming in just for the trophies, you can't let the moment pass you by. Bambi's dad steps into your sights, it's your duty to drop him.

Pleasureofthehunt replies: Certainly good points. Climate change is valid. Who wants to talk trophy vs. food?

trophyhunter says: There wouldn't be any trophies if everyone shot antlerless. Best to have patience, let one go.

blazer says: Antlerless taste better. How much wall space can you give to hang a trophy? My wife will eat it, but she won't look at it holding up the walls.

Hunterman says: That's what you got a basement for. Load her up.

Pleasureofthehunt says: Eating venison is an art. We'll talk preparation next week.

☙

25 - LIBBY

...the partial will pass away

Jordan found a recipe for pheasant on the Internet, using one of his and Nona's favorite sites. Vic didn't comment on how much time Jordan and Nona spent together to find the recipe this time. He and Jordan made Thanksgiving dinner together, asking only for me to interpret an unfamiliar measurement. "What's a pinch?" Jordan asked. "Like, maybe a half a teaspoon?" At least he was in the ball park.

They shooed me out when I wandered too close to the range where they stood side by side, stirring individual pots. The aroma made me hungry for the first time in a month. I settled in the family room pretending to read *Good Housekeeping* while Vic's question of two days earlier still rambled in my mind. What would I pray for, if I had the energy? Did I still pray for Vic to be safe, even though I know God does whatever He wants? I pray for my son, of course. For my father to be comfortable. For Nona to be happy and want to stay with us always. I suppose I pray for my friends whenever I know they need an extra hand. Church, of course. We pray on Sundays. What did it mean to Vic, to pray all those beads on his rosary? He told me about it of course, but I struggled with the concept of saying the same thing over and over, until my brain numbed. He said it was comforting.

Praying for myself seemed sinful, selfish. Still, if I ask God to let me die in peace, is that a prayer?

Vic came out a half hour later with a glass for me. "Here, try this. Mulled cider."

I sniffed and swirled, smiling at the amusement that crinkled the corners of his eyes. "Mulled, hmm?"

"Your son actually tied little cloth baggies with pieces of cinnamon stick and cloves, then steeped it in cider in a warm kettle."

"This is good," I told him, after he watched me drink. "Nona would love it."

"You're sure you don't know where she went?"

"She has her cell phone, I think. You can call if you're worried."

"No," Vic said. "I wouldn't interrupt her. How are you feeling now?"

Jordan came into the room. I don't know what I would have said, anyway. I dreaded the shopping excursion with Greer tomorrow. We usually spent an entire day on the hunt for bargains, topping the evening with a show or a movie. I already told her I couldn't stay out that late this year.

"Mom, Dad said he would take me to see the cryo tanks at City Memorial tomorrow. You're gone all day, anyway, with Abby's mom, right?" My son turned away before seeing how I would respond. "Dad, Dad, we could go up with Ryan and his dad to their cabin they rented. End of gun-deer season, and you promised."

I felt Vic look at me, but I would not meet his question. They needed to learn how to go on together. "We'll talk some more about it after dinner, son." Vic put his hand on Jordan's shoulder. "We'd better take another look at the pheasant. We don't want it to dry out."

Vic would step into his new role with ease. From guiding millions of dollars' worth of precious medical equipment with the hundreds of decisions to the daily guidance of his son, Vic would figure out how to give Jordan what I could not. Nona would stay, at least for a while, I was pretty sure. I tried not to worry about her disappearing act this weekend.

I must have dozed, for I blinked and had to stretch my neck stiffened in an unnatural crook when the aroma of Thanksgiving dinner touched my subconscious.

"Libby!"

"Mom!"

The summons to dinner echoed in our house. I felt like a guest in my dining room. We had the room decorated formally, in raised oak paneling and Austrian crystal light fixtures. The table was a massive plank of wood we had found in a German market and shipped home. The antique dealer pointed out details he said made it five hundred years old. I didn't care, for I loved the arches and swirls carved along the skirt. I waxed and buffed the oak to a deep responsive glow. Vic found a craftsman who made eighteen chairs with carved backs to match the middle Gothic style. When we had been home those early years, we had entertained.

Vic pulled out my chair. I sat, fingering the brass napkin rings and smiling at the place setting. I looked up to see Jordan staring in my direction. I felt invisible. When Vic asked Jordan to pray, Jordan bent his head, and with a mechanical cadence, rattled off the supper prayer Nona had taught him. "God is great," he began and we joined in by the time he reached "Let us thank him for our food."

Jordan joined his father in the sign of the cross afterward, something Vic did not remark upon.

"Dad and I looked around, but the only glass we had was the cake plate. You know, for pheasant under glass. So we decided not to use that. In case it bothered you."

I reached for the heavy platter, only to find Vic's fingers there ahead of me, helping to support it. He set it next to me on the

• • •

table, then helped himself to sweet potatoes.

"Did you find the sweet potato recipe on the same website, Jordan?" I asked.

"On the can."

Vic smiled. "Jordan noticed the recipe while we were in the store."

Another male-bonding ritual: I had sent them to grocery shop together yesterday afternoon, as Jordan had early release from school and Vic picked him up. We attended the Thanksgiving Eve service at Northbay together after dinner. Jordan had seemed fine then.

After our family meal was over, I told my men that I would clean up, since they had cooked. When Vic announced that he would help me anyway, Jordan went up to his room. I wished I could be a mouse in the corner up there, watching him. Or maybe an angel, looking down from above, protecting him from dangers I wanted to snatch away.

Ↄ

26 - ABLE

When I was a child...

Thanksgiving Day was not a high holy day, but Able enjoyed the festive Mass at Our Lady of Sorrows before he divided the day between the pediatric wing and the adult building. Families wanted to be together this time of year, when it was so hard to be thankful for the devastating situations thrust upon them. Able did what he could to offer comfort and encouragement. If God granted him the ability to bring mercy from such a sin-ridden heart as his own, then he would continue to serve as long as he had strength and breath.

Able had visited many parishes during his early years in southern California, never quite feeling at home, until he found Our Lady. The tile roofed and stucco building was without the comfort of padded pews or carpeting or expensive video and sound equipment. Father Diego Torres's lilt gave the Mass a magical rolling feel, like ocean waves. The words echoed in murmurs under the arched and vaulted roof of the sanctuary, and along the Stations of the Cross. Twenty benches were arrayed around the altar. Father Diego wore the plain robe and sandals of his Capuchin order. He enjoyed a good meal, Able knew, as well as many local wines. The robe looked comfortable around his barrel-shaped body.

Able stuck a finger behind his collar to loosen it. As he spent more time learning about Torres, he discovered that the Father lived in two rooms attached to the back of the chapel. Torres swept the stone tile floor of the church daily, celebrated Mass for a dozen or so faithful, heard confession, and continued a routine of visits with his people, devoted prayer times, meetings, more prayer, dinner, an occasional outing, and sleep. Sundays usually found the chapel full of congregants; holidays usually meant people standing at the back.

Father Diego kept the grounds of the chapel in simplicity as well. The nearby golf course paid dearly in water ration, a commodity Able agreed was too precious to waste. Instead of a green lawn and lush plant life, Diego collected interesting rocks and driftwood. A few potted plants were kept near the entry, fed with wastewater from his laundry or dishes. Sometimes Able confessed his covetousness of his friend's simple lifestyle, for which Diego chuckled and bade him say penance with the rosary of Our Lady of Sorrows and its unique prayers.

This morning the little chapel was packed full with visiting family come from northern climates, judging by the paleness of their faces and arms; come to be thankful in the warmth of southern California. Able perched on a folding chair placed near the door, which was left open to allow fragrant humidity from the ocean and the golf course to waft inside.

Able studied backs and profiles and listened to the whispers and rustling of the people. He went forward to help with the Eucharist. "The blood of Christ," Able repeated over and over as they came with bowed heads and outstretched hands and open mouths. "The blood of Christ, shed for—"

"Amen. Thank you, Brother," the woman whispered and reached for the cup to help herself after he halted in surprise.

Able swallowed and forced himself to carry on while his heart and mind threatened to crush him with fear and longing.

Nona.

CB

27 - LIBBY

...I spoke like a child...

"Libby, pardon my French, but you look terrible."

Greer Wendell was one of those people with a pet phrase that made me just want to hit her after I heard it for the third time in three hours. Greer was my closest confidant, not counting Nona, but she could stop saying "pardon my French" unless we were shopping on the Rue Montorgueil in Paris instead of at the Bayshore Mall in Wisconsin. Or she was using foul language.

"Come to think of it, you haven't looked good most of the fall. Have you been to see your doctor? It hasn't been that long since...you know."

With my eyes closed, I could pretend the Cheesecake Factory where we were having lunch substituted for La Cocarde. I just wouldn't ever say it out loud.

"And you said Nona was taking the weekend off. Do you need me to call someone?"

I was proud of the fact that I'd lasted three hours on my feet. Right now, though, after we had ordered the soup and salad, I didn't think I could even get up to use the ladies room. I opened one eye. "Thanks, Greer. That's just what I need to hear to lift my spirits."

"Come on, Libby. You know what I mean. Are you sick? We can go home."

"Let's have lunch, regroup. I know you're not ready to be done. This place is busy, so we'll have time to rest up. Or I can sit while you finish shopping."

"Of course I wouldn't enjoy shopping without you. I'm nearly done, anyway. How about you? I can come back anytime."

"I just have the children's tree gift to get." Social Services offered a few handfuls of gift requests every year to at least fifty local churches. Each tag had the name of a child, gender, age, size, and a wish gift, along with basic needs like a nightgown, or toothbrush or socks. I usually picked a girl's name to buy for, since I had a son of my own. "I think, after we eat, I'll be recharged enough for one more loop."

Greer gave me a narrow-eyed study. "Okay." She thanked the waiter who brought our coffees. "What about the doctor? Something you're not telling me? You asked for prayers the other night at church."

"I'm leaving next week for a new therapy study. In Texas."

"Oh, honey—"

"Yes, it's back. And, if you don't mind, let's talk about something else, okay? I see you're on the Christmas party committee for the ladies group. I thought, after last year, you swore you'd never do it again."

Greer sat back in the booth, looked aside and dabbed under her eyes with the maroon cloth napkin. She picked up her coffee, jiggling it. She cleared her throat. "Yes, well, I'm not doing decorations again. I got the entertainment."

I took a deep breath and pasted on a grin. "What is it?"

"I'm not telling. You'll just have to…" Her grin turned upside down. "But you won't be there, will you?"

I looked at the table and fiddled with the napkin on my lap. Breathe, deep and slow… "Just tell me about it."

The waiter came with our salads. Over lunch, Greer told me about hiring the Academy's string octet. "Anything less wasn't ready for public venue, the director told me." We ate our soup. I did feel a little better as we sat and talked. I liked her too much to want to be a drag on our outing. She wore her dyed hair bobbed in the usual simple round cut that women of our age like to get. We wear it to take the first glance away from the wrinkles of our necks and the fine lines around our eyes. We prefer to emphasize our earrings, which dangled or jingled or were classic heavy rings. Greer was a comfortable companion and would do what I asked, which meant not talk about me. She wasn't shallow, and I knew she wasn't ignoring my problem, just trying to hold us together in public. I would miss her too. She was one of those truly sweet and dear people, a real innocent who God would hear. She brought joy to everyone in her circle and I was blessed. Maybe...

"Abby and Jordan might be able to hang out, um, after church or if they have homework. Sometimes, right?" I asked.

Greer got the hint, that I respected her as a mother, a mother good enough to spend time with my child when I was gone. She squeezed my arm and rose. "Ladies room. Be right back."

I paid the check before she returned and she didn't even protest. We finished our shopping less than an hour later.

When we got home that afternoon, before Greer let me out of her car, she grabbed my hands and started to pray. By the time she had moved on from begging for healing to comforting those around me, we were both in tears we didn't have to control. Vic and Jordan were still gone, so I indulged myself in a good crying jag. I did not allow us to get to the weeping stage, though. I'd feel terrible and headachy all night, and I could not allow my men to see me with eyes swollen and red like that.

I hugged her hard after she helped bring my bags into the house. "Thank you, Greer. I'll trust you to be discreet, right? What I asked for in church was the wisdom to make good decisions for my family, and that's still my desire. My father's needs are being met, but I'll miss seeing him. Vic's home for a while, so Jordan will have his father and Nona for support. I—we—haven't told him anything yet. So, it would not be in his best interest to hear it at school, instead of from us."

"I understand. I promise not to tell Abby anything, and I won't. I'll pray for you all."

"Thank you, Greer. And I'm sorry we cut our day short."

I walked her out. "I'm not that sorry," she said. "I just miss your company. Tell me what else I can do for you and your family, okay? I'll pry Jordan away whenever I can. And I know the other parents will be there too, for him and Vic."

We waved good-bye. Our friendship extended beyond basic social needs, to the personal touch of prayers or a favorite snack or sharing a movie rental. I spent the rest of the afternoon slowly labeling my purchases and putting them in Vic's closet with notes about their distribution.

28 - WEBCHAT: SHAREMYDISEASE

Surviving11 says: What is the joke about stem cells these days. Some people make it sound like using these not quite human parts are a cure-all to replace sick parts. Others cite this as the ultimate evil, a sort of monstrous combination, like Frankenstein's creation, or something.

How am I supposed to answer if someone suggests stem cell therapy as a part of treatment, sort of like some crazed psychoanalysis of diseased parts of the human animal? Is it moral to let a person manipulate the most private aspects of your individuality? Even if they use pieces that have no individualized purpose?

When I looked deeper into DNA manipulation, no one even tries to hide the information that they use enzymes to cut hunks out of the structure. No one is even embarrassed to say that viruses are used to plug holes. We are creating entire new species. Let's not mix metaphors, here, people. Are the rest of you as afraid as I am?

The Phoenix says: It's not all that bad. There are protocols, safety features in place for research labs. It's not like we're going to turn the human race into zombies, or something. Give it a rest and do your homework from the right sources. Ask experts if you have questions, and quit frightening the children.

Surviving11 says: I'm not a child.

Tin man says: Nobody said anything to you. I'm having gene therapy right now, for leukemia. I'd be dead if I didn't try it.

Anonymous says: I didn't know that about viruses. They really do that?

Tin man says: Only harmless retroviruses are used to take on the chromosomal DNA of its host cell.

The Phoenix says: Nature uses enzymes to cut out bad

segments of DNA. It's called a nuclease. Get a grip.

Anonymous says: Yeah, whatever that means. How about in English?

The Phoenix says: Your body continually repairs itself. Your genetic information is wounded constantly any number of ways, even through exposure to the sun or pollution. Your DNA strands constantly clean themselves up by chopping out the hurt bits and inserting fresh information.

Tin man says: What about turning skin cells into different cells? That's creepy, like turning tin into gold. Alchemy.

Anonymous says: There's this 3D printer...

Surviving 11 says: Cut it out. That's just plastic.

The Phoenix says: Haven't got the real procedure perfected yet, except for some tissue, like skin built around a frame. Tends to mutate.

Surviving11 says: That's what I'm talking about. The fact of the matter is, we are putting stuff together that the creators never thought of. No good can come of that.

℘

29 - ABLE

...I acted like a child...

Able waited at the back of the chapel, sitting quietly and alone, thinking, thinking, thinking, until after the building emptied of its corporeal occupants. Even Father Diego left after Able asked for a season of solitude.

The first time had been an accident.

That first time he slipped, Able had not expected to be paid anything for his introductory talk twenty years ago to the Habilus Rotarians about hospice services. When he had been handed a signed rectangle of paper after lunch, he tried to give it back, explaining that he could not accept any money. Certainly not a check made out to him for three hundred dollars.

They told Able to give it to the hospice. That was on a Tuesday. He had tucked the check in his notebook with full intentions to turn it over to Rich the next day. The phone call that night changed everything. How clearly he remembered those agonizing words from halfway across the continent, echoing after two decades.

"I almost lost her today."

"Who? You mean Emily? What happened?"

"She choked. And no one was there to help her. I want so badly to move her to a better facility, but..."

"What do you need?"

"Nothing you can give me, Able. I'm sorry to even complain. I was so frightened. I wished you were here. I'm sorry. Don't listen to me."

"How is she now?" Able asked.

"We took her to the hospital. I needed to give them five hundred dollars down before they would keep her overnight."

"Listen. I have a check here, made out to me for a talk I gave today. I was going to give it to the hospice, but I'll send it to you right away."

"Able, you can't."

"I'll tell them, don't worry. You need it. Rich Bernard doesn't."

"We talked about this before."

"And we'll keep talking about it. She's my child, too."

"I should have let her die."

"Don't ever, ever say that."

"It would have been more kind, I think."

"Please, Nona. God is in control."

"Do you really believe that?"

"I must."

"You see so much suffering. Don't you ever pray God to take them?"

"Don't ever think that. We pray for God's great mercy, his will to be done."

"God should not allow suffering."

"Sometimes he does."

"How can you believe that?"

"Because, Nona, I believe in a greater picture than the time and place we occupy this moment. I believe that the mosaic of the past and the future makes a pattern we can see only when we look back from our place in the kingdom of heaven."

The great sin. Able Fenwick made a child during his postulate period. When he confessed and left the order, Nona Roland, the Alexian Associate who worked with him at the Village, who comforted Able after the slow, painful AIDS death of his brother, refused to marry him. She told him their child had died.

Able wondered then what kind of father he would have made. With his call still loud in his heart, he returned to the Alexians. With his education complete, and forgiven, he took his final vows.

Three years later, while on rounds with a colleague working on alternative methods of communication with young children unable to vocalize, he met Emily. Her stringy reddish wisps of hair and a pushed-out face grabbed his heart. On closer look, the child had Nona's peat-moss colored eyes. She was severely dysfunctional and wheelchair bound, being cared for at a county nursing home. This little girl had barely enough coordination to point to pictures. The colleague hoped she could eventually learn phonemes and piece together words, but right now, the professionals were unsure about her ability to grasp more than basic wants. Able thought he might visit Emily again and checked her full name to write in his notebook. Emily Louise Roland.

That was the first Tuesday of the rest of his life. The shock wore off after two hours. Able bound Nona to update him regularly on Emily's progress. Each call was like a stripe across his back, a reminder of his failings, and of his helplessness. Until that first check. He had followed it with others, given to him as honorariums, and passed quietly on to Nona. Em took his name and moved to Green Willow, a privately run center which also hired a staff of highly-qualified educators.

Two years after that talk to the Rotarians Rich Bernard called Able to his office one Saturday. Rich had been to an international conference on hospices in Switzerland. He had run into a National Institutes of Health representative who had heard Able speak a few months earlier. The representative wondered what branch of Rich's work was in Milwaukee, Wisconsin, where the check given Able for a donation to Rich's foundation had been cashed.

Rich would have helped. Deep down, Able knew that. Perhaps a character flaw led him to continue a life of sin, using that money, unrepentant, too full of pride to ask another man to do for his child what he could not. Though God asked Able to live in poverty because of his religious order vow, Able would not allow the child to suffer.

Rich never censured him, nor dangled the secret in petty small favors. The honorariums were allowed to be sent to Green Willow but Able knew Rich did not keep his secret freely. When Rich felt the need to bypass the more lengthy process of getting FDA approval on certain experimental tests on human subjects, Rich chose Able to act as his conscience. Able had no choice and no way to legally object without hurting Emily.

Strange concepts flittered in Able's head while he sat at the back of the little chapel, alone, on this day of celebrating family. He stretched his feet into the patch of sunshine thrown on the stone floor and wondered what it would feel like to remove his shoes and socks and let that warmth caress the skin of his toes. His subconscious registered the reverberation of a car horn and crunching gravel as he contemplated an ant carefully feeling its way along a crevasse. A shadow interrupted the view.

Able raised his head to see Nona's outline showing dark with a nimbus of light from the window.

"I tried to call you." She stepped forward into focus and dropped onto the pew beside him. "I'm sorry to just show up like this."

"Is Emily all right?"

"Oh yes. I called her this morning. She said to wish you a Happy Thanksgiving."

Able waited.

Nona fiddled with the wooden handles of her crocheted handbag. "You're probably wondering why I'm here."

Able closed his eyes. He wished Nona was on the other end of a telephone link, not here, where he could smell her lavender scented soap and feel the warmth of her presence. He opened his lids again, to meet her stare. "Are you all right?"

"Yes."

Four seconds of silence seemed to be Nona's limit. "It's like this. I just needed to get away for a few days. Things are pretty tense at the house. I had to take a break before it started again."

"It?"

"Her cancer resurfaced."

"How bad is it?"

"I don't think she's going to make it. She doesn't want to."

They could have been colleagues discussing a case, except for the lack of names or details. As medical professionals in a world made microscopic by lightning-speed electronic information that somehow sent a person's name and status around the world in seconds, both Able and Nona agreed never to mention specifics. Able still did not know the street address where she resided, or the name of her employer. She picked up her mail at a post office box and had a personal cell phone.

"'Not wanting to' is a pretty serious charge, Nona."

"Look, I don't want to argue, not after all this time. Can't we pretend we're on a phone call?"

"About Emily?"

"About us. We've talked about ourselves, too, Able."

Able watched her look high into the rafters of the chapel, then set her face toward the altar. "It's beautiful here. I can see why you chose this church to worship."

"I'm surprised to hear you say that, Nona. From what you've described to me about your current practice, you seemed to remark on the décor more than the service."

"I've never been impressed by the ornate. You know that. Seasonal décor changes. What lies underneath is permanent. My heart will always follow the true church, no matter where my body attends."

"You don't have to lie to me."

Nona turned to look at him. Able felt shame at the disappointment he had planted in the line between her eyebrows. "I'm not," she said quietly. "I see where I worship now as an opportunity to see others in service."

They no longer argued weekly, or even monthly, about salvation. Able caused Nona to adapt nearly everything in her life to protect and nurture their child. How could he fault her for the choices she had to make? There were no stones to throw. Nona chose to be a single parent to access government services that would otherwise be denied a family of mid-range salary. She had decided to keep Emily's existence a secret to make it easier for her to work. Gender and family concerns were not to be weighed by an employer, but Able knew that when it came to a decision between hiring a single, unattached woman or a woman with a disabled child who might need her mother to take a lot of time off for her care, the unattached person would win every time.

Able had taken the hospice assignment shortly before he had found out about Emily. By then, anything he could do to help Nona would be detrimental to Emily and the astronomical cost of her care. The government would deny them aid if Emily had access to any more money than Nona made at her job. Nona had made opportunities out of situations that would crush lesser people.

"Yes, I feel that God has led me here," Able said. "I participate in daily Mass when I am in Habilus. This is a good place for me to be refreshed in spirit."

Nona sighed and faced the altar. She closed her eyes. Able wondered how this woman could live as an extra limb in a household that seemed replete with a set of functional parents and well child. She had been so fiercely independent once that she had refused to share his life. Why had she needed him this time? What could he give her?

Nona opened her eyes. "Maybe that's what I need right now. A time of refreshment before I go back." Able hurt when he saw the sea of tears spilling over. "But, Able, what I really need to know is how you help someone face death."

ᘓ

30 – LIBBY

...I thought like a child...

I startled awake to the sound of clattering dishes and smells of breakfast in the morning. Nona must have come in late last night. Vic's deeper tones complemented hers and Jordan's in muffled conversation. After a squinty-eyed look at the clock, I knew once again I'd have to hustle to not look like a complete failure as a parent before my son left for school.

Alarms never worked for me. In fact, before the cancer I never had a problem getting up when I needed to. Since my treatments, I turned alarms off in my sleep before they could sound. Anna had no answer for the problem. Nona had offered to come and wake me, but that seemed beyond the bounds of decency.

The sun had only begun to light up the horizon over Lake Michigan. I wormed my way into my housecoat and stumbled, barefoot, down the stairs. The three of them looked like the quintessential happy family, adjusted, talking about happy family business. I watched for a moment, even though Nona gave me the eye. She frowned when I half-smiled and shook my head. I went into the room, brushing against Vic's shoulder on the way to the coffee pot. I knew better than to touch Jordan.

"You look like you had a great vacation, Nona. Welcome back." I brought my mug to the table. Vic had made his signature French toast. I wished I was hungry. Jordan had only toast, for he would not eat anything made with eggs, unless they were mixed in batter, like cake, or brownies.

"Good morning, Libby. I was just telling your men about the coastal sight-seeing cruise I took in southern California."

"Ahh. So you went someplace warm before the snow flies." I saluted her with my mug. "Good for you." We'd have time to talk later, and I didn't ask her to repeat her story for me.

Vic would drive Jordan to school while he was home. "Five minutes, Jordan."

Jordan jumped up and left the room. Nona and I sat quietly at the table. Ever since I had told Vic about the study, I knew that I needed to come clean with Nona, too, and ask her advice. She seemed contemplative this morning, although she could just be tired from her long travels yesterday, if she had come all the way from California.

Vic went for his jacket and car keys. "I have a couple of things to do this morning, so I won't be back until lunch," Vic told us. "Tell your mother good-bye, Jordan."

Jordan mumbled in my direction and left a chill in his wake as he opened the door to the garage. Vic narrowed his eyes and smiled weakly at us, then followed.

Vic's time away on errands would give Nona and me plenty of time to talk. I got up to get another cup of coffee and gestured at her with the pot. "Want some more? No? Okay." I returned to the table, trying not to shuffle. "So, you went on a cruise?"

"A two-hour one. The gray whales are starting to head back from Alaska to Mexico. We saw two, although it's a little early for them. Global warming is affecting everything, the guide said. Soon, they'll have to change their migration patterns."

She said all this in a rote way, as if she had practiced what she would report about her trip. "I'm glad you got to do something fun," I said. "How was the weather?"

"Perfect, of course."

"Did you stay with someone you knew?"

Her eyes regained a sharp focus and zeroed in on me, as if searching.

I gnawed my bottom lip. "I'm sorry. I didn't mean to pry."

"Oh, honestly, Libby. You're not prying."

"It must be like living in a fishbowl here, sometimes. I want you to have room to live your own life, and not have to account for your actions to us. It's not like we—"

"Libby, I just needed to go and see someone, okay? An old friend I hadn't seen in a long time, catch up, that kind of thing. We had a good time, and now I'm home." She leaned across the expanse of the tabletop and grasped my forearm with cold fingers. "I need to hear about you."

Time for truths. Should we stay here, chatting in the brick kitchen, with Nona's ivies curling around the window and my copperware gleaming on their hooks, or go somewhere else? If we were able to be more intimate I might be tempted to stray from my carefully orchestrated plans, the finality of which not even my husband knew.

We stayed.

"Vic will take Jordan away for Christmas. I think Hawaii. The last three weeks of December and over New Year's." Nona opened her mouth, so I rushed on. "So, you should just go to visit your cousin whenever you want. There won't be anything here for you to worry...nothing here to keep you."

"Nothing?" She sat back. "No one to worry about?"

Her silent study condemned me. "You know it's back. You knew before I did." I tried not to make it an accusation.

Nona cleared her throat. "Libby, I'm sorry." Her words still came out hoarse. I couldn't bear to look at her, in case her expression matched some of that sorrow from her voice. "Where are you going?"

Not, "what are you going to do," or, "how do I help you?"

"Anna gave me some options for study groups. I looked at them. I decided on one at the University of Texas, but I...was hoping you'd check it out with me."

"Vic agreed to this?"

"I didn't give him a choice. I'm not asking you, either, for permission. Just for...support."

"Like you asked me to take your husband."

"No!" I scraped my chair back and got to my feet. The picture of the three of them, Vic and Nona, with Jordan, at this table an hour earlier, stung. "Maybe."

She got up, too, and came around the table. "Libby, this isn't fair. You did everything you were supposed to do. I thought we'd beaten it."

"I did too."

"Do you want to tell me more?"

I pursed my lips and trembled. "No. I just don't want to fight anymore." I looked at her, unable to keep the tears back. "Does that make me a bad person?"

She folded me in her arms. "Of course not, Libby." I didn't want to cry again, so soon after yesterday, but I couldn't stop. Nona had just as much right to grief as I.

When our mutual bout of weeping calmed, she pulled away. "You've been through a lot. And you're right. You should decide what to do. But the fact that you want to participate in a study leaves room for hope. Even if that's not the reason you're going."

I snorted and ducked my head.

"Come on, show me what you got."

She led the way to my work room. Only later, when I thought back about that day, did I wonder how Nona knew I kept the information about my condition and the study groups there.

• • •

31 - ABLE

...I reasoned like a child

Nona's question haunted Able all through the weekend as he sat at Helen Harding's bedside. Helen had grown unresponsive, clearly entering that period of grace when a timely whisper releases the imprisoned soul. Her death naturally followed her disease. Rich's attempt to manipulate her cell structure had little effect on the course of her cancer, but had he gained enough information from his studies to make sure her journey had not been in vain? Able prayed it was so.

He'd sat at many bedsides of the lonely, watching carefully, wondering how it felt for the tortured to find that moment of peace. He thought about how he helped others face death. When the time came for each of them, he preferred to think that he walked alongside of them, a companion on the journey, rather than the counselor he was. Death was certainly one experience for which he had no firsthand knowledge.

In this building with the lab, where Rich kept his private patients he officially released from hospice, Able was the only person from the main complex allowed in. Rich kept this side of the business separate, so not even Director Liz Carrelton could justify her presence or control. He had no board of operations, no checks or balances. Regular federal inspectors found nothing out of place.

Helen sighed. The crepitating sound from her chest signaled the end. Able leaned closer. Her eyelids fluttered. How did he walk her to the end of her life with dignity and peace? With prayer?

"Helen, if you can hear me, know this: you are loved and forgiven. You are welcomed into the kingdom."

Her eyelids quivered again. Her chest moved once, twice. Able held her hand, which already seemed intangible. He had to look to see whether or not he really touched a part of her. He did not call Father Diego, or any of the others who could give last rites. They were not administered here to the already dead. Helen Harding ceased to exist when she was released from the main hospice to take part in Rich's work.

Facing death meant something different for everyone, especially the loved ones, he'd told Nona. Comforting the dying was not an easy gift, as he had experienced most recently with Daniel Kestwick. And had tried to tell Nona.

"So you fight death?" Nona had asked him.

Able thought about that daily. "Now that's like telling God he's wrong."

"All of our medical training teaches us to defy illness, to overcome disease and find a cure for every wrong."

"Did you ever consider how arrogant we sound?"

"When do you draw a line?" Nona had asked.

In Rich's case, the issue had become how far across the line anyone should step. Helen sighed again, then did not take another breath. Able folded her hands upon her chest, closed his eyes, made the sign of the cross and prayed. He next summoned Mary and Rich. They each did their part to prepare Helen's body for cremation. Rich had arrangements with the Tucker Brothers Funeral and Cremation Services in San Diego. Often accompanied by Brother Able, Rich brought in the bodies and filed the proper electronic death certificates. Paper certificates were no longer issued. Rich subscribed to the California Electronic Death Registration System, the EDRS, for filing. He'd already completed the necessary segments, including the manner of body disposition. The Tuckers had no reason to question him. Everything was in order. Rich Bernard's hospice was well-reputed, known to take in anyone, even the indigent. The fact that sometimes Rich paid for the cremations from his own funds, and not those of the hospice, was considered an unusually nice gesture of respect. If, upon occasion, Rich brought in a body a couple of weeks after the death certificate had been electronically signed, Able saw Rich write "waiting for family confirmation" on the authorization forms at the crematorium.

Able next brought in a chlorine-scented laundry cart and removed the linens from the room. He took it back to the main complex for regular pick up with the rest of the laundry.

Was this all part of helping someone die? Or part of helping Rich find a cure so no one else would have to die like that? Perhaps, Able conceded, he meant to assuage his own guilt.

The peace on Helen's face brought both joy and remonstrance to Able's tortured conscience. Keeping watch had to include some of hoping for a greater good, and helping a soul reach Paradise.

☙

32 - LIBBY

When I became a man...

Vic and I went to Jordan's school together to pick him up. We arrived before classes were over for the day to speak to Principal Findley regarding our plan to take him out of school two weeks ahead of the scheduled holiday break. The Principal's secretary, Marie, showed us into his office, a large room with equally large and pretentious looming cherry wood furniture, to wait.

Our request wasn't unusual amongst our set. Often, families went skiing in Europe or some such thing. We had rarely made special arrangements like this, and never for so long of a time.

"What are you thinking about so furiously?" Vic whispered, interrupting my train of thought.

"Just silly things."

Vic raised his brows and opened his mouth to say something when Findley's door opened. Seeing Mrs. Stokes, the counselor for Jordan's grade, accompanying the principal, made me glad Vic was with me.

"Mrs. Davis. And Mr. Davis, too. It's good to see you." Findley shook hands with us, and waved his hand at Stokes. "You know Mrs. Stokes, of course, Jordan's school counselor."

I watched Vic bob his head toward her. "Of course. Nice to see you again."

I just smiled and said nothing, but hoped it was nice to see her, too. I did not recall having to deal with a counselor the last time we requested a release for our son. She was one of those seemingly well-adjusted, firm types, with character lines on either side of her nose, nice eyes and a classic short wavy hairstyle. I thought she was around my age, and married to Northbay's assistant chief of police. I could imagine the dinner conversations at their house.

Findley sat behind his desk and picked up the form we had filled out. Stokes sat beside Vic. Findley reminded me of a dried-up cowboy with stick-out ears to hold up his ten-gallon hat. He fiddled with the paper, the only thing besides the phone and computer on the shiny expanse of his desk, and pretended to read it. He looked up at Vic and me. His muted yellow polka dot tie puffed up under his neck, arching out from his lemony colored sweater vest. I made a mental note to buy the man a tie clasp for a Christmas gift. "I understand you want to remove Jordan from school for approximately a month."

I could feel that something was bothering him, something that didn't have to do with our request. "Only two and a half weeks, really, considering Christmas vacation." I said. "I saw his last report. Mr. Hasselberg seems to think he's doing well with his work."

Findley punched up a file on the computer. "He may be doing well, but surely you've noticed a general downward trend in his overall grade average?" Findley turned the screen toward us. Vic leaned in to study it. I fiddled with the pleat of my slacks.

My husband sat back after a few moments and crossed his legs. "I'm glad you're keeping an eye on this. Apparently this year, he's dropped a quarter point on average grade in the academics. Is that what I understand from this report? It's only the first semester. We can watch him, give him help when he needs it."

A quarter of a point. I glanced at Stokes, who was frowning. Ah, not the entire story. I didn't think so. Stokes faced us. "A quarter of a point average grade reduction might not normally be cause for alarm. What concerns us most is a shift in attitude from Jordan."

Vic sat up. "Attitude? Is he—"

"If he's been rude, we'll speak to him," I said.

"It's not that." Stokes looked at Findley, who shrugged. "The gym teacher found blood on his towel," she said. "He refused to say where it came from, or let us look at him. It wasn't that much, but—"

"When was this? Why didn't you call us right away?"

I felt Vic's anger vibes and reached over to put my hand on his. *But, blood?* "How much? Where? He was hurt in class?"

Findley looked at me. "Just a swipe, Mrs. Davis. Like from a scratch or something. And Mr. Schultz said no, nothing happened in class. Not even in the locker room, as far as he knew. Normally, we immediately call in the police if we suspect any kind of abuse. From any source," Findley said.

"Wait just a minute!" My husband surged to his feet. "What are you trying to say?"

I watched Stokes's reaction. She looked alarmed, as though she hadn't seen that coming from Findley.

"Where is my son?" Vic thundered.

"Vic!" I jumped to my feet, too, and touched his arm. "Please, let's hear what they have to say. No one's made any accusations, yet."

Vic sat, slowly. I did too.

Mrs. Stokes regained her calm, concerned expression. "Has anything unusual happened at home?"

I felt Vic's deep breath. "I just finished a long job overseas." He looked at me, almost willing the admission about my latest diagnosis.

I would not give in. "Mr. Davis will be spending more time at home. I think the change will be good for Jordan. For all of us. Can you explain more about what you think is bothering Jordan? Or can we speak to Mr. Schultz? If Jordan's hurt, do you think we need to take him to his pediatrician?"

"Mr. Schultz showed us the towel," Stokes said.

I nodded, impatient. "You said that. But I'd like to see it too. What did Jordan say?"

"He said he accidentally cut himself with a sharp edge of his belt buckle when he was getting dressed after class. The boys sometimes get a little foolish, Mr. Schultz told us."

Findley sighed. "He promised to be more diligent in his observations in the future."

Vic cast his assessing gaze at Findley, then at Stokes. I had seen this look for years, usually in determining whether a piece of equipment would fit in the allotted space, or whether someone would follow through on what was promised. If I could capture this scenario on canvas, I would have added some layers of light to chase away the heaviness of fear. "You said you were concerned about Jordan's attitude."

Stokes answered him without a glance at her boss. "He's been withdrawn. The teachers make reports on all the students at least once a quarter, more often when there is any hint of the slightest concern. Jordan has never been very...outgoing?" Why did she look at me? This was her show. "Lately, I've had a report of belligerence—"

"What?" Vic asked.

"In class, where he refused to respond to a direct question and a direct request in English class. And one incident in the lunchroom, where he threw another student's full lunch tray across a table."

The anger resurged in Vic's voice. "Why didn't you call us?"

Findley held up his hand. "Jordan claimed it was an accident, that there was some roughhousing going on, and he got carried away. The other student agreed."

"We want to help get to the bottom of this," Stokes said. "If there's anything you can tell us that would help us understand and work with you, please, say so."

Vic looked at me again. I felt the blood drain from my face. "I'm having some medical issues." I kept my eyes on Vic. "I want Jordan kept away from all of this. Until it's over."

The counselor apparently disagreed. "But, don't you see? Not being told what's happening might be just the problem here."

❧

33 - ABLE

...I gave up childish ways

"How do people decide on hospice care? And what draws them here?" Brother Able led the workshop portion of the weekly staff meeting in the beginning of December.

Liz Carrelton asked him to spend time at each gathering to foster enthusiasm amongst the workers, whether they liked it or not. "A successful business must employ a spirit of camaraderie. If nothing else, let them complain about how much they hate being enthused instead of other petty issues. Just make us proud to be partners in this work environment," she had ordered.

Able complied, to the best of his abilities. Starting off with quotes, jokes, a few non-threatening statistics, he managed to fill a half hour without resorting to a team cheer.

Dr. Kasey Salisbury, the new psychotherapist, sat attentively. She had been hired to fill in for Dr. O'Brien's maternity leave, but would most likely stay to complement the staff. Able cringed at the disservice to the patients and families of revolving therapists, with Brother Michael and Dr. Hernandez's quick departures.

Able clicked through the organization's website. "In the electronic age, it's easy to pass ourselves off as a two-dimensional pretty place to spend your final days. People choose us because they not only see that we can give them good care, they feel the sense of privilege we have been given to share the last moments of life. Our reputation is not just from statistics, or beautiful surroundings, or even good reports from inspectors, but relies on word of mouth based on how we treat our honored guests.

"Let's face it, no one wants to die. But if they know we'll do what we can to make their passing dignified and comfortable, they will choose us to help them on their journey from this life to the next."

When the meeting was over, Able walked Dr. Salisbury to the cafeteria for lunch. After they took their trays to a table and settled in, Able asked about her adjustment to the complex and her new job. "Do you have any questions?"

Dr. Salisbury chuckled. "I'm just getting to the point where I can figure out what to ask. But nothing specific right now, thanks."

"I think you'll find June a good person to talk to."

"I enjoy having someone to bounce around treatment options with again. June has been very kind helping me as I learn how to deal with whole families at once."

During the initial interview Able guessed Dr. Salisbury to be in her early forties, and was later gratified to learn she was closer to his own age. She was a psychotherapist, then finished her PhD after her husband's death. Over the other candidates he had interviewed, she had the unfortunate benefit of having dealt with family suffering at close range. "You had a private practice, I understand."

"Yes, with my husband. We had couple's therapy, but occasionally a family would come in to try and work out issues. It's a different challenge to help all the members of a family unit engage in working through their emotions as they say good-bye to their loved ones."

Able picked the mandarin oranges out of his dish of cottage

● ● ●

cheese to eat first. "Do you find your own experiences helpful?"

Dr. Salisbury swallowed her bite of chef's salad and wiped her mouth. "Because of my husband's death? Some people would say that because I've been through the loss of a loved one, I should understand what they're going through. But what I've come to know is that every human being reacts differently in any situation. No one can figure out how he'll respond to the news of impending death, let alone the process. That's the patient. The family is even more unpredictable. Even if a wife already lost a spouse through divorce or death, she can't expect to feel and react the same way if it happens a second time." Dr. Salisbury smiled. "But I'm sure you have discovered as much yourself."

"The only formula in family counseling is that nothing is constant. Emotions fluctuate moment by moment." He studied the woman. She was a professional, from her elegant hand gestures, to the tailored suit she wore, to the discreet earrings tucked inside black shoulder-length hair. "It's difficult to watch people die. Especially if you have the chance to get to know them.

"Eighteen patients have died since I came on staff. I counseled with three, one of them only once. I can cry, Brother Able. I hope I'll know when to ask for a break. I also appreciate the liberty to stay with a family in need, even if my shift is over."

"Scheduling death is beyond anyone's means. We are obligated to care for each other, as well as our patients. Be assured, we watch carefully. The debriefings after a death help."

"That's a good idea. Since I'm so new, those meetings did help me get to know how some of the other staff members participate in care."

"I noticed you've made an effort to get to know a good cross section of the staff."

"My parents both worked at a city hospital. My dad was a

night custodian. My mom worked her way up from cook to switchboard. I learned early on from listening to them that any place worth beans runs on a happy staff. You can tell how happy the employees are by how clean the corners are and how good the food is. The first time I visited, I checked the corners."

"And how did you find them?"

"Sparkling."

"Food?"

"Excellent—not just dumped from cans. I knew then that I wanted to work in a place where people take pride in what they do."

"Even if the events make for an emotional joy ride?"

Dr. Salisbury leaned back in her chair and glanced around the room. Able followed her assessment. Blinds were half set against the early afternoon glare. The same wood-like vinyl was laid throughout, with tiled paths winding around tables and along the food counter. The walls were a lighter version of the maroon in the lobby with a dusting of silver weaving through.

"Life is an emotional joy ride," she said. "Shouldn't we expect the same of death?"

Able laughed. "Absolutely!"

34 – LIBBY

O my people, what have I done to you?

"**N**ot being told?" I was incredulous at the audacity of Jordan's school counselor. Only Vic's warning hand on my arm kept me in my seat. What could be going through this woman's mind that she could possibly ask a question like that. "Do you have children of your own, Mrs. Stokes? I don't think you understand what we went through the last time."

"But I do. I was here three years ago. I don't think you understand fully how much he suffered."

"We had him in therapy."

The school bell rang. I looked at the clock. Three thirty. The sound of a thousand feet tromping through corridors seeped underneath closed doors.

"Mr. and Mrs. Davis, you have my deepest sympathies," Mr. Findley said. "I think it would be good for Jordan to spend time with you." He signed the paper and handed it to Stokes. "I'll send the request to his teachers so that Jordan will be able to keep up with his work during his absence." Findley stood, saying, "My secretary sent a note to have Jordan meet you here. Thank you both for coming in, and I hope we'll all continue to work together. Please let us know if there's anything else we can do to help."

I watched his back through narrowed eyes, wondering if I was supposed to laugh or scream. Vic looked like he'd been blindsided and Stokes studied us as if we were lab rats in a maze. Yep, bad parents. I would not have been surprised to see the child welfare people coming through the door next.

I tried to alleviate some of the tension in the room. "I...we are grateful for your concern, Mrs. Stokes. We all have Jordan's best interest at heart. I can see that. If you have any suggestions—"

Findley's door opened at that point. Jordan came through, coat in arms, backpack slung over a shoulder. A whiff of excitement whirled in with him, adrenaline-fueled anticipation that piled up behind an invisible wall when he noticed Mrs. Stokes sitting next to his father.

"Mrs. Stokes was telling us disturbing news about your recent behavior," Vic said.

"Vic, we should go," I said.

"Son, I'd like to see the place where you cut yourself."

"This isn't the place or the time, Vic. Let's go," I repeated.

"Jordan."

I watched my son take a step backward from his father and my heart ached for them.

"Dad, it's nothing. We were just goofing off. It was an accident."

"Is anyone trying to hurt you?"

"No, Dad. It's nothing like that, honest. It's just a little cut, here," he hitched the coat up higher on his right arm and pointed to his left side. "Just by my hip, that's all. I didn't mean to get the towel messed up. I-I'll take it home and wash it."

"Jordan, we're not worried about the towel," Mrs. Stokes said. "We're concerned about you."

"I already told you, in your office when you were making me miss history, that there's no bullying going on."

"Jordan!" I hissed at him.

Vic's voice was stern, like my father's once had been. "And that's another thing, son. What's this about refusing to answer a question in class? When adults address you, you answer back. Politely, and with the correct information."

"I already apologized. I just wasn't paying attention."

I jumped up, awkwardly. "It's all right, Jordan. I'm glad you apologized. We should be going." I turned to reach for my coat, which I'd slung over the back of my chair. "Thank you for your time, Mrs. Stokes. We'll be in touch."

Vic moved slowly. He towered over the guidance counselor. Usually he made me feel secure. Mrs. Stokes craned her neck to look at him while he shook her hand. "You must let us know immediately if you or Jordan have any difficulties of any kind," he told her.

"We will."

The ride home took place in the eye of the storm. Once there, Jordan tossed his coat on his hook and made for the steps.

Vic's tone was soft. "Jordan."

Jordan didn't turn around. "Can I start my homework? Please."

"Later. Come in here, first."

My husband led the way into the family room. He and Jordan sat in wing chairs while I took the sofa. Vic looked at me, not for permission, or in accusation, but in resignation. "I want to talk about why we're letting you get out of school before Christmas vacation. Jordan, this trip is going to serve a couple of purposes. Your mother won't be coming with us."

"Are you getting a divorce?" Jordan asked.

"Of course not," Vic said. He frowned as his cheeks lit. "Where did you...never mind."

I wasn't surprised at Jordan's thinking because so many of his friends' parents had split up. Maybe divorce was easier to wonder about than another round of visiting his mother in the hospital.

Vic's sigh went clear to my bones. "Jordan, the main point I want to make is that this behavior cannot continue. Cannot. Do you understand me?"

"It's not my fault, Dad. I don't know what everybody's so upset about. I had a couple of accidents. I'm a growing kid. Awkward teenager. Things happen. I didn't mean it."

"That kind of attitude will not make me sympathetic to your case, young man. If we're going to be spending the next few weeks in close company, we're going to have to make some adjustments. The first of which is I will never hear the words 'it's not my fault' from your lips again. Do I make myself clear?"

"Yes, Dad." Jordan said the words while staring straight ahead.

"Mrs. Stokes had a point, Libby."

I knew it was coming. As soon as the woman uttered the words, I knew Vic would take her side. Maybe they were right. But my son would hear this from me.

"Jordan," I said, looking at his left cheek, "I'm going to be in Texas while you and Dad go away for Christmas. I'm taking part in a cancer treatment study."

Vic broke the silence first. "Jordan?"

"So, will Nona be here for Christmas?" he asked.

"Jordan! Your mother—"

"Don't worry, Jordan. I already got your present. Dad will give it to you." I stood up and approached him. I wrapped my hand around his head and drew it to my hip, resisting his attempt to pull away. "I love you, Jordan. Everything will be okay. You'll see." I released him. "Vic, why don't you two call for take-out for supper? I have some packing to do."

I cringed at the last words I heard from the room as I put my

* * *

foot on the first riser.

"Jordan, I need to see that cut."

I heard my husband's footfalls before he rapped at my bedroom door. I was folding a bathrobe into my suitcase and looked up when he came into the room.

"He didn't mean it, Lib."

"I know."

"We're all worried about you."

"But that's just the problem." I tossed the garment toward the suitcase and plopped on my bed. "I don't want any of this to be happening at all. I don't want anyone to have to be worried about me. I'm the mom. I'm supposed to be worried about everyone else." I pursed my mouth. "Speaking of which, did you see Jordan's cut?"

His own mouth mirrored mine. "Yes. Just a little scratch below his bellybutton, so he was embarrassed to show anyone."

"You think that's all?"

"No." Vic pushed the case out of his way and sat next to me. "Are you sure you're doing the right thing, Libby?"

"How can I be? I thought we were doing the right thing last time and look what happened."

"Can I talk to Anna?"

"Sure. I'll call the office and sign off to let you see any test results." At this point, I didn't care. No one knew what I had planned after I spent a little time in Texas.

I wanted to leave before noon on Saturday so that I wouldn't make myself too tired on the drive. I planned to arrive in Texas on Sunday evening, settle in and show up at the university hospital on Monday morning. I had a good map, a reservation about half way for the first night, and my bags packed.

Vic set my luggage in the back of the Corolla Nona usually drove when she was home. Since she flew to South Carolina, she wouldn't need the car so I would take it to Texas. I figured she could drive mine when she returned. Or Vic could get her whatever she wanted. Vic wouldn't find out about my little tryst with our lawyer and the trust money I rearranged until he had our tax consultant look over the last year's income and damages closer to March. I should be long cold by then, anyway. "You have Nona's cousin's number, too, don't you?"

His lips barely moved. "Yes." I could see by the tautness of his shoulders and the mask of his face that he was on auto pilot for emotional control. He had always been good at that. I needed to be physically separate from the stress to be successful with that kind of effort. All that psychology stuff—you know, think up a place for yourself, imagine yourself there, that kind of thing, made me impatient. I jumped when Vic called for Jordan.

"He knew you were getting ready to go," Vic muttered. "I'll go see what's keeping him."

"Vic, wait." I wanted this memory of him alone, like we used to be. But when he turned to me with brows raised, I felt shy. "I just wanted to say…to tell you that I'm…thankful. For everything you've done. You're a good man, given me everything I've ever wanted."

His silence was unnerving.

"That's all." I looked at my booted feet. Silly. I wouldn't want to wear winter boots in Texas. "And that I know you and Jordan will have a good holiday." I braved a look at his face again. "Thank you for letting me do this too. And, be patient with Jordan. He's a teenager. Maybe you weren't like him when you were that age—"

The pressure of his lips against mine stopped my flow of last-minute whispered instructions. "This isn't good-bye, Libby. I'll call you tonight. Like always." He took my hand and led me back in the house. "Come, talk to our son."

Jordan stood on the other side of the island in the kitchen. He gave me a crooked smile. "Just giving you guys a chance to be alone." The smile didn't reach his dark eyes. For the first time since I gave in to Nona and Anna, I felt a chill of despair. In motherhood, I had failed to create a lasting bond with my child. I hoped God wouldn't judge me too harshly for that. Perhaps this cancer study would help someone else eventually. Maybe God would accept that for penance.

"Jordan, come. Let's have a family prayer." Vic held out his arm. I will always remember that smile Jordan had, a dead, fake twist of his mouth. He came to us, even allowed his father to put an arm around him as Vic held us both and said words of petition, of comfort, of feeling. "It's your turn, Jordan."

"Lord, when you take my mom home to heaven, let her know she's in good hands. Amen."

I swayed, held up by Vic's strength. I kept my eyes closed while I listened to Vic say, "That's enough, Jordan. Go up to your room. Now."

After I knew Jordan was gone, I pulled away. "Time to go." My voice was too bright, too brittle. I turned toward the garage.

"Libby, don't leave like this. He doesn't mean it. He's confused. I'll help him understand. Please."

"I know. You'll be all right. Maybe you should consider some more therapy, though. You'll be the father Jordan needs right now. He's always just wanted you, ever since he was a baby, remember? I couldn't even nurse him."

"The doctor said it happened occasionally, remember? It's

not your fault. He got over being so sick once we switched to soy."
Vic followed me to the garage.

"But he wanted the bottle from you. You'll check in on Dad once in a while, won't you?"

"Of course. I'll call you every day, just like always."

I opened the car door and got in. "I might not be in good enough shape to talk," I warned him. "The guide said there could be side effects."

"Then you'll just have to listen to my voice, won't you?"

As good last words as any.

● ● ●

35 - CONFIRMATION JOURNAL: NOTMYGRANDMASGOD

Liberty has cancer. We could be talking about America, what with all the laws about everything else. The only thing eighteen-year-old adults can do anymore is get killed in war. Or get married, and only the stupid do that. Old enough to vote and enlist and get kicked out of the house legally, but not old enough to drink or even rent a car. This country is nuts.

So we get to "how does the resurrection of the body comfort you."

Any sane person says resurrection can't comfort anyone. Who'd want that? I mean, there's got to be some comfort in knowing when the pain is over, when you let enough of it out, it's not coming back. People die when they can't stand themselves anymore, or when stuff wears out or doesn't work right.

And that's a whole other thing. Not work right. Is it still not working right wherever you go when you get resurrected? All these people walking around all disgusting and sick or crippled or shot up or hung. Then again, kinda cool. Who knows? Maybe god thinks that's normal.

"My very flesh"? That's nuts. Who'd want the same body? Who'd want christ's body—all busted and gross from nailing and getting speared and spiked. And be like that forever? How would you do anything?

Oh, yeah, right: you sit around and praise god all day. So you don't actually do anything anyway. I'm telling you, this is a lose-lose situation we got going here. I'm not the only one seeing this, am I?

Tony asked a good question—does everyone get resurrected? And Tom, who's really a good guy at heart, even if he's on the side of the righteous, says, yeah, only some of those go to heaven, and some don't. Well, that just goes to show you, it doesn't really matter what you do, right? But, no! He backs himself up. If you're chosen, you want to act frozen. I mean, religious. It's a natural state of humans, or something. This just gets badder all the time.

One thing I can be religious about. If someone has to be resurrected, it should be my mom. I should pray god to end her pain on earth so she can be resurrected. At last—I have a reason that's good for liberty to die.

I'm sorry, confirmation class, I'll be missing the next month, because my dad's making me go to Hawaii with him. Sayonara, everybody!

36 - ABLE

How have I wearied you?

"**A**men."

Able finished his morning prayers in his room and prepared for the rest of the day. Did the hospice's website attract patients? Although he had touted the site as a friendly introduction, he was troubled by the idea that people would choose a place to come based on what they saw on a computer screen. How about the man Able met on the way home from the China conference—Victor, the one whose wife was sick?—how would he determine what to do for her, if, please God no, she should need end-of-life care? Able might have told Victor about Habilus. The man had not even known how ill his wife had become, though, so surely promoting a hospice on the plane ride hadn't been the right thing to do at the time.

Able returned to his room and noted a message in the holder near the door. He put away his things and went to return the call to Brother Harold in Milwaukee. After exchanging pleasantries, Able confirmed his plans to give his annual report on the work of the hospice to the Brothers. He would fly to Wisconsin next week for a few days.

Perhaps he could follow up with Victor. The man with the leaky soul had rarely been far from Able's prayers. Even seeing Nona hadn't driven Victor completely from his mind. Able could make time to try to locate him, if just to ask about the wife and offer more prayers. Someone at Hayden International might be able to help connect them, depending on how closely they guarded their staff. He could explain who he was, and ask if Victor could be given a message.

Able had time to visit the solarium before the evening meal. He stopped in the entrance to survey the room's current occupants. Corinne Peters's nine-year-old daughter was visiting her mother. Able had reviewed Corinne's file when she'd been admitted last week. Pregnant, the woman had delayed treating her breast cancer when she first received her devastating diagnosis. She'd done valiant battle against the disease for the past decade. When it attacked her brain, the New Jersey family decided to come to California to wait out the end in a more temperate climate.

Able treated families here, not diseases. Whole families were affected by an illness, not just patients who were dying. For half of a generation, Able and Rich used this philosophy to provide comfort to those who needed it most; those who, quite often, were not the patients themselves. Helen, who had no one, was one of the exceptions.

Over the years the work became penance for Able and, lately, furious determination for Rich to duplicate the miracle of Joanie's cure. Corinne's daughter, Lorna, had been born with spina bifida. Lorna bore her condition well, just as she had grown up with the knowledge that her mother would not always be part of her life. Lorna held her mother's hand.

Able thought about his daughter Emily at age nine in a wheelchair. Emily couldn't control her fingers enough to grasp anything.

Doug Peters, accompanied by Dr. Kasey Salisbury, entered the solarium from the outside door and joined his wife and daughter. Dr. Salisbury beckoned Able over.

"Hi, Brother Able." Lorna wriggled in the chair, and twisted the hand control so it appeared as though she did a little jig.

Able took the little girl's other hand and two-stepped in a jerky circle while Doug clapped. Kasey laughed and joined in, and even Corinne managed to force her swollen and cracked lips into a smile.

"Does Dr. Rich know about St. Nicholas?" Lorna said after their impromptu dance.

Able had lived on the east coast of Wisconsin long enough to know about the custom Dutch immigrants brought with them. "Let's see." He pulled a mauve padded chair from around a nearby table to sit with them. "You must mean the night when Dutch children fill their shoes with hay for the reindeer and wake up the next morning to find gifts there instead."

Lorna's wide-eyed enthusiasm made him smile. He met Dr. Salisbury's puzzled expression. Able winked at Lorna. "I don't think Dr. Salisbury is Dutch. Are you Dutch?" Lorna bobbed her head vigorously and giggled. Able sat back in the chair. "I always thought Santa Claus came on Christmas Eve, December twenty-fourth. If he comes tonight—"

"That's what I say," Doug cut in.

Lorna crossed her thin arms over her chest. "But we do it at home!"

Able leaned forward and put a finger beside his nose. "I think Dr. Rich knows St. Nicholas personally. And it is the night." Able bent close to Lorna. "Reindeer don't like the heat," he whispered. "But they know the way."

"I wondered why the staff began decorating for the holidays today," Dr. Salisbury said. "Does St. Nicholas Day have anything to do with it?"

"Dr. Rich likes all things in their proper seasons," Able said.

"It's hard enough to anticipate the change of seasons in southern California."

"Wait...wait...." Corinne Peters whispered.

Doug leaned over his wife, brushing the thin hair across her forehead. "What, honey? What did you say?"

"Wait...for Christ...mas."

"She says she wants to wait for Santa to come on the twenty-fourth," Lorna said. "Don't worry, Mom. We'll wait with you. We love you."

Amen, Able thought.

෬

37 - LIBBY

Answer me!

Did I ever mention that I keep "ignorance is bliss" as a back pocket motto? There was no way I could prepare for the experience of participating in a treatment research study. I didn't go online and check other sites; I didn't ask Anna if there was someone I could talk to who had gone through this already. All the laws governing privacy would certainly affect giving out that kind of information. In my heart I didn't want to know what would happen, or how I might feel, or if I should be afraid or hopeful. What kind of people might I encounter, either at the clinic, or in the study. I expected the medical professionals would be typical distanced scientific types, perhaps with poor bedside manners. I could stand that, since I never planned to complete the whole three months the study was supposed to last. Maybe that was unfair, but it was the best I could do at this point in time.

After checking in to the clinical study area and filling out the other forms they don't tell you about when you're filling out the initial forms, and taking the required physical, I was shown into the lead researcher's office. Four huge rubber trees grew to the ceiling in front of two floor-to-ceiling windows. I liked the shade they made, flanking each other. There was some lingering odor I could not immediately identify and it stuck in the back of my mind like that tune you cannot stop from playing over and over. By the time I had counted the rubber trees, tried to think what the smell was and noticed that not all the books on his wall shelf were medical texts, he burst into the room like a waterspout over Lake Michigan.

"Hi, I'm Tom," he said, and squeezed my hand more tightly than I thought polite. "You're Liberty? Nice to meet you. I read in your file that you're from Milwaukee. My name is famous there." It turned out that Dr. Tom Schlitz was neither distant nor poorly mannered.

He could not have been thirty years old. Reddish, sandy hair, too long and too wavy, a wide mouth and way too thin of a build wrapped in a white lab coat did nothing for my peace of mind. But Anna had agreed this would be a professional, securely run cancer study, and I trusted her.

"First of all, do you have any questions?" The doctor called Tom sat behind a big desk, folded his hands on top of it and leaned forward.

"I don't know what to ask," I said. I frowned when I realized his tie was decorated with tiny test tubes and bubbling beakers.

He sat back, crossed a leg over his knee and cocked his head. "Liberty. That's an unusual name."

"Everyone calls me Libby. Libby Taylor." Yes, I had dropped Vic's name on purpose. Although Davis was fairly common, Vic's name was well-known in medical circles due to his work. It was also the step I needed to take to redact myself from life.

"What do you expect to get out of this study?"

"Get out of it? I thought I was helping you," I replied. The past two days of driving, trying to reassure Vic that I was fine, and today, the check-in process with the whirl of sights and names and hospital smells was starting to make me cranky.

"Most people think they might be cured."

After a moment I realized I was supposed to respond. "Oh." Maybe I should have made it a question.

"I hope you understand that my study is for treatment development. That's different from drug trial phase. We're not there, yet."

"Yes." I cleared my throat. "My oncologist explained that."

His beeper went off. He checked it, then got to his feet. "What I mean is, what do you think will happen? What do you really want?"

"I really want you to be able to help someone else beat this disease."

"Fair enough. I'm sorry, I have an emergency. I would like to talk some more, though." He grinned.

I realized he was not that young, after all, for there were crinkles around his eyes and gray threaded in the sandiness of his hair. "I expect I'll be seeing you." I got up and preceded him out the door.

There were two hundred and ninety-seven patients enrolled in the Phase I research study, many here now, but most in shifts of about two dozen at various stages. I no longer felt isolated in my disease. We had been warned that if our disease progressed, we would be removed from the study. Adverse reactions during any part of the study and treatment were to be expected. Imagine dozens of women without uteruses spending time together. What would we have to talk about, besides where else in our bodies the cancer had metastasized?

As it turned out, none of us were ever together, could not know each other's names or anything else. The treatment room doors where I reported each day were identified by the doctor's name and my case number. The nurses and other professionals were calm and friendly as they took samples, ran the machines, asked about symptoms. I had never felt more anonymous. The study was double-blind, which meant not even Dr. Tom with the famous last name of one of the legendary Milwaukee beer barons knew exactly who would benefit from his concoctions while we were enrolled.

For the next two weeks I traveled either once or twice a day from the hotel room the drug company paid for to the hospital to participate in the study, the name and nature of which I had agreed not to disclose. No fears there. I couldn't pronounce the scientific terminology, anyway. I lounged in the half-lit impersonal room on a padded chaise where I received infusions over the course of a quiet hour. I could watch television, but I chose not to while the IV bag of drugs were emptied and replaced with saline to flush the tubing for another half an hour. I had way too much time to think. I suppose I could have brought a book or puzzle to work. The atmosphere seemed too dim even for that and I doubted I could concentrate. I wondered what my son was doing now, if Vic was really listening to him, how Nona was getting along with her cousin and whether she'd stay with Jordan when she got back. I think she knew I wouldn't come home again.

A tidbit of information Nona had dropped in casual conversation, long before the school year began, surfaced. She mentioned that Jordan asked her if he could do his own laundry, and would she show him how to do it?

At the time, I had appreciated my son's growing independence. Why did my brain red-flag the memory now? I chalked it up to too much saline.

A professional checked my blood pressure constantly, measured my breathing, scanned my leg—it was my *leg*, not a tumor-carrying piece of meat—and I submitted to filling vials of blood both before and after treatment to check for toxicity, as well as other effects of Tom's treatment. I responded to more personal questions about my elimination habits and appetite and dreams than I ever had before in my life.

About day three, I began to suspect that another woman staying at the same hotel was involved in the study group. I guessed her to be a decade older than me, with one of those fuss free round beige permanents that women like to wear. She sat alone at supper, reading. I had seen her come and go a couple of times, around the same time as I. Once I caught the white of a bandage under the sleeve of her sweater. Should I approach her?

That evening, as I hustled out of my room during commercial time for fresh ice, I saw her leaving her room at the same time. At least, I assumed it was her own room, four doors down on the other side of the green-carpeted hall. She had an ice bucket too.

"I've seen you around," she said, by way of greeting while I waited beside her at the ice machine. She filled her bucket, then hesitated. "We're not supposed to know each other, but I bet we have something in common."

"You haven't, by any chance, been spending time at the University clinic, have you?" I asked. I felt like we were talking in signals, like spies who hadn't met, testing the secret language.

"Yes. Would you like to talk? Come on. Stop in my room."

We spent the first night coming up with code names for each other according to our professed fantasy flower life. She was Daisy, for the Shasta daisies she said she used to pick and play the "loves me, loves me not" game. For this period of time, I would be nothing like the Liberty Taylor Davis anyone knew in Wisconsin. I was Lily, for the dark red daylilies my mother let run wild all around the Door County property. The speckled trumpets bloomed one day a year, scenting the air with memories of opening the cabin for the season, of meeting Vic for the first time and falling in love before he could even see me. I talked to her about anything but my home, and entertained my new friend with stories of my trips overseas. I seemed exotic even to my own ears. Of course, she had no way of knowing if I told the truth or not. I listened to her tales, too, trying to decipher reality from wishing.

Of the study itself, the expected outcomes, I cared nothing. I told Dr. Schlitz the truth—that I hoped he would help other people, but I did not need to be cured. I felt no guilt that I would drop out after this first treatment and head for California. The only activity I allowed myself of my old life was a small sketchpad I began to fill with little pencil drawings of parts of things: the IV pole and bag and snaking tubing, the dials on the machines next to my cot, the table setting of the evening meal in the hotel, the nurses' hands while they capped the tubes of blood. My drawings were black and white. Never faces or other identifying characteristics, of course. After I began to photograph, I had trouble with perspectives of people's faces, anyway. My craft business was limited to nonhuman aspects.

Had been. I probably should have cleaned out my office before I left. At least I had finished all the work before I stopped accepting new projects, though I hadn't made any such announcement on the website. Maybe Nona and Vic would give my supplies to some group home or something.

Vic called each evening like he promised. I imagined Hawaii in the shining afternoon, the smooth lap of ocean on the beach, the pungent scent of hibiscus on the air. Vic took Jordan to a luau, he said, the other night. Jordan seemed less anxious, calmer in manner, Vic said. I knew that the main thing Jordan needed was to be away from the thing that fed on my bones.

We test subjects ate well enough. The sponsor gave us vouchers to eat lunch in the hospital cafeteria, which wasn't bad.

The hospital had to set a good example and served tasty, greaseless fare.

Daisy seemed obsessed by the tests. She constantly telephoned the hospital and hung around the lab, even though she said they shooed her away. She knew she couldn't find out individual responses. "I just want to know how the whole thing is going in general. Doing this is so much better than sitting in the hospital at home, twiddling my thumbs or staring at my doctor who didn't know what to do next." Daisy and her bitten fingernails were from Ottawa, Ontario but she had a son who lived an hour outside of Houston.

Daisy expected to be cured. There were nine projected responses to the study: complete; partial; stable disease, progressive disease, early death from malignancy, early death from toxicity, early death from other causes, or unknown due to insufficient data. I wondered which she would fall into. I already knew my outcome, and it didn't have anything to do with the study.

Over the weekend, I unplugged the phone, turned on the room air conditioner for background noise, and slept. Daisy went to be with her son's family. I had a PET scan at the beginning of the second week to determine changes in tumor metabolism. At the end of the first session, I would have my tumor biopsied.

For the biopsy procedure, I had been prepped, mildly sedated and draped, just like the last time in Anna's room. I lay, enjoying the sensation of weightlessness and feeling totally unconcerned about much of anything. A gowned figure came into the room.

"Libby, I'm sorry I haven't been able to finish our talk when you first arrived," the figure said.

"Talk arrived?" I parroted. I tried to frown in recollection but breathed out a laugh instead. "I don't know."

The figure leaned over me. "I'm Dr. Schlitz, Libby. Remember?"

I had not seen him during the previous days, except for the briefest of helloes during one of my infusion sessions. I had not expected him and was unprepared to recognize his masked face. "Sorry." I tried to stop the inane laugh and succeeded in making a choking cough.

"How are you feeling?" The mask loomed in my face. I could not focus and blinked.

"I'm fine. How are you?"

"I'm all right. Let's get this over with, shall we? Can you be still for a few minutes?"

"I think so."

The next thing I remember is waking slowly in a darkened room, not the same place as the biopsy. Someone shifted in a nearby chair when I moved. The person got up and came toward me. I felt cool hands on my forehead.

"How are you, Libby? You had an unhappy reaction to the sedation, but you'll be fine in the morning."

"Dr. Schlitz. I have a headache. What time is it?" I squinted toward the window.

The hand moved from my head to an IV bag hung above the bed. "I'll give you something for the headache. It's about two thirty."

"In the afternoon? I shouldn't—"

"In the morning."

Startled, I blinked the rest of the sleep from my eyes. "What happened? Why are you here? Shouldn't you be in bed?" In my woozy state I must have sounded like his mother. A splash of heat crossed my cheeks.

● ● ●

"You stopped breathing, but you'll be all right. Just a bad reaction." His voice was warm, smiley-sounding. The tone made me want to check for Snoopy bandages. I faced the direction of the voice and tried to make out his form in the mostly dark room. My eyes adjusted to the dim lights of the pieces of equipment stationed around me. "Thank you for your concern, but I wanted to check on you. You should try and sleep now."

"Did you save my life?"

"Nothing so dramatic, Libby. You just needed a little jump start."

I don't know why I asked the next question. "Are you okay?"

I heard him sigh. "I will be."

In the morning before I left the hospital for the hotel, I was told that the study was to be terminated. I was thanked, told I should come for a final interview and afterward, could leave.

As I left the hotel for the final time, I saw a heavyset young man with thinning hair come out of Daisy's room, carrying a suitcase. He wiped his face with a handkerchief. I studied my key card, debating, while he fiddled with the latch on the door.

"Excuse me, but did you happen to know the woman who stayed in that room?" I asked.

He did not turn around. "She was my mother."

"Was? Oh, no."

"I'm so-sorry. I can't talk right now." He walked away, as if afraid I might chase him down and ask him more questions.

I was glad that I didn't have to feel guilty about checking out of the hotel and starting for California later in the day.

The concierge arranged a bus ticket for me with the cash I had withdrawn on my credit card. I mailed the card back to Vic after that. I threw my cell phone in the garbage at the hotel after I erased all the call lists and other information. I parked the car around the side of the hotel in the employee lot and took all the papers out of it. I put my dirty clothes and suitcase in the dumpster, taking only a change for the three days it would take to travel to my planned destination. I figured I'd die in a hospital gown.

A city bus would take me to the Dallas Park and Ride for a four thirty p.m. departure. I never slept well anymore, so the thought of spending an interrupted night on a cross-country adventure didn't bother me. The occasional jolt on the bus was excruciating, but during the layover in Abilene, I bought a cushion. We passengers blinked like owls during the transfer at Amarillo. I drank coffee so I wouldn't fall asleep during the hour I spent in the terminal. I guarded my bag, although in truth, I didn't care that much if it went missing. I wore the paperwork from my lawyer under my shirt.

At Vegas I checked into a motel and, with the help of pharmaceuticals from the nearby free clinic, slept like the dead. I gathered my strength during the next day for the last leg of my journey, which would end in San Diego. That, too, would take the better part of a day. I threw out my dirty clothes the next morning, and at lunch time, steeled myself for another ride. We reached San Diego at nine o'clock that night. I checked into a dingy little adobe motel with a neon sign that flashed alternating palm and Joshua trees.

In the morning, I went for a last walk on the beach.

38 - WEB CHAT: SHAREMYDISEASE

Surviving11 says: Some information about research studies came up the other day. How can the federal government allow these experiments?

Tinman says: Doctors gotta find medicine that works somehow. How else are they going to do it?

GraceofGod says: My cousin Laverle was in one of those. For a new kind of heart medicine. He died.

Anonymous says: Someone really has to be desperate to be a guinea pig like that.

Tinman says: Usually. No place else to go.

Sixfeetunder says: I checked the side effects on the one my doc wanted to set me up in, and no way. I'd rather go peaceable.

Tin man says: Not everyone has that choice.

Surviving11 says: How would you make it peaceable?

GraceofGod says: My grandma stopped eating and drinking. We sat by her bed. We prayed and sang hymns. It was beautiful. She woke up a little at the end and said I'm coming home, Jesus! We clapped and laughed and sang her home.

raynchar574 says: That sounds rude. I want it quiet. What about the person next door.

Sixfeetunder says: I wouldn't let them humiliate me with tubes in every orifice and bags and needles and stupid violins everywhere. People prodding you every minute. Everyone standing around crying. No, sir. No way.

Surviving11 says: What would you do?

raynchar574 says: My wife is quite comfortable. I don't know where you got your information, six feet under.

Surviving11 says: Where are you, raynchar574?

raynchar574 says: That's private. But I can tell you, I don't think she's suffering.

Tinman says: Good to know.

GraceofGod says: I'm praying for you, Ray. God is holding you in his hands. Precious Lord, keep that poor man's wife and his own soul in perfect peace.

Surviving11 says: Are you talking about euthanasia, sixfeetunder?

Surviving11 says: Are you?

Surviving11 says: Are you all so scared to talk about it? It's legal in some states.

GraceofGod says: We're praying for you.

39 – ABLE

For I brought you up from the land of Egypt...

After morning prayers, Able had breakfast with Dr. Salisbury in the lonely wing set aside for Alexian Brothers and traveling associates. He was currently the only occupant.

"I apologize for having to leave you so soon, Dr. Salisbury. I'm confident you're going to do a fine job. Dr. Henderson will help you in any way that you need. I don't expect to be away more than five days, and you may call me any time of the day or night with any questions."

"Thank you, Brother Able. I'm not one of those overly confident types. If I don't feel comfortable, I'll certainly ask Dr. Henderson's advice."

"Mrs. Carrelton and Dr. Bernard, of course, will be here to help you out, as well."

They took their empty dishes to the kitchen.

Dr. Salisbury's demeanor reassured Able that he had made the right recommendation in her hire. "Thank you for your time, Brother Able. I wish you a pleasant journey. I have some appointments this morning,"

Bobby from the grounds crew took him to the terminal with plenty of time to check in. Able's flight to Milwaukee took place in the lull between busy Thanksgiving and the rush of Christmas. A three-hour layover in Kansas City gave him time to contemplate his report to the Brothers. And a strategy to track down Victor at Hayden International.

Able's flight arrived late at Mitchell International Airport in Milwaukee. Brother Philip, a second-year Novice to whom Able had been introduced last year, met him.

"Brother Philip. I thank you for your service at this late hour."

"My pleasure, Brother Able. You had a good journey, I trust? The cold of Wisconsin must be disconcerting after southern California. I'm parked down this way. This is your bag? May I?"

Able allowed the angular young man to take his carry-on bag and followed him through the whooshing glass doors to the parking area. "Do I detect a note of nostalgia for a warmer climate?" Able's escort, who originally hailed from Oklahoma, would earn a master's degree in Human Resource Management next spring.

Philip smiled widely as he stowed Able's bag in the trunk. "I go where I am sent, Brother."

Able laughed. "Well said, Brother. Amen." He did not expect anyone to meet him after midnight at the Community House. He thanked Philip and they said good night.

Communal morning prayer and Mass refreshed Able's spirit. He missed Brother Michael's fellow Alexian presence in California. Not that Able felt exiled in any way. He looked forward to spending time in community here and giving his report tomorrow.

"Brother Harold, what can I do?" Able asked after breakfast. Brother Harold Schowalter, current director of Alexian Village Manor, showed him a few clerical tasks where he could lend a hand. Harold was a square chunk of very German-looking man. Swarthy with square black glasses decorating the middle of his face, he looked as though he would be more at home in a beer tent rather than the black and white collar of his profession.

"Tomorrow, of course, will be a day filled with meetings," Brother Harold said.

Able smiled to himself as he sorted through documents and folders in Brother Harold's office. No one liked to file. Not even Associates. No matter how Able tried in California, he could not convince Gert the task would not be so odious if she took care of each item on a regular basis instead of saving up the work until it took on a life of its own.

The rote duty allowed Able to consider his schedule. Perhaps he could visit Emily before the evening meal. If he finished the filing quickly, he could take the time to look up the telephone number for Hayden International.

After inserting the last letter into its folder, Able pushed the metal drawer shut and checked his watch. Two forty. He returned to his room and dialed Emily's care facility. Yes, his daughter was available for a visit that afternoon, he was told. Yes, they would expect him around three thirty. He wondered if he would run into Nona, who usually visited during the week. Able changed into casual slacks and sweater while he contemplated his next call.

Finding a number for Hayden International was not as difficult as he feared. However, he could only locate a general toll-free number that would, no doubt, feature a list of impersonal choices.

Able held the phone to his ear without much hope.

"Thank you for calling Hayden International Medical Group. This is Deborah. What can I do for you?"

Startled, Able gripped his handset tighter so the instrument would not slip through his fingers. "Pardon me, Deborah. My name is Able Fenwick. A few months ago, late October, you, well, not you personally, allowed me to take one of your charter flights

• • •

to return to the United States after a conference in China."

"Yes, Mr. Fenwick."

Able heard the clicks of a keyboard. "Brother Fenwick. My apologies. How can I be of service?"

Able blinked. He had been prepared for a circuitous route to a human, if that had been possible. This immediate contact put him out of sorts. What did he want? "There was a passenger with me, one of your employees, a Victor Davis, I believe?"

"Yes, sir. Mr. Victor Davis. That's right."

"We had a good journey. And thank you, by the way."

"You're welcome, sir."

"I wondered if there was some way you could get a message to him. From me? I'm in Milwaukee for a few days and hoped we could connect."

"I regret to inform you that Mr. Davis is away from the office for the next month. But I'd be happy to relay your message."

"Oh." Able reviewed the options. "Yes, thank you. When Mr. Davis is next available, perhaps he'd like to contact me. He mentioned his concerns about his wife, and I hoped to hear good news."

"I'll tell him for you, sir."

"Thank you. I appreciate your help, Deborah." He gave the woman the number of his portable, as well as the extension at the hospice. Perhaps Victor would contact him in California. He wouldn't miss a chance to pray for the Davises, even during a telephone call. A leave of absence or even a vacation this early before Christmas could be a sign. Either they were taking advantage of the time Mrs. Davis had left, or celebrating good news.

Able let Brother Harold know that he would be out for the remainder of the afternoon, but would return for the evening meal. He had not seen Emily for a year. He borrowed a community car and drove to Green Willow, the private facility where she'd lived most of her life. Em would be thirty next year, the age most women dedicated their lives either to their careers or family. Was it easier not to have a choice?

Her room was empty. Able stopped a passing aide. "Excuse me. Do you happen to know where my daughter, Emily, is?"

The woman eyed his ID badge carefully before relaying the information. Able didn't recall seeing her before, which was not unusual, and she apparently hadn't recognize him, either. "Emily is in the common room."

Would Emily remember him? He didn't know why the thought that she would forget him between visits plagued him. She always responded to him whenever he came, and for that he thanked her mother. Able stood in the door for a moment to watch her. She sat in her wheelchair in front of large windows overlooking a natural area of green and water. Bird feeders attracted feathered entertainment, which several residents seemed to enjoy.

Emily's muddy brown eyes flashed when he came into her range of vision. Able wondered if she wanted to jump up and run. "Hi, Emily. Remember me?" He pulled a chair up close to hers.

Emily began to roll her head and shoulders and rock. Her mouth worked around a harsh k-k-k.

"What can I do for you?" Able asked. He straightened her board, then wiped her mouth. "Do you want me to get something for you? Are you cold?" Should he call for help? She might be experiencing a seizure, for all he knew. Perplexed, he turned to seek a nurse or doctor.

A character straight out of Victor Hugo approached them. A little gnome of a person with wild hair and prominent hunch said, "She means Koko."

"Thank you. She wants some hot cocoa?"

The person's cackle was evocative. "No, no. Not to drink. Kitten. To play with."

"Ah. I see. Would you like to…" He and Emily were alone again. Emily made wild jabs at the picture board on her lap. Able leaned in to see that, yes, one of the pictures Emily hit more than the others was a cat. "There's a kitten here at Green Willow?"

"K-k-k-k."

"You like the kitten, I can tell, Emily. What color is it?"

Able stared at his daughter, bemused at the transformation from his visit last year when he wondered if she would turn to stone.

"Here we are," a young lady said at his side. She held a tiger-striped kitten in both hands and squatted in front of Emily. "Look who's come to see Emily. It's Koko."

Emily stopped her odd rocking motion and stared, bright-eyed. Able smiled at the next sound coming from Emily's lips. His daughter's purr matched Koko's.

Pet power worked another miracle. Able had considered introducing pets as part of the hospice care. Patients and their families often brought their non-human friends from home. Able had attended a workshop on the topic. Rich remained nonplussed at the concept of having animals live at the hospice.

Able didn't watch the clock which would only remind him that at some point he'd have to leave again. Emily's eyes drooped soon after her exciting visit with Koko. "Do you want to go back to your room before supper?" Able asked her.

Emily struggled to push her palm over the picture for bed. "M-m-m."

Able unlocked the brakes of the chair and rolled her down

the hall. Once there, Emily's caregiver, Betsy, came to help. "Hi, Mr. Fenwick. How are you?" she asked, politely glossing over the fact that he hadn't visited Green Willows for a long time.

"Fine, thank you. And you?" Here, Able could be Emily's mostly absent parent, not some sorry excuse for a religious Brother. *Ah, Lord God. Forgive me.*

Able brushed Emily's bronzy wisps from her forehead and kissed her. "Good-bye. I love you, Em."

"See you around, Mr. Fenwick."

"See you around, Betsy."

Able drove back to the community house in time to set the table for the evening meal. Afterward, he accepted Brother Harold's chess challenge and played to an audience of Brothers who loudly debated their every move.

Able kept his report on the Habilus hospice complex with its award-winning counseling program to a half hour. He brought his slide show which featured Alexian Associate Gert Berry. Perhaps more associates would be interested in coming to California, even for a short term. He chose not to mention Brother Michael's brief sojourn at the complex.

While Able listened to Brother Harold introduce Father Roland Jaciewiscz from Hungary and the medical mission, he felt the buzz of his phone. He checked the incoming number. Local, 414 area code, but not one he recognized as Green Willow or Nona. Heeding the sense of urgency, and hoping at the same time he was not being irresponsible, he excused himself quietly to answer.

"Yes? Able Fenwick."

"Brother Able? I hope I'm not disturbing you. This is Vic

Davis. The timing of your message cannot be coincidence. I believe we must talk."

40 - CONFIRMATION JOURNAL: NOTMYGRANDMASGOD

Christmas bites. Vacations suck. All Dad did was call her, worry about her, make me say stupid things I didn't mean. And now, just because her phone's dead or something stupid, we have to leave early. Man, I even prayed for the plane to crash into the ocean on the way back, or something cool like that, just for excitement. There wasn't even any turbulence. It's not like we were doing anything exciting in Hawaii anyway.

How boring is sand? It's not like I'm some little kid who gets a kick out of building sand castles or anything. We went to the black sand beach, but it hurt to walk on.

Dad went snorkeling exactly once. Had to wear the long-sleeved shirt, but I could let up for a while, maybe stop. I could stop, if I wanted to. It's not bad. It could just be scratches now.

Dad wouldn't let me go surfing just because of some shark warnings. C'mon! Had some kind of barbecue thing, wore the stupid flowers. Hey, Beecher'll get a kick out of this: I got lei'd in Hawaii. Get it? Haw, haw. They had skeet shooting, but we had to go call the hospital, or something. Rented motor scooters one day, but to do what? Visit a pineapple farm. I kid you not. I gotta get dad lessons for the guy.

Went to Mass twice. I thought they just did some island religion kind of thing here. I mean, I remember there were missionaries, or something, but I thought they all got eaten. Mass is okay. I'm trying to do what he does, but how can I just copy him? I wish he'd tell me what to do that's right so I don't feel like

* * *

a moron who gets everything wrong.

This is not, repeat not, what I signed up for. Oh, but that's just it, isn't it? I didn't get a choice.

Had to do it again, let out some of the bad stuff. But not too deep. Just enough to sting, to remind me that I survived. Next to the other ones under my arm. I covered it with that europaper excuse for TP they use in planes. Is there a mile-high club for slicers?

Ↄ

41 - ABLE

...I have redeemed you from the house of slavery

"Mr. Davis," Able said. He sank into a chair and, holding his cell phone to his ear with a clammy hand. "I was informed you were on vacation with your family."

"I've just returned. My son and I, that is. Can we meet? How soon?"

Able closed his eyes to bring up the rest of the day's scheduled events. He could not miss the reception for the Brothers from Hungary, nor the special evening Mass where Brother Charles Enderly would say his final vows. "I sense you have an emergency, Victor."

"I don't know about that."

"I have obligations to my Order today. Perhaps we could breakfast together tomorrow?"

"Yes, yes. That will give me time to sort out some things. Thank you. Would you come to my home?"

Able agreed, and got directions.

Brother Able stood on the driveway of Victor's brick home after the taxi dropped him off outside a high gate at seven thirty the next morning. A red brick Queen Anne cottage-style home and four-car garage confirmed his suspicion that money had not been enough to grant Victor Davis the desires of his heart. Able walked through the opening and up to opulent front patio.

Victor opened the door. "Brother Able. Thank you for coming. This way. Can I pour you a cup of coffee?"

"Good morning, Victor. It's good to see you again. Yes, coffee would be welcome."

Able followed his host along a brick-lined interior hall, making him feel as though he were passing through a covered courtyard. He glanced into a large living area, white, with classic oak floor and a mantle over the fireplace. Able squinted. There might have been family photographs on the mantle, but he was too far away to see. Large framed artwork, mostly nature close-ups, hung on the walls.

Victor indicated a heavy chair in the dining area. "Please, be seated. How do you take your coffee?"

Victor waited at a heavily carved sideboard, a carafe in hand.

"Black, thank you." The room was just as impersonal as the entryway. Elegant, not cold, but formal, as if staged for a decorating magazine.

"I'm expecting to hear from the police any time," Victor said. "So, forgive me if I have to leave you suddenly."

"This must be devastating for you. If I understood you correctly, you said your wife went somewhere for treatment while you took your son on vacation?"

Victor brought his own cup to the table and sat. "She wished it."

"So your fears were realized."

Victor bowed his head. "Yes."

"And now you haven't heard from her."

"I can't understand it. I learned that her program was cut short. She should have called me and returned home, but I heard nothing. I called the police, of course. When they located her personal belongings and informed me that her car was still at the hotel where she'd been staying, but that she'd checked out, I came home immediately."

"With your son."

"Yes. I'm having trouble with him, or I'd travel south myself and find out what's going on. My son has taken the news very badly. I'm worried about him. He locks himself away in his room with his computers."

"How old is he?"

"Fourteen."

Able sipped at the coffee. "That's not such unusual behavior for a teenaged boy, surely?"

"Perhaps you're right. I'm afraid I haven't been around him as much as I should. I'll be semi-retiring from my position at Hayden, though, in the new year. I hope to spend more time with him."

Able took a deep cleansing breath. "You're probably wondering why I contacted you. I felt compelled to look you up. I've been thinking about you and your family since we met. How can I pray for you?"

"Thank you, Brother Able." Vic gave a deprecatory wave at the room. "It must seem to you that I have the financial resources at my disposal to hire any type of help. And that would be true enough. But, Brother, my faith in Christ is the only thing I can count on right now. My wife is missing and my son has struggles that are beyond my ability to understand. I do not consider prayer to be my last recourse, but my first and best. If it is the Lord's will, I pray my wife be found. Safe. I ask for guidance to deal with my son."

Able cringed inside at Victor's barely perceptible smile, a haunted, choking twist of his lips. "I understand. But, first, if I may, do I remember correctly that you told me your wife has a companion? Perhaps she knows the whereabouts of your wife?"

Victor nodded. "Yes, of course I called her. She is away, too, on leave for the holiday. But she says she's heard nothing. I tried to convince her not to cut her own vacation short, but she'll be arriving at the airport at noon today."

Able drained his cup. "Is there something I can do? Perhaps pick her up?"

"No, no, thank you. But I appreciate the offer."

"Shall we pray, my friend?"

"Please."

Able spoke the first words, "Our Father," when the telephone rang.

"Forgive me," Victor said. He checked a cell phone and rushed into another room.

Able used the interruption to stand and stretch and inspect some of the furnishings. A huge painting of a water lily in greens and rusts decorated the wall opposite the massive side board. He had just bent close to examine the artist's signature when Victor strode back into the room. "I must collect Jordan and see the detectives. Please, excuse me."

"Of course." Able set his hand on Victor's forearm. "Rest assured, I will continue to hold you and your family in prayer. You have my number? I keep my phone with me. Even after I return to California tomorrow, I hope you will contact me and let me know the outcome."

"Yes. Yes, I will. Thank you for coming."

Able didn't want to disturb Victor further and called for a taxi from outside the house.

. . .

❧

42 - LIBBY

You shall eat, but not be satisfied...

I suppose not too many people walk cold into a hospice. Patients, I mean. As soon as Alonzo, the taxi driver, heard my destination and determined I was not a visitor, he began to tell me stories about his mother-in-law who took two years to die in hospice. I laughed at what I thought were the appropriate moments, until I realized that my mirth became real. I gave him a huge tip. I stood on the curb watching the green and white van pull away and felt as though my best friend had dumped me in a strange city where I couldn't speak the language.

I made myself go in the front entrance and ask to be admitted. The poodle-looking woman whose name tag read "Billie" gave me a calculating stare. I probably come across like I belonged at the county mental institution instead, but I was tired. Really, really tired. And if I ended up at the county institution instead, who would care what I said?

I handed my thick portfolio over to Billie who asked me politely enough to have a seat in the elegant maroon and silver waiting area. I shuffled with a cane I picked up in Flagstaff to a padded oxblood leather recliner and hoped I wouldn't fall asleep while waiting. The calm wash of the fake waterfall on moss-green granite, gliding two stories to a pool with circling koi, lulled me to a daze.

"Miss Taylor?"

I should not have been able to set Vic's name aside so easily, but the weeks I'd been away from Milwaukee living as Libby Taylor conditioned me to respond. I opened my lids reluctantly to a pair of eyes that reminded me instantly of the waterfall. I glanced over for a second, hating to lose contact, yet needing to check. Yes. A misty ocean blue with brilliant-flecked granite. Above them were a man's stubby black lashes and thick dark eyebrows with a little round scar under the right one. The man wore a light-colored suede suit coat.

He took my hand and helped me sit up. I squirmed at the sight of the little crowd of people clustered around my chair. Billie from the desk stood there, with a tall slender blonde who was probably a movie star, and an older salt-and-pepper haired woman grasping a clipboard to her chest.

"I hoped I wouldn't fall asleep. I'm sorry." I reached for my cane, which apparently had slipped to the floor. The irreverent thought flashed through my mind: if a cane clattered to the floor of a hospice and no one heard, did it really make a sound?

The man picked up the cane and helped me to my feet as if finding strays in the waiting room were normal procedure. "Would you like to come this way, please?" He motioned down a hall to the left. I blinked myself awake and watched Billie return to her station before I noticed that the older woman also carried the teal-colored file I'd given to Billie with other material. We stopped before a door marked "Richard Bernard MD" and entered an office suite that featured windows facing the far-off seashore, comfortable sofas, and shelves lined with pamphlets and brochures. The faint crash of waves seemed to permeate the entire facility, and I wondered if the sound was shipped in live.

I supposed we were at the security area and I would be escorted out as soon as they figured out where to escort me to. The hospice complex was a good mile off any main road.

● ● ●

The tall woman brought me water in a beautiful glass. I thanked her and looked out of the windows while the others seated themselves. The same woman pulled out a tape recorder from the nearby desk and set it on the coffee table in front of us.

"Do you object to having this conversation recorded?" the man asked.

I shook my head. The woman pushed the "record" button.

"I should introduce myself. I'm Dr. Rich Bernard. This is Dr. June Henderson, and to her left, my assistant, Laura Reeves."

The surprise must have shown on my face, for the doctor smiled. "We don't usually get walk-ins," he said. "We'll need to confirm your records." He indicated the file in Dr. Henderson's hands. "Make some calls and do an exam. But we do not turn away anyone in need."

"That's what your website said," I replied. "I would have called, but I didn't know what to say."

"That's quite all right." Dr. Bernard sat back in his chair and crossed his legs.

"Why don't you tell us about yourself and why you're here?" Dr. Henderson asked. She poised her pen over her clipboard despite the recorder.

I cleared my throat and took another sip of water. "When I learned that my cancer had returned, and was aggressive, I began to research end-of-life care." I flicked my eyes again toward the window that faced the ocean. "Anyway, you have a nice website."

Reeves brought over a small plate of some kind of flat brown cookie, as if my response earned a reward. I sniffed. Ginger.

"Can you tell us about your situation?" Dr. Bernard asked next.

My situation. What should I say? I stared out the window.

• • •

Walking paths wound around the grounds close to the buildings. There were birdfeeders and bushes out there, and pergolas for shady resting spots. I had wondered if I lost my sense of smell on the way to California, but I realized that in the dry states, there had been little of the lushness of verdant growth, exotic flowers, spice of cinnamon and ginger, to entice me. This sense was a double-edged sword of temptation. Perhaps thinking my senses were deserting me was one of the coping mechanisms I needed to help myself turn off. Realizing there were still wondrous things to explore might make me sad to leave.

"Miss Taylor?"

"I'm sorry. My situation is simple. The cancer that attacked my uterus three years ago, for which I had surgery—you can read my case in there," I pointed to Dr. Henderson, "came back." I touched my hip and leg. "Here. It's spread. Metastasized. I don't want to deal with more radiation or anything else. I was in Texas for a while, at a research study that was shut down. I'm tired. I want to die in peace. On my own terms."

I looked up from my leg in time to see the glance between the doctors. Henderson got up. "It was nice to meet you, Miss Taylor. We'll talk again."

Reeves left her desk, too, and accompanied Henderson out of the office.

Dr. Bernard reached for a cookie. "Why do you want to stay here, with us?"

"I told you. I'm from the Midwest, so California seemed like a good choice. Definitely warmer this time of year."

"What about your family?"

"There's no one," I said, proud that I'd prepared myself to answer so smoothly.

"Your husband?" Dr. Bernard bit into the cookie.

So, the rings I'd worn for over twenty years left a dent. Even the month I'd been without hadn't made a difference. "He's no longer in the picture," I told him.

"No children?"

"This is about me," I told him firmly. I tried to cross my legs, but forgot for the moment how numb I was and my leg slipped down my shin. I ploughed on, ignoring my embarrassment. "I have money. My—I have a trust fund worth half a million dollars to give you. I probably won't last long enough to use it up. I don't expect to, but you can have it all." I grinned. "No strings attached."

Dr. Bernard chuckled. "We don't have financial concerns here."

I deflated some at the gentle chastisement. "Oh."

"We have several levels of care. We'll want to give you a physical, as I mentioned, since we have no referral, as well as a psychological evaluation."

"That's it? I'm in?"

Dr. Bernard's smile washed over me gently. "That's it. We'll get you settled and schedule the exams, perhaps even today." He stood and bent toward me. He bore the aroma of ginger from the cookie, not the usual harsh fake spice of men's personal care products. His hands were strong-looking, tanned and matched his fit-looking frame. I let him help me stand. "Are you currently experiencing any pain?"

"Not much." I had held off on anything stronger than the prescription extra-strength acetaminophen I'd gotten at the clinic in Vegas, wanting to stay as clear-headed as possible until I got here. I took a step forward, again forgetting how numb with exhaustion I had made myself walking up the steps to this place. My leg collapsed completely. The doctor caught me around the waist before letting me slide back down to the chair.

• • •

"Sorry, sorry," I mumbled. "I'm more tired than I thought."

"Billie didn't recall having you ask to move a vehicle. Did you come by taxi?"

"Yes. I had a last walk on a beach this morning after I woke. I got in a little late last night from Texas." My face grew hot, especially when he laughed. "I'm planning to regret it under the comfort of narcotics."

Dr. Bernard reached for the buzzer on his assistant's desk. To the voice that answered, he said, "Can you bring a wheelchair to my office, Consuelo? Thank you."

He watched me, as he leaned on the desk. He cocked his head. "We'll do what we can to help you through this, Liberty," he said, using the name on my file. "You're not alone here."

"Thank you. Call me Libby."

"I'm Rich."

The chair arrived, pushed by a copper haired Latina woman with a swaying walk. After both of them helped me in, I tried twice to lift my left foot onto the rest. Rich knelt in front of me and took my foot in his hands. After gently setting it on the rest, he looked at me. This close, I could see the lines around his mouth, the white hair at his temples and a freckle at the outside edge of his right eye. "We'll take care of you, Libby."

"Thank you," I whispered. I folded my hands and bit my lip, looking at my lap while they wheeled me to a room. I paid no attention where we went. My sense of direction had never been keen to begin with and I figured now others would be responsible to get me where I needed to go. The thought of Peter in the Bible talking about being led where he did not want to go flowed through my thoughts.

"Where are your things, Miz Libby?" Consuelo asked.

Even Rich stopped his motions of checking the bedside

connections to look at me.

"I didn't bring anything with me."

"No other clothes?" Consuelo looked at me as if I'd lost my mind, not just my possessions.

"I didn't think I needed anything," I said.

Bernard dismissed Consuelo, who turned and left the room.

"It's just that most people find their own clothing or books or pictures comforting. We'll get you some things to wear."

I hitched myself into a reclining chair set near a small round table with a vase of some orangey flower and wispy ferns. A woman in a white smock with daisies and yellow pants came in. "Hi, Dr. Rich. Who do we have here?"

"Vi, this is Libby. Libby, Vi will help you today. When we get you settled, we'll tell you about our care system. You'll always be able to call on at least three people if you need anything. Vi, right now, Libby could use a change of clothes."

Vi's eyebrows rose so briefly I doubted I saw her reaction. She sized me up. "I'll just step out for a moment. Be right back."

"I'll have our staff get your appointments set up. Our intake coordinator, Mary, will have some paperwork for you. And we photograph everyone, for security purposes."

I watched him fiddle with the remote for a discreetly tucked away large-screen television. He put it down at the sound of a soft buzz of the pager in his belt that even I could hear. He checked it. "Excuse me, Libby. I am needed elsewhere. But, I hope you'll feel comfortable here at Paradise House."

• • •

43 - WEBPOST: THEPLEASUREOFTHEHUNT

For those of you needing to keep your hand in during off seasons, of which there are few, particularly late winter or early spring for most game but coyote and snowshoe hare particularly here in Wisconsin, today we'll talk about opportunities to maintain hand-eye coordination and the pleasure of using a weapon indoors.

I say "a weapon" because, unless you're content with indoor target practice at some nearby club with such a facility, I've found paintball to be the next best thing. We have an indoor paintball gaming center nearby—good for practice. Even better to hunt human prey, which act unpredictably, sometimes like game in the wild. Prices are generally reasonable, and there's usually no problem getting a party together. You decide on your own equipment, or you can rent. Serious gamers think the funds are worth the price of play. The weapons can be realistic, if you're willing to pay. I use the Tippmann X-7. Eyes? You bet. The best ones are the new ones that only go off when they sense a target.

And wear the proper clothing. Some guys go extreme and do the face paint thing *under the mask*, but that's unnecessary, IMHO.

Woodsball is obviously the gaming choice for our purposes. Patience is the key. As my friend DanMan says, "it's all about the waiting." If you can do an outdoor facility, so much the better. No sweating in heavy clothes indoors. I hate the music they sometimes play. It's better if you just listen to yourself breathe through your mask, and it's easier to hear your target's motion if it's quiet.

Reward yourself with a brewski afterward. Hard day's hunt can still be fun indoors. Just be wary of the passionate party dudes.

Rifleman says: Crazy. Don't know what to think. Scratching my head.

manandhisgun says: Crazy is right. So, do you go for the standard CO2 or are you into N2?

pleasureofthehunt says: N2's better. If you're not doing speed ball, you don't need it to last.

manandhisgun says: Front pack or back?

pleasureofthehunt says: Front's more flexible. Plus, you can lean back on the bunkers or a tree better while you wait.

walkingtrigger says: You ain't done nothing till you do true speed.

pleasureofthehunt says: I assume you mean the game.

walkingtrigger says: Whatever.

laser34 says: Camo paint or neon?

pleasureofthehunt says: Camo.

laser34 says: I got a new Spyder MR3 with eyes. Where you at?

pleasureofthehunt says: A buddy has that model. Shoots straight.

SharraT says: Can you still bring your dog?

Camoman says: What do you mean hunt human prey?

pleasureofthehunt says: I misspoke, obviously. Grow up.

$$\text{\large ℭ}$$

44 - ABLE

...and there shall be a hunger within you...

Echoing whispers of hushed conversation rushed toward Able when he stopped outside the laundry after lunch to take care of his personal wash.

"She brought nothing with her."

"Nothing at all? What does she think, that this is some kind of nudist colony?"

Gossip was disallowed on the campus, although he knew he could not entirely forbid the workers from talking privately. The most he could do was ensure it never happened on the patient floors or where families could hear. He gave them fair warning before he entered the room. "Good afternoon, Consuelo, Margarethe," he called out as he pushed open the swinging doors.

Margarethe, the wizened department head, recovered her composure first. "Good afternoon, Brother Able."

"A new patient?" Able smiled at her. "I must check the census."

Consuelo, through her flush, said, "Yes, Brother. Forgive me. Vi told me to ask Margarethe for a supply of clothing for Miz Taylor, who arrived today with nothing but the clothes on her back."

"Oh? And where is she from?"

Margarethe bit her lip, while Consuelo tried to look affronted. "I'm sure I don't know, Brother Able." She turned back to the laundress. "So, I can look in the store?"

"Yes, yes, go ahead. I'll be with you momentarily." Margarethe waved her colleague to the back. "You sure I can't help you with your laundry, Brother? There's no need for you to take the time, you know." Able followed Margarethe's long gray skirt and orthopedic shoes through the door behind her desk.

"I am thankful for the kindnesses I know you already perform for everyone, Margarethe. I can't begin to imagine how you sort out rashes and allergies and scents as it is. Not to mention the even less pleasant aspects of what must be dealt with. You go ahead with Consuelo." Able watched the tiny German woman depart. She was the first and only laundress Rich had hired. The "store" was what they called the stockpile of little-used items left behind by patients and families who did not care to have them back. Most were made into rags or burned, but it was wise to have an emergency cache for times like this.

A new patient? Who came with nothing? Even Able admitted curiosity. He checked the patient roster on his mobile data unit after setting the machine to wash. He'd return later to finish up. Usually Rich notified him personally of new patients at their morning meetings, but Rich had been pre-occupied with an international teleconference. Ah, well, he could go and see Miss Liberty Taylor himself. And ask about her intriguing name.

Able wandered the halls, greeting patients and families until he found the new patient's assigned room. He knocked. And knocked again. Had she fallen asleep? He decided to push the door open a few inches and peek inside.

"Good afternoon, Miss Taylor. Am I disturbing you? I'm Brother Able Fenwick, a family counselor here at Paradise House. I try to meet all of the new patients."

"Come in. I guess I didn't expect anyone to knock."

Really? He stopped at the threshold and studied her as quickly as he could before entering her spacious room. Miss Taylor surprised him. This woman had secrets to haunt her deeper than the death eating her insides. Her dark blond hair was the same color as Joanie's. He wondered if she was alone, or who she had left behind.

"Hello, Fa-Brother. Sorry. No, you're not disturbing me. Please, sit."

Having not had a chance to check her intake forms, he wondered about her faith. No feeling at all escaped from the woman who wore the late Mrs. Harper's white padded satin robe. For someone who was dying, she seemed oddly apathetic in her lack of preparation for the last days or weeks of her life by not bringing any comfortable prized possessions along. Initial apathy often made dealing with a patient harder toward the end. Such a person might turn violent. He had seen it happen.

Able wondered what she had been like in her vitality, for now she appeared a faded copy of a refined woman who would probably wouldn't have been caught dead wearing white with her already pale coloring. Miss Taylor turned a sketchpad face down on her lap as he approached.

"Perhaps there's some confusion, Brother. I have no family with me."

"'Family' is the title, not the requirement. We work with everyone."

"I don't believe I need any counseling, Brother. I told that to Dr. Henderson. I'm well aware of my circumstances."

The patient's response usually clued Able to the direction of conversation. Liberty Taylor did not provide him a working map. Yet. "Everyone else around here will ask you how you feel on the outside." He invited her to smile with him. Her mouth made the slight curve that he imagined she showed to a telemarketer on the other end of the line. "I was going to ask how you feel on the inside," Able said, pretending he knew where this conversation was going. "But I'm more curious about why you're here."

❧

45 - LIBBY

You shall put away but not preserve...

Why was I here?

I sat in the lounger in my pastel-themed room. I closed my eyes and let my head fall back.

I used a gel ink pen with the Paradise House logo to sketch the vine on the little patio outside the French doors. I had never cared much for a leitmotif of pastel. It seemed weak. The mauve swirls on the walls looked so pale I thought of old bismuth pills that I had left in my travel bag a decade ago. The blues made me look twice to see if they were really there. Patternless daubs of color were probably soothing to those who no longer saw well enough to care. Knowing the last thing I would see would probably be a washed-out abstract by an anonymous wallpaper designer almost made me change my mind about the whole thing.

Just kidding.

The sound of the surf in the background was nice, though. I could pretend this was a condo on Maui.

Brother Able asked if I felt all right, not "How are you?", the one question I could answer in at least four different languages. Was my petulance part of second childhood? The last stage before death?

"Yes, yes. I'm fine. You surprised me, that's all. I could have told you how I felt. I just went through that with the other doctor. Henderson. Why am I here? Letting myself die at home seemed so messy, so burdensome."

Maybe I should lighten up. I looked around the ugly room. "I had no choice of room."

I wanted to shock him out of therapist mode, see what he was really like. "I could have killed myself."

What did it matter what he thought? He must have heard it a thousand times already.

Able confirmed my suspicion. "You say you're letting yourself die. How is that different from killing yourself?"

"Ah." Did he just say that in Vic's voice? "Call me Libby. No one told me this was a Catholic-run organization."

"It's not. Are you Catholic?"

"No. My—someone I know, is." Oops, thinking of Vic would have to stop. I was Libby Taylor, the last one standing, the anonymous one, soon to be a memory. But for whom?

"Would you not have come otherwise, Libby?"

Would I? Would all of Vic's rites and ceremonies have changed anything? The oil at Northbay Christian Family Center had done no good, either. "I don't know. I didn't think anything mattered, except that you promised to make me comfortable. I'm allowed that, aren't I? This last little bit of selfishness?"

"There's no one we can contact for you? No one, perhaps, you'd like to talk to?"

No one around here knew Libby Taylor. "I've mended all the fences I could, Brother Able." How hard had it been to erase Liberty Davis? Not terribly. One visit with the lawyer. The remainder, like my personal stuff at the house, was out of my control. I had said good-bye to my family the easiest way I knew.

"You have an unusual first name, even for California."

"My mother was a wanna-be hippie, I think. Giving me this name was as close as she could come to doing something unexpected in Wisconsin."

"I interrupted you earlier. I should leave."

His eyes went to the sketch pad. I could tell he couldn't resist one more question. I didn't want him to go, yet, either. Why was I feeling so obtuse, so contrary? It wouldn't hurt to be polite.

"You were drawing something, perhaps? Are you an artist, or just a hobbyist?"

"I am an artist." That came out too easily for a dead woman. *Try again, Lib.* "Or, at least I was, in my, well, it's not even 'other life,' is it? When I lived."

"That was in Wisconsin? I have ties to Wisconsin, you know." *Oh, God, please.*

Frigid apprehension rippled down my spine, followed immediately by the white hot gut poke of guilt. California wasn't far enough away to be lost, was it? If God found Jonah, he would certainly find me. Was this my whale experience? "Oh?"

"Yes." Brother Able got to his feet. I noticed a little hitch, as if he favored a leg. Perhaps I noticed things like that more because of my own troubles. I wouldn't ask personal questions. Not yet.

"I'm at extension four on the house phone, Libby. Part of what we do here at Paradise House is help you work through this experience. It can be uncomfortable, even messy. But we've been doing this a long time, and conversation helps. You'll be assigned to a counselor who will contact you shortly."

If I was forced to talk at someone, I wanted it to be him. "Can't it be you?"

"I'm sorry?"

"Can't I talk to you about...all this?"

"I'm not always available. I travel."

Was he trying to ditch me now? "But you'll still be here tomorrow, won't you?" Tomorrow was as far as I would look.

● ● ●

"Yes. Would you like to talk again?"

"If it fits your schedule, Brother Able. I wouldn't want to make unfair demands upon your time. I'm sure other patients who have been here longer need you." Lots and lots of patients, who all took his secrets to their graves, if he told them. I decided he had some memory of Wisconsin that he wanted to share with me. As long as he didn't find out anything more about me, I could at least do him the courtesy of listening to him.

"I'm here for you, Libby Taylor. I'll see you tomorrow sometime, then."

He left, a shadowy figure that wafted out the door. I turned the sketch over. Rich Bernard's eyes stared back at me through tangled vines.

46 - ABLE

...and what you preserve I shall give to the sword

"**I** know what you're thinking. I met her, and I know."

Able forced out the words while punishing his right quadriceps and hamstring prior to running.

Rich's eyes hooded against the brilliant flashes of sun off the waves coursing onto the beach near Paradise House. "Perhaps." He paused. "Does it matter?"

Able and Rich continued to stretch. Able had not run on the beach with Rich since summer. Still, he shouldn't take his irritation with his muscles out on Rich. Able twisted his torso. As he lifted the repaired knee toward the brightening sky, he bit back the groan. He should, however, check Rich's delusion that curing every cancer would dissolve the pain of losing his wife. "You can't bring her back, Rich."

"You're the one harping on that old theme. I've always known it. But I've moved on. You're the one with the problem. I wonder if you weren't a little in love with Joanie, yourself."

"I respected your wife, Rich. I made my choice long before my order assigned me to Paradise House."

"A choice that didn't include your daughter."

Able flexed his fist which had clenched of its own accord. Rich had never taunted him before, never used Emily as a weapon. Blinking away the tension, Able recited the words of forgiveness in his heart. Out loud, he said, "Life would be different if everyone knew all the secrets, wouldn't it?"

Rich straightened. He waved his right hand at the complex in the distance. "I've not forgotten them or the sacrifices they made to help others conquer disease. That's why I keep the photographs on the walls of the lab, where I see them every day." The doctor took a few experimental strides before moving to firmer sand closer to the briny water's edge.

Able followed in Rich's wake before coming alongside. "But you didn't talk to them first, Rich. You never asked them what their dreams were, what they hoped for. You didn't know them."

"You're wrong. I never forced anyone to take part in the research. They all volunteered of their own free will." Rich dodged a bold seagull. "They accepted their fate, and wished that others would never have to suffer the same insult." Rich's glare impaled Able. "The insult of your God upon their bodies."

"Helen was a real person, with dreams of a happy life."

"She was already dead when she came here. She was too afraid to be examined for the disease before it was too late to cure it by standard means. But her sacrifice will help others."

"Rich, wait. Slow down."

Rich wheeled to trot backwards.

"Libby Taylor isn't alone. I'm sure of it. She has a family."

"She will soon reach exactly the stage of disease I need for the latest trial. She has the same cancer I cured before. And she's already past conventional treatment. She knows it. I don't force them, Able," he repeated, as if Able had not understood him the first time.

"She has a history," Able insisted with breaths he should have saved for running. "She's not somebody whose epitaph will read 'Nobody will miss me,' or 'I sang but no one listened.'"

"I only know what they want to tell me."

"When can I see her file?"

• • •

"When I'm finished with it."

"What do you really want, Rich? What's your real goal? To know love again? You won't have it among the dead."

"She came alone."

Able huffed, knowing he was close to the end of his endurance. "That doesn't mean she'll want to fill the emptiness with you for whatever time she has left," he shouted with the last of his strength to Rich's back.

"I have never forced anyone to do anything. For any reason."

Able flailed his arms as he came to a halt. He watched Rich run on. The demons of hell had no cause to torment the doctor here on earth. They'd get their turn soon enough if Rich continued on this path. The demons of this world, those who dwelt in his heart and mind, turned Rich Bernard into a man who chased his own soul. Able turned and ran in the opposite direction for half an hour, urging his body on and reveling in the pain until it blocked out other more disturbing thoughts.

Brother Able attended early morning Mass at Our Lady of Sorrows, then breakfasted back at Paradise House. He had appointments with three families soon and two of the staffers after lunch who begged his indulgence to sort out the gift-giving dilemma in their department. Ten days stretched until Christmas Day. Decorations at Paradise House were tasteful and discreet, and included other traditions beside the Christian one. Able couldn't object, nor did he want to. He had ample opportunity to explain the way of Christ through the differing practices. Rich had become blasé about the holiday since Joanie.

What is it that you really want? What's your real goal? The question he'd asked Rich that morning repeated throughout the day.

At suppertime, he caught Mardell, one of the many kitchen aides, delivering a meal to Libby Taylor. He took the tray. "Hello, Mardell. I'll take this for you."

The woman dipped her chin and hurried on, pushing her squeaking cart down the hall.

Able balanced the tray in one hand and knocked on Libby's door. At her summons, he pushed it wide. "Hello, Libby. It's Brother Able with your supper." He sniffed. "Smells fishy."

"I didn't realize you were called upon so widely." Libby set her magazine next to her on the couch.

Able pulled the wheeled tray toward her. "I'm a man of many talents. You don't appear to be a fan of bed."

"When you know you're going to be flat on your back forever soon enough, bed doesn't hold much appeal."

"Ah. I see your point." Able lingered, debating whether or not to ask to join her for the talk she asked for yesterday. She made no hurried move to eat, not unusual with the clientele at Paradise House. Dressed in a loose brown pullover and khaki slacks, she looked tense and pale. Her sketchbook lay on the round table. "How are you feeling?"

"About like that fish, I suppose. Especially if it's parboiled to a soft glob."

"That good?" Able cocked his head, then checked her white board out of the corner of his eye for the name of her caregiver. "Did you tell Laurie? She should be able to make you more comfortable."

Libby's mouth puckered before she spoke. "I don't want to be too comfortable. Not yet. Somehow, I just..." She shook her head. "Brother Able, I'm ready, but I'm not, you know? Of course you don't know. I'm being silly. I apologize. I'm sure your own supper is waiting for you somewhere."

Able rocked on his heels. "Actually, I'd love to join you, if I may be so bold as to invite myself."

Libby looked at the tray. She lifted the cover. "Looks like there's plenty for two here."

"Ha! I prefer my fish baked."

Mardell brought another tray shortly after he called the kitchen. Able opened the cover right away, as Libby had been waiting for him. He sniffed again. "Well, I'd really rather have it fried. I miss Friday night fish fries, back in Wisconsin." He took a deep breath. "Who am I to talk about what's good for you and what's not? May I offer thanks?"

Libby inclined her head. "Please."

Able wove his fingers and leaned over. "Lord God, let us be truly thankful for all of your blessings. Guard and guide Libby during this time. Grant her dignity and peace. Amen." He looked up at her, wondering what she thought. She clearly was not hungry. Able could not ask the Lord for health in this situation. She reached for a cup of applesauce and a spoon with a tremulous hand. Able bit back the offer to help.

"Thank you," she said.

"For what?"

She smiled. The lines on either side of her mouth showed white. "For not trying to feed me."

Able understood then that she meant more than food. The time for the faith talk would come later. He took a bite of the soft fish, baked with pepper seasoning and lemon wedges. Marion gave meals her best shot in a place where appetites were iffy at best, and most often scorned or declined on purpose. "Where are you from, Libby?"

Libby swallowed with the help of her tea. "Oh, I've been all over. The last place, I guess, was Texas."

"You have family there?"

"No. I was in a research study."

"Oh. Why did you participate?" *What is your goal, Rich? What do you really want?*

Libby shifted restlessly on the couch. She put the empty sauce cup back on the tray and stared out of the window. "Everyone was pushing me to do something. My doctor, my friends. It seemed easier to give in to them. At least pretend I tried."

"Tried?"

She folded her arms and looked at him straight on. "To care. This is the second time, Able. The last time. I didn't win the first time I had cancer and I don't want to go through the treatment again. You said it yourself, 'grant her dignity.' That's all I want right now."

Able snapped a carrot stick in two. "What about your family?"

"My father suffers from Alzheimer's disease and has been institutionalized for several years. The people there understand my situation and know what to do."

Able tried another tactic. "Your friends, Libby? The ones who pushed you into action."

"Action I wasn't comfortable taking. True friends don't make you do things you can't do."

Libby wasn't like the typical end-stage patient who came to Paradise House simply to die, Able thought. She was not angry enough, despite her professed disillusionment with her friends. Surely she had other family besides her father. She might be sick enough to die, but Able came back to her comment that she was ready, yet she wasn't. What did she need to do before she could

. . .

finish her race? "Were some of these friends from your church?" he asked on a whim.

"Yes. They prayed and believed I would be healed the first time."

"How did you expect prayer to work?"

Libby raised her chin and offered another mirthless smile. "Maybe they expected too much."

"Healing can take many forms."

Her gaze settled on the sketchbook that lay open on the round table. "I suppose it depends on your goal," she said. "Will you let me draw you? Not now, I'm tired. But soon?"

"Of course."

Libby pushed the tray away.

"That's all you can eat?" Able clicked his tongue as he tsked.

"Eating, like bed, doesn't hold the same interest as it used to."

"Do you have some favorite food? Marion can make pretty much anything."

"Marion? That's who?"

"Our head cook. We should call her a chef, I suppose. She's been here twelve years."

"The food is good."

"So, do you?"

Frown lines marred Libby's forehead. "I don't know. I used to cook a little at home. With my friend." Her eyes fluttered again. "Let's see. We had pheasant for Thanksgiving." She yawned. Mardell returned quietly to take their trays.

Able could not bring himself to press her about the "we."

Laurie poked her head around the door. "How are things?" Able motioned her forward. He got to his feet and touched Libby's arm. "I'll be back tomorrow."

* * *

47 - WEBPOST: THEPLEASUREOFTHEHUNT

An e-mail from Chuck asks "What's your favorite type of hunting?"

The answer, of course, has to do with your target, or your goal. What do you want? Are you out for the meat? The death shot to drop a wounded prey? The skill of wielding a weapon? Or the thrill of bagging a trophy?

Let's take a look at each of these aspects.

Generally, you're not going to find vegans shooting things. Unless it's varmints in their garden patches. If you like wild game, which is getting harder to find, you're going to have to get it for yourself. I mean, you might find venison donated to food pantries, and you might find farmed ground and packaged buffalo or elk in the grocery store, but stalking the frozen food section with a basket to find food that who knows where it's been or who touched it, is pretty gross. A true meat lover will take pride in the hunt, the clean kill and the butchering.

Then there's the skill demanded of a hunter. Weaponry is just part of the process. You have to learn the signs in the woods or the field. Animal habits and habitats. The seasons are important. Even learning the regs. What kind of gun or bow and how to handle it can be learned. Often, a true hunter has some inborn talent for finding a target. Patience may be a virtue, but not everyone can learn it. It takes time and energy to learn the ways of your weapon, matching the type to the target animal, not trying to impress anybody but yourself when you practice.

What about the trophy hunters? Man, I hope you go out with someone who can take the meat. A head's all good and done, but don't waste the rest. Me, I'm not much into trophies, so I turn you over to my buddy lonesomedove457 for his take.

lonesomedove457 says: I love anticipation. I wait for opening day of hunting season, and wait for a deer to walk out, and wait for a good shot. There is something awesome about knowing I have a good chance to bag an animal bigger than me. Then there is the big buck factor. Antlers make me giddy, and at least twelve points are a personal goal and bragging rights.

So you see, patience is a common denominator in the thrill of the hunt. Decide why you're out there. Learn what it takes to reach your goal. Then be patient, and all good things will come to you.

fortuitoushunter says: I agree, man. There is a lot to it that is inexplicable. There are lots of different things rolled into one. What's my favorite type? Well, it's gotta be a trophy. But I hear you about the meat. I guess I never thought of that before.

SharraT says: You forgot something. Some people think that hunting is a really good bonding experience, from being in the woods to trying to stay warm together in your camp.

pleasureofthehunt says: Others prefer to be alone. My one good partner waxes poetic with this sentiment: It's a chance to be the still thing in the woods, like a tree with eyes, taking in all the normal activities and goings on that would normally be disrupted by me if I weren't hunting. And then when a deer walks into view the adrenaline is pumping so hard that my whole body is shaking and my heart is pounding so much that I'm afraid the deer will hear it. Then I take aim, waiting for just the right shot. The one that will make a good clean kill and alleviate its suffering.

☙

48 – LIBBY

The voice of the Lord cries to the city—

The swirls on the wallpaper made me dizzy. I tried to keep things I knew straight in my mind. I recited birthdays and first and last names. Places I'd been, although I couldn't often remember the years.

Next week was Christmas. I knew that much. I wondered if Vic would give Jordan his Christmas gifts early. I hoped they would put up the big tree in the living room, to the left of the fireplace, like always. We hadn't put stockings out for a while now. Vic, me, Dad, Jordan, and Nona. Sometimes Dad was well enough to spend part of the day with us. I never knew until I saw him.

No, wait, that wasn't right. Nona was visiting her cousin. Vic and Jordan were in Hawaii. Did they decorate palm trees in Hawaii? Vic and I should have gone there on our twentieth anniversary instead of to the hospital when I got cancer. Our anniversary was soon. Had I remembered a gift for him?

Someone put little lights on the patio outside my room. My nurse brought in a poinsettia plant yesterday. She asked if I wanted any kind of holiday music or decorations in my room, or whether or not I had any kind of religion. I said I'd get back to her. Then I called her again and asked for a Bible. I carried it with my sketchpad out to the perpetual sunshine of the yard outside the patio doors.

Patient rooms overlooked the distant shoreline. Family

rooms were clustered on the inside of the complex. The sound of waves and gulls were piped in everywhere, unless you wanted to turn it off, or preferred something different in your own space. Sometimes I forgot which button was for the light and which the music. Not much mattered. I hadn't gotten out a whole lot, even though I was beginning to hate this wallpaper with a passion. Was I afraid I'd run into someone who knew me? Or afraid to be seen in a dead woman's clothes? I only knew that I didn't want to meet another person who would die before me, like Daisy, or talk to anyone besides Brother Able or the nurses who came in regularly.

The doctor found me on my patio. I couldn't recall how long I'd sat there. He looked more tired than I felt. Not on the outside, but in his soul. I didn't know if everyone else saw that about him. I couldn't imagine what it would be like to work with the dying. Would it have made my heart hard? My spirit calloused?

"May I join you?" he asked.

"Of course."

Rich pulled up another lounge chair and plopped himself down, faced the sun and closed his eyes. He had not asked me how I felt today, a small favor which pleased me immensely; a lovely change from the same routine of every other person who entered my realm.

The two of us lolled precious time away, not feeling the need to break into the hum of bees or twitter of birds with human sounds. A squirrel ran across the grass a few yards from me. I jumped when Rich spoke.

"Libby, do you ever wonder why some marriages last forever and others don't?"

He opened his eyes to mine when I let the silence stretch. This was not a subject I would talk about to a shuttered expression.

"Maybe you should stick to asking the patients how they feel," I said.

He blinked. A slow grin erased the tired lines between his brows. "You feel fine," he declared.

"How do you know?"

"You haven't started on the heavy stuff, despite the fact that you eat very little." He pointed to my lap. "You're reading a really long book, and you're still drawing. You're out here. You don't care if Christmas comes for you and you haven't let them decorate much. So you can share some of your wisdom." He relaxed into the chair and closed his eyes again, a self-satisfied smile on his lips.

"Maybe I just hate the wallpaper."

"Me, too. Liz Carrelton thought it was soothing."

"The woman who likes the glaring mauve and glittering silver in the entry?"

"Yep. Administrator. My question."

"I'll answer yours if you answer mine."

He flicked the forefinger of his left hand as if that was all he could manage. "Sure."

"Well, this may come as a shock to you, Dr. Bernard, but the decisions of the parties involved are rarely the most important determining factors in said everlasting marriage."

"Hmmm. Makes sense to me."

I smacked my thighs with my sketchpad, making them sting and ache. "I just made an enormously profound statement and you brush it off."

"I'm not brushing it off. I'm digesting it."

"I'm not lunch. Things happen. Things beyond our control."

"I loved my wife," Rich said. He sat up and stared at me. "We would have lasted forever, but we didn't get to decide. Your profundity is comforting. And righteously true."

"Oh? You don't poll all your patients?"

"No."

"Why me?"

"You're not really finished yet, are you?"

I pretended he meant my drawing. I held up the sketchpad and showed him the bold lines of the trellis and the light among the bougainvillea. "I could be."

"You came here for a reason."

I sat back, took a deep breath and let my tension ebb. "I always thought I'd like to die in a snowy, cold winter."

"We don't have snowy winters in southern California."

"Really?"

• • •

ϣ

49 - ABLE

...and it is sound wisdom to fear your name

Laura Reeves brought a stack of files to Able before she went home for the day. Able thanked Rich's assistant and wished her a pleasant evening. He gave in to temptation and took the first five files outside. Never tired of winter California-style, he sat at one of the picnic tables used for employee break time, although the sky would soon grow too dark to allow him to read. Two files later, the light was nearly gone. He listened to Marion directing the symphony of supper in the kitchen behind him while he debated whether or not to go inside.

One more patient file. Able picked it up.

Davis, Liberty Taylor.

Before he opened the cover he tried to convince himself that Davis was a common last name. But when he turned the page, Libby's photograph cured him of his foolish notion. Extra material in the file had been brought from the University of Texas, where the patient had participated in a research study under the principal investigation of Thomas M. Schlitz, MD. Able skipped to the end where Rich typically put the background checks necessitated by past fraudulent insurance claims. He read through the information which danced and pranced on the page with a life of its own. Married December 23, twenty-three years ago, to Victor Arthur Davis, aged fifty-four, who was employed by Hayden International Medical Group.

Able read the words over and over until they burned in his

mind and made no more sense than the first time he had seen them. They made no sense, yet Able knew they were true. Able had not mentioned his encounter with Victor Davis to Rich. Therefore, Rich could not, would not, be playing this game of cosmic coincidence.

Able gathered the files and returned to his room, where he shut the door and tossed them onto his bed. He didn't turn on the light but went straight to kneel before God.

The "speak, O Lord, for your servant is listening" came in waves of anger, disappointment and irreverence he had not felt since accidentally discovering his daughter had not died, after all. He shouldn't care so much about one man and his wife who had a sadistic need to abandon her loved ones as if they were worn-out garments, too threadbare to make a good rag.

Victor's distress over his sick wife's disappearance had been real; Able was certain of it. Their son struggled with his mother's illness and absence.

"Your son, Libby! How could you?"

Anger nearly lifted him off the *prie dieu.*

Remember, Able, you noticed right away that my daughter has unfinished business.

Repulsed, Able leapt to his feet this time. "No, Lord God! You cannot mean for a mother to leave her child."

My ways are not your ways.

"Why am I here?"

To listen. That's what I ask. Listen. Watch. Learn.

"How can I?"

With my strength, Able. With my presence. Abide in me.

"I would never leave Emily like she abandoned Jordan."

I know.

Able ignored the evening meal at Paradise House for a visit

to Our Lady of Sorrows and Father Diego, who might speak with more reason than God.

Able sat in the shadow of the bell tower, three rows back of the last parishioners who filled the middle pews. Diego said Mass twice daily during Advent. Able had continued his observance in the morning, rarely attending in the evening. He didn't know if Father Diego noticed his presence until the Eucharist.

☙

50 - LIBBY

Hear of the rod and of him who appointed it!

Rich stretched on his patio chair and crooked his arms back to cradle his head. The small grin he wore though his eyes remained closed irked me.

"So, you promised to answer a question of mine," I reminded him.

"Shoot."

"What makes you do this?"

"I'm obsessed." He took a deep breath. "I can do nothing else, and believe me, I've wanted to just walk away more than once. But when a patient comes here because conventional medicine fails her, I want her to know that someone else in the medical field cares."

"That's pretty harsh, Rich. Surely you don't believe that no one should get sick and die. There are instances when there's nothing to be done."

I knew that he didn't mean to hurt me when he squeezed my hand. "Perhaps. When we use terrible weapons to maim and destroy as many lives as possible."

"What caused your devotion?" If he noticed that I had changed his wording from obsession to devotion he didn't correct me.

"I research. That's how I started in oncology. We don't know enough about how the body works. I want to change that."

"Do you still research?"

"When I can."

"Do you have any family?"

He opened his eyes then, and made a gentle curve with his lips. "All this. Everyone here is my family."

"That's not really an answer."

"Ah, but you didn't define family."

I thought about Nona, and realized he was right. A family didn't always mean blood ties. "All right. You're not married now, but you were, once. Will you tell me about her?"

The doctor swung his legs to the ground and reached for my left hand. He traced the lines on my palm before he turned it over and rubbed his thumb along the indent where Vic's ring had once shone on my finger. "Tell you what. I'll tell you about Joanie, if you tell me about your husband."

What had I said the first night I came, more than a week ago? The seasons didn't change so perceptively here on the western seashore as in the northern inland lakeshore. Passing time meant nothing. I'd forgotten Vic for an hour and shivered in the breeze. What had I said? That there was no one, no one in the picture, yet he knew I was married. "How will you know if I'm telling the truth?"

He gazed at me with the ghost of a smile. "The same way you'll decide whether to believe in me."

I quaked, hypnotized and strangely drained by the magnetism of his presence. Did it matter what I believed? He could tell me he'd been married to some famous movie star, or even had found the cure for cancer in his research, and I would have believed.

Though we maintained physical contact, I knew Rich left me when he began to speak. He eyed the ocean as though he retrieved his words from its depths. "I should have given up the research. I should have stopped practicing after Joanie, my wife, died. She had cancer. Like you, like so many others. But for her, I found the answer. We'd been married a dozen years. We had difficulty conceiving, and by the time we realized why, it was so late. Stage three."

He dropped my hand and stood, anchoring his hands on his hips. He touched the beeper at his waist, whether because he felt its summons or merely wished a welcome interruption, I didn't know.

"A doctor should figure these things out sooner," he said.

"We see what we want to see, find what we set ourselves up to look for."

A breeze ruffled the hair along Rich's forehead. He turned back to me. "Ah. I was right seeking your wisdom."

I smiled to forestall some of the sting of my question. "What happened?"

"She went into remission. Three years later, I arranged to have a month's leave. We went to Istanbul for a second honeymoon. A celebration, you know? Joanie wanted to see Turkey. Why, I can't understand, but she'd talked about it so often…. Anyway, she picked up an infection."

He stopped speaking. His mouth pinched and he swallowed as though fighting a gag reflex. He went to tuck a piece of vine inside the lattice.

"How long has it been, Rich?" I asked after a while. The wind gusted, cool and damp from the ocean. Maybe it would rain later.

"Five years."

I watched him lean into the breeze, fighting for control, and wondered what else was wrong with me, that I couldn't suffer the same sense of despair over the loss of Vic. My husband hadn't died, to be sure, but we had lost each other even so, those years

●　●　●

of suffering. I'd been self-centered then, through radiation and hormone therapy, unable to stand anyone's touch. Especially not from my husband. My distance was not his fault. He wanted me, tried to keep our bond taut, but I felt another strand break every time he flew away and I had to stay home with a dying mother and a child who looked through me. No marriage in heaven, Pastor Grant told us once, quoting scripture somewhere in the book of Matthew, where Jesus's authority was constantly being challenged by those Pharisees. Should I tell this news to Rich? Would it comfort him? Vic had his faith and Jordan to comfort him. Rich had no one.

"I planned to give up the research after I lost her," Rich said. "Why didn't you?"

"In a way, I'm still doing it for her." Even over the rattle of the windscreen, I heard Rich's beeper. "You owe me a question and answer next. Don't forget," he said. "See you later."

Maybe Rich had found his comfort after all.

☙

51 - ABLE

Can I forget any longer the treasures of wickedness...

Able's guilt and shame bound him to the worn pew while the faithful partook of Holy Communion. Father Diego peered into the shadow and waited in between the groups from the congregation that he served alone. Able couldn't lift himself from his seat. Diego served the last parishioners and waited again. His patience turned to long-faced moroseness as he faced Able's direction. A few people turned to stare into the shadows. Able closed his eyes. Perhaps they would forgive sleep more readily than an unresolved matter of confession that kept him from partaking of the Eucharist.

When the rustling of clothes marked the exit of the participants, and long after young Sister Domitia who occasionally brought her portable keyboard from the nearby Sisters of Charity convent had ceased her wheezy postlude, Able opened his eyes. Before him was the back of Diego's cowl. Heavy, clingy frankincense which Diego had burned before the service still hung in the air. Able said nothing. Diego said nothing. After a time, Diego pushed to his sandaled feet, paid obeisance to the Eucharist on the altar, and shuffled out.

Able stared at Christ. Christ stared at his own pierced and bloody feet. The numbness of despair persisted after another person kicked some pebbles at the door of the chapel before entering. A man walked straight to the altar. He lifted his face to the lit figure of the suffering Jesus. Able recognized the favorite stance of Rich Bernard. Defiant, in control, hands on either hip under the spread wings of his jacket. Pretending to think about what a person said to him while knowing all along that he would still do as he thought best.

Rich heaved a breath and turned around. He went to sit in the first pew on the opposite aisle from Able. Able couldn't tell if Rich had seen him or knew that he was there. Maybe Able had become part of the shadows that hid him.

"Joanie believed in you," Rich said to the Christ. Rich's voice was raw, the syllables choked. "The only thing I ever asked you was not for myself, but for her. To save her."

Able felt a tingle in his feet, as if they were coming back to life after being deprived of blood.

"You were the one to save her, all right. For yourself," Rich told the crucifix. Rich enunciated each word, then garbled a barked laugh.

Able had feeling in his fingers. He flexed them. Did Rich mean what he said? That he believed Joanie went to heaven?

"What kind of a perverted salvation is that?" Rich jumped up and began to stalk around the base of the altar. "She did so much good for everyone else. Everyone. No one has been able to replace her. You took her, and it cost the lives of countless others. How could you?"

Able reminded himself that anger was a natural stage of grief even if it took Rich five years to get there. Able hoped it was a good sign. Why now? And would Rich be able to accept God's grace and mercy?

Rich wagged his finger at the bleeding Christ. "Ah. But I see now you're trying to make amends."

What was this?

"I can accept that. I accept your apology." He laughed again, a short yelp of defiance. "I even thank you. How's that? Thank you. And I take your challenge."

Challenge? Surely Rich could not mean—

"I will make sure she lives. Despite you."

Rich strode down the aisle, angels nipping at his heels. "Despite you, too, old man," Rich hissed furiously as he passed Able.

The tingles of life turned to stabs of pain as Able rolled to his feet, feeling as old as Rich accused. Why now, after all these years, would the Holy Spirit reveal the depth of Able's stain? Was this some kind of divine litmus test?

Ask me.

What, Lord?

Ask me why now.

Able shook life back into his wrists and arms. Chill raised his hackles. A nightmare vision of Joanie Bernard entered Our Lady of Sorrows and processed up the aisle. Able blinked once, and again, to shake the image, as ephemeral as Rich had been solid a moment before. He did not believe the spirits of those who died came back to haunt the living.

Life coursed through his limbs and he no longer felt too heavy to move.

Able wanted to leave the chapel. Or at least run from the awful daydream. His feet were welded to the floor. Was he projecting his own guilt after Rich's accusations? The specter of Joanie sat on the steps to the altar and faced him. She began to speak, confessing all sorts of disillusioning sins Able had never guessed. Wanting other men to father a child if Rich could not, blaming him for her illness. Searching the sources of Able's quotes before his workshops to make herself look smart in front of the others. Making vapid fun of patients after she pretended to care while listening to them.

No, no, no! Able was not Joanie's Father Confessor. He did not want to hear this. Joanie had been good and kind.

Hadn't she?

Even when he caught her in his office?

Listened to her at lunch?

And, too late, when she told him…told him about…

As Able watched, hands over his ears, the phantom Joanie's skin and clothes became saturated with spreading darkness which ate through her until he could only hear her voice. Able felt the tingle again in his hands and held them away to see the same black covering them.

But, Father, I confessed.

Not everything.

Father Diego touched Able's sleeve. "The Blessed Mother told me it was time to return."

Able whispered, "Forgive me, Father, for I have sinned."

"Our sin is ever before Him, Able. Somehow I am convinced any absolution I can give you tonight will never be enough. You must also forgive yourself."

Able still faced the altar. "My sin has a face, Diego. I spoke to the man in his grief over his wife. I know him. I prayed with and for him. I prayed with his wife, not knowing who she was. This time, I accept that what we are doing is wrong. I cannot allow the doctor to continue to use people, no matter the cost."

"Admitting you have trouble is the first step, my friend. Come, let us reason together."

Able followed Diego to his apartment.

When rosy brush strokes marked the crest of each ocean wave,

Able returned to his room at Paradise House. Instead of disillusionment over Libby's choice of action, he feared for her. Rich Bernard was a brilliant doctor. And he had a point in his conversation with God. The Lord took Joanie home far too soon. For what reason? Joanie had been a vivacious woman who had eased the suffering of patients and their families with her listening skills. Able did not need to know the depth of her depravity any more than he needed to know Diego's. The Lord looked upon the heart. Able did not need to.

Problem-solving for the dead and dying involved assurances that the living would not suffer in the aftermath. Emily must not lose her quality of care if Able took action. Government authorities would not be the answer here. Able must stop Rich. They had both pushed the limits of morality far too long.

52 – LIBBY

...and the scant measure that is accursed...

Rich pointed out that I had chosen a really long book. I opened to the stories of Genesis in the Bible and read as if I had never seen them before. In the early mornings, I found that I could collect myself enough for a few hours of coherency before the fog of pain and narcotics billowed across my mind.

When someone knocked at the door of my room. I called "come in."

I held up the Bible. "Brother Able, you look like Jacob, who wrestled with the angel all night long." He didn't respond, or even smile. "Are you feeling all right?"

In a rasping tone I didn't associate with him, Able said, "I thought I was supposed to ask you that question. I see you're in bed. Perhaps you're the one not feeling all right?"

I squinted at the clock. He'd probably been up all night and was tired. "Considering the fact that it's six fifteen in the morning, I wonder why you're not in bed. Were you with a patient?" The chill of déjà vu shivered up my spine at a remembered fragment of conversation with Dr. Schlitz. "Are you all right?" I'd asked the doctor after he resurrected me, when the study shut down.

"Just getting an early start on the day," Able said. "May I sit?"

"Of course."

Able pulled up a chair.

"I'm afraid my fingers are stiff yet, Brother Able. I don't think I can do you justice."

Able looked startled out of his contemplative mood. "What?"

"I don't think I can make a sketch of you until my hands are more awake." I wondered why he'd come. He obviously needed to tell me something. Perhaps it was about Milwaukee, as I had guessed when we first met. "Did something happen?" I asked.

"Something?" Able jumped to his feet. "Forgive me for disturbing you so early, Libby. I just recalled...another appointment. May I return later?"

"Yes." I watched him leave. Even his clothes looked rumpled. I hadn't noticed he wore wrinkled jackets in our previous meetings. I sniffed the scent of pre-dawn sky in his wake.

For the first time since I left home, I felt compelled to pray for someone other than my family. I took my time finding the right words. The mechanism that directed my prayer life had rusted somewhat, but I soon found a comfortable rhythm to oil the machine. I began with the Lord's Prayer and eased into the habit of following the acronym for "pray." Praise came easy enough after reading of the creation earlier, in Genesis. A phrase of a song buzzed through my thoughts, weaving words together. *Lord, you are...more precious to me than anything.*

Repentance used to be easier. What horrible things had I done recently besides ditch my family and friends? I had been a model patient so far. My growing admiration...maybe more...for Rich Bernard would not hurt anyone, would it? Who was going to know, anyway?

I really ought to be more sincere about confessing my shortcomings, since I planned to meet the Lord face to face sooner than later. *All right, I'm sorry! I just didn't know what else to do. I failed as a wife and mother. I failed them, and I just couldn't deal with...with...inconveniencing them anymore. Surely you'll forgive me for wanting what's best.*

I hurried on to the part I really wanted to spend time on. "Ask."

Able needs you, Lord. He needs your wisdom and guidance. He is so important to the people of this place. I've heard talk. Everyone loves him almost as much as they revere Rich. Brother Able has the appearance of one who is suffering greatly, and I ask you please to lift his heavy spirits, or, at least, to help him carry whatever burden you have given him to bear.

I spent a few more minutes on the attributes I associated with Brother Able Fenwick personally: his kindness and patience. His self-sacrifice to serve God in this place. I asked God to bless Rich's work. Then I let loose for Vic and Jordan and Nona and my father. Vic...what was he doing now? I was sorry for leaving the way I did, truly, but thoroughly convinced this was best. I did not want to think they'd suffer on my behalf. I was the only one to suffer this time.

I had a legitimate reason to skip the last letter, "y," or "you," which meant I could pray for myself.

Vi brought my breakfast, a welcome interruption. It seemed wrong to waste God's blessings on the remainder of my lifespan. He would be better off showering them elsewhere. Maybe on Nona. Definitely on my son. Stomach juices stirred when I smelled the cinnamon of thinly sliced coffeecake.

"Good morning, Libby. What's going on?" Vi asked. She set the tray beside me. "Not up yet, I see."

"I have a confession to make," I told her.

She stood next to me, monitoring my pulse and making notes in her portable electronic log. Then she looked at me and smiled. "What's that?"

"I'm hungry."

Vi squeezed my forearm. "That's okay, honey. There's

nothing wrong with that. You haven't eaten much at all, anyway." She began to back away. "You tell me how you like that, and I'll let Marion know. See you after while."

I eyed the tea and grimaced. Bathroom first. I maneuvered my numb left side and stood, shaking, to grab the walker. I dragged myself the few steps. No one had yet told me I shouldn't attempt to take care of my personal needs on my own, and so far I thought I masked how hard it was becoming for me to walk. Once I bathed and dressed in the mornings, I parked myself on the sofa or the recliner.

I washed my face and tried to pull a comb through my hair while I checked in the mirror. The areas around my corneas looked more like poached egg whites and my skin appeared grayish. I stuck my tongue out at my reflection and pushed the steel frame walker back toward my bed. Perhaps I would be lazy today and stay there.

I was startled by the sight of a visitor.

"Brother Able!" He sat in the same chair he had vacated an hour earlier. He looked refreshed, maybe damp from a shower, and wore clean clothes. "You're back."

Able watched me settle, offering no hand to help, which perversely annoyed me. "Would you like some of this delicious coffeecake?" I asked him.

"No, thank you. Libby, I know about your husband. And your son."

I smeared the butter I had been about to spread on my bread on the back of my hand instead. My fingers were so clumsy when I first woke up. I bent my head against the nausea that butterfly-kissed my stomach.

"I read your file," he said, as if he needed to divulge his sources.

I took shallow breaths through my nostrils. I looked up and noticed for the first time that he held a folder on his lap. My shaking fingers were no longer able to grasp the butter knife and I set it down carefully. Why now? Why did Brother Able feel it necessary to torment me at this stage of my death? Tingles trotted up and down my neck. "The information I brought from Texas had no personal details."

"Rich does background checks on everyone. We've had issues with insurance in the past. Not everyone who comes to Paradise House understands that this is the end. Grief comes in stages that affects the entire family."

"My family isn't involved. If you read my file, you also know that I turned over a generous trust fund."

"It's not about money, Libby. You lied about your circumstances."

"I never did. I'm in the last stages of metastasized cancer. Rich knows I'm married."

Able closed his eyes and stroked his mustache. "I see."

"I don't think you do. What are you accusing me of? And why is this any of your business? Why bother me now?"

"Does your husband know what you're doing?"

"Vic knows my choice."

Able stared at me. I shivered, for at this moment his eyes had the same cast as Jordan's.

"You have a teenaged son. Don't you care about how this is affecting him?"

"I care deeply. That's why I'm not letting him be around me, to watch it again. He was a little boy the first time, only eleven years old. There's nothing I can do this time. No promises that it will be better, nothing he can do about it. A powerless young man suffers more than a helpless child. I was never the kind of mother

* * *

he needed. And he has—"

"A boy needs his mother and his father."

"Let me see that folder."

Able handed it over. I breezed through the report from the University of Texas, Dr. Schlitz's study and the findings of my physical here at Paradise House. Dr. Henderson's personality profile of me was there. I merely glanced at it. The last page was the background check. I looked up at Brother Able with narrowed eyes. Anger painted my tone with a hue I did not like. "There's nothing here about my son."

Able pursed his mouth and shifted a little in the seat, but kept me skewered with his accusatory expression.

"How do you know about my son?"

When he remained dumb, but dropped the look, I had to say something. "You must have guessed." I pushed my breakfast tray away. "What, is this some kind of therapy to make me feel bad about my inadequacies and sins before I die? Leave me alone, Able. Get out of here."

He seemed to deflate, all the righteous indignation sucked out by some celestial vacuum.

"You're right," he said. "I don't know what's come over me. Please, forgive me. I had no right to talk to you like this."

I wiped the butter off my hand and took a bite of the coffeecake, which now tasted like dust. I tossed it back on the plate. I had just prayed for him. Why was he treating me like he had the right to judge me?

Able folded his hands. "You told me that you had mended the fences that you could. Do you want to talk about it?"

"No." I bit my lip. If Vic had wanted, he would've found me. He could have come here if he tried hard enough. He was more resourceful than anyone I've ever known. Summoning tears felt like clawing my eyeballs out with Marion's fork.

"One of the other stages is denial, Libby. I learned something last night, something about myself. Would you like to hear it?"

What—he thought I would say no? As if it mattered. I folded my arms and stared out the window.

"God showed me how I look at other people and only see what I think they should be, instead of how he sees them."

"That doesn't sound so terrible."

"It's not real. If I only see what I want, I hurt you when I do not look at what you really need."

53 - WEB CHAT: SHAREMYDISEASE

Surviving11 says: I can't let this nature versus nurture thing go. I just did a paper for school on genetic engineering. How could the natural world allow so many mistakes to happen? And then they copy over and over, while other things stay the same. Like crocodiles. They've around for, like, billions of years, just the same.

Gammatate says: Are you talking genetic engineering, evolution or natural selection?

Surviving11 says: Does it matter?

Gammatate says: Those are all entirely different disciplines. Some of those things man has control over. Other aspects are in God's hands.

Tinman says: God again. I knew someone would bring that up again.

Surviving11 says: god is just another name for nature.

rainmaker says: don't insult nature.

John316 says: God loves the world he created.

Surviving11: Then why is it so messed up? Why are people so messed up? And don't say anything about sin and Adam, man, that's so old.

John316 says: So, what's your take, surviving11? You must have a theory about why people get sick.

Surviving11: Radiation. It messes with our building blocks. Discovering DNA was such an accident. I wish no one ever heard of it.

Tinman says: But don't you want to see how it's messed up.

EchoEcho says: That's what I was telling you about. Energy swirls around in currents it's attracted to. Too much energy, and the thing it's attracted to goes haywire.

gftckt.mxsouth says: or too little

Surviving11 says: But what about the people who say they can fix nature's mistakes? Make a person go back to normal?

John316 says: Define normal.

Surviving11 says: not you.

gftckt.mxsouth says: There's no need for that. Let's practice maturity here. We're all trying to help each other through the worst time of our lives. So, has anyone tried gene therapy?

John316 says: I haven't come to a conclusion whether it's God's will for me. My physician recommended trying it for my Parkinson's. There have been good study results reported.

Surviving11 says: Then why don't you do it?

John316 says: I'm not normally disposed to present that kind of vulnerability to strangers.

Tinman says: We talked about stem cells earlier. It's working well with my leukemia.

gftckt.mxsouth says: There are certain diseases that seem to do well with such therapy. Advances in genetics are being made all of the time.

Surviving11: What about cord blood?

Tinman says: That's one of the better sources of stem cells. They used that on me.

Surviving11: What, your own?

Tinman says: No. Something the doctor had.

Surviving11 says: That's gross. How could you let them put stuff from a stranger inside you? Aren't you afraid of mutating or something?

The Phoenix says: I've got to step in here. Kid, I don't think you belong here. This is a place for people to share legitimate concerns about their own health. I'm going to ask the webhost to monitor your posts and remove you if you become disruptive.

● ● ●

Surviving11 says: That's not fair! I have a right to free speech. Come on, everyone. Can't you see what's happening? Cancer is supposed to clear out the inferior genes from the human race. There are a lot of worried people who agree that people will cease to—

John3:16 says: Thank you, webhost.

EchoEcho says: Yes. Poor kid, though. Must be really mixed up.

Tinman says: How do you know he was a kid?

The Phoenix says: Speech patterns are typical of a youth. Other identifiers, such as "doing a paper for school" and immature analytical skills.

EchoEcho says: He must have come on site for a reason. Do you suppose he was sick?

John316 says: Or someone he loves, and he just wanted to know how to deal with it.

EchoEcho says: Kids these days are so hooked into computer stuff, they don't even think about real people. All that virtual stuff is crazy.

54 - ABLE

Shall I acquit the man with wicked scales...

"**I** carried denial for the past thirty years, Libby. I speak from experience."

Libby lay back on the white pillow. In the white robe, against the white sheets with her pale hair and ashen face, she looked like a child's drawing discernable only by an irregularly penciled outline.

Able had not seen what Joanie Bernard needed, deep in her heart. He had never tried to fully understand what Rich wanted to do here at Paradise House. For years Able had whispered to himself that Rich harbored delusions of godhood. The doctor was capable of doing anything to get his wife back.

But was that all? Able had wanted to see Rich's shortcomings so that he wouldn't have to examine the sin in his own life. Rich didn't deserve Able's disrespect. Able's self-delusion that he was a better, forgiven person proved how little esteem he held for God's grace and mercy. No one—no one—deserved that mercy.

"I don't want to hear anything about it, Able," she said. "Please, let me remember you as I want."

"Libby...what about Jordan?"

"Jordan has all the right people in his life to take care of him now," she said. "I'm doing this for him. He can't be allowed to see me like this. I love him too much. Vic knows. He understands and will do the right thing. I'm so tired, Brother Able. I woke up too early. Can we talk later?"

Shame washed over Able. His own troubles were nothing compared to Libby's. "I'm sorry, Libby. I'll look in on you later."

Able pulled himself to his feet and left her room. Even if he convinced himself that he had only Libby's family's best interests at heart, he didn't need to badger her at this point. He could seek out Victor, try to offer whatever help the man would accept.

Gert Berry turned around at Able's approach to the office, message in hand. "Oh, there you are, Brother Able. Where have you been?"

"Out and about, Gert. How are you this fine morning?"

"Well enough, Brother, well enough."

"What do you have for me?"

"Oh! Right. Mrs. Carrelton requested the honor of your presence at a lunch meeting." Gert unfolded the note. "At Frigo's." She cocked her head at him. "That's sort of unusual, isn't it?"

Able's heart skipped a beat. He smiled at Gert. "My boss's generosity moves me." He held out his hand and glanced at Gert's round letters. "Could you respond, please? Tell Mrs. Carrelton I will meet her there at one o'clock."

Gert hesitated, as if she had something else to say. Able didn't encourage her. He had reports to finish and appointments this morning. They would keep him too busy to consider Mrs. Carrelton's intent.

When Able entered the casual brick and glass family restaurant, the hostess directed him to the corner banquette where Mrs. Carrelton had already been seated, along with Kasey Salisbury.

"Good afternoon, Brother Able. I thought you and Dr. Salisbury and I should take the time to talk outside of Paradise House. Please, sit."

Able slid in opposite Dr. Salisbury, away from the window's glare. Meeting off campus like this was an unexpected twist on Mrs. Carrelton's usual handling of touchy subjects. What was it this time? Dr. Salisbury was a smart woman. Able believed her to be a person who wanted to know how things worked. A person who wanted to know how things worked would most likely have searched past records in an effort to discern patterns in patient and family care. Paradise House policy was very open to constant improvement in quality care through staff and patient recommendation. Following the patient census would show very slight discrepancies in room assignments. While it might be necessary to move patients to a new section of Paradise House for safety reasons if a rare and unexpected change in condition occurred, the event was, or should have been, well documented.

Discharging a patient, like, say, Helen Harding, from the patient census, yet treating her case in Rich's lab wing for three weeks before her death, would justify an investigation. That is, if the patient had any family who called for such an investigation. Auditors seemed to find nothing unusual. At Paradise House, the counselors were actively involved in patient care and served a dual role for patient advocacy in any social work considerations.

The waitress brought them water then left them to decide their order.

Carrelton said, "Paradise House runs as smoothly as a frosted cake, where the only bumps and ridges are part of the decorator's master plan."

Able recognized the speech from a workshop held last summer and tuned her out to watch Dr. Salisbury's reaction. Able appreciated Liz Carrelton's directorship. At every opportunity she publicly praised Dr. Bernard, whose talents supplied the majority of operating expenses and who gave his life's energy to working himself out of a job. If Rich Bernard succeeded, the need for hospice services like Paradise House would be vastly reduced. Mrs. Carrelton knew when to ask questions, and how to analyze the answers. Paradise House flourished with a growing international reputation for quality of care. The workshops that Able and Rich were called upon to provide, as well as the symposiums and published papers proved the program worked. The complex could not grow any more at the current site.

He came back to the moment with Carrelton's typical statement: "Paradise House, by nature, is a place where people seek comfort when other avenues to recovery, or cure, are no longer available. It is our best therapy to help them physically, emotionally, and spiritually meet that end in dignity and peace."

Dr. Salisbury's eyes flashed. She sipped at the water, and gave her salad order in clipped tones when the waitress returned. After the young uniformed woman left with her pad, Dr. Salisbury said, "There are a few discrepancies in the records, Brother, that I don't understand. I know this is a big place, with a constantly revolving patient census, but certain pieces of information don't make sense to me. Perhaps you could explain them."

Carrelton spoke first. "Rich Bernard is well respected in the medical community. Paradise House is always at the top of polls for family satisfaction in the care of their loved ones. In fact, we plan to expand in the near future."

Interesting. Rich would be ultra-cautious about setting up another branch or getting involved in a franchise that would take a certain amount of operating control out of his hands. Because of Rich's real goal, the work he did in his lab to eradicate cancer, he'd never allow more people to examine the close workings of Paradise House and raise questions or criticism. Able ignored

Carrelton.

"What do you think is happening?" Able asked Salisbury.

With a quick intake of breath and a side look at the director, Dr. Salisbury said in a rush, "There are some ethical courses of action that disturb me."

Able jumped in before Carrelton could. "Such as?"

"I read of a number of patients who have been discharged over the past several years. Not all have been followed, which I find odd. While I understand the difference between treatment and palliative care, both of which are offered, I can't help but wonder if there's a successful treatment, why isn't it written up? One patient had lab work done. When I went to ask about some results, Dr. Bernard's assistant—"

"Mary was less than courteous, I'm afraid, Brother Able," Carrelton said.

"Did you bring this up with Dr. Bernard? I'm sure he would accommodate you, Dr. Salisbury," Able said.

"He's been unavailable. I tried to see him over a week ago. Then I made two appointments, both of which he broke."

"He's a busy man," Carrelton asserted.

The waitress brought their food. Able offered thanks. He watched the others, who ate as though they wished they were somewhere else, avoiding eye contact. He wondered how much Carrelton knew about Rich's work. The doctor had spent time in Wisconsin several years ago, learning cutting-edge techniques of genetic manipulation pioneered at the venerable University. In the early days of controversy over the rights of humans to mess with the nature of humanity, Wisconsin had been given permission to experiment with genetic therapies and stem cell research. Rich had recorded some successes, even been able to send eight patients home over the past six years, as Dr. Salisbury had discovered. None had recovered as completely as Joanie Bernard. All the other patients had been unattached and had given their permission to Rich for his experimental treatments. Mary Schumacher, who specialized in harvesting a patient's own stem cells, had sped the research into individual cure genetic therapies when she came to work in Rich's lab.

The UW research had been controversial and recent changes in the political arena forced the closure of several of the studies, especially those involving recovered human tissue. Able did not know if Joanie had divulged her secret to Rich before her cancer diagnosis. Joanie told Able about the coming baby. At the time, the thought never crossed his mind that Joanie had told her husband. No mention of a pregnancy had been brought up after her recovery, and Able wondered later if the suspected pregnancy had merely been a false hope in light of the disease. After her tragic death, and when the stem cell research began in Rich's lab, Able wasn't so certain what had happened to the pregnancy or even whether it had been real.

Dr. Salisbury put her fork down halfway through the greens and chicken on her plate. "Is Dr. Bernard doing research in genetic therapy?"

Mrs. Carrelton's soup spoon splashed some of her chowder against the pale green wool of her suit. Her quick breath and snort of displeasure was obviously twofold. While she dabbed at the stain, Able answered. "Yes."

"Are certain patients being singled out for experimentation?"

Carrelton gasped and looked around them. "Dr. Salisbury!"

Able met Carrelton's look, then touched her hand in warning and empathy. "That would be a terrible rumor to start, Dr. Salisbury."

* * *

"You said it yourself," Dr. Salisbury said. She pulled her hand away. "People come to Paradise House to prepare to die. Treatment may be offered but never guaranteed. Why single some out to give them false hope?"

"What, in your opinion, is false hope?" Able countered. "If you examined their files, you saw that those patients were given extra good years of quality life."

"They still died."

"No one lives forever." Able brushed at his mustache with the linen napkin. He sat back against the seat, appetite gone.

"If the state and federal inspectors are satisfied with the lab and the hospice, if the research and treatment being offered are prudent and beneficial, what are your specific concerns?" Carrelton asked.

"I don't like being kept in the dark about procedure. What if a patient begged me to help her live, instead of die?"

"Surely you've been in that position before," Able said.

"Not when I might have the means to make it happen."

The waitress approached, hesitantly, as if the fear of interrupting overrode her code of good service. "How is everything? Can I get anyone anything else?"

Carrelton scared the girl away with a fierce glare and harsh tone. "No, thank you. We'll call you when we require the check."

Able frowned at Carrelton. "Today, with ongoing advances in science, many cancers are being cured daily."

Dr. Salisbury gave up any pretense of eating after that. She set her napkin on the table. "Why isn't Dr. Bernard publishing his findings?"

Able leveled a look at Carrelton then answered. "Our lab is small and privately funded. Dr. Bernard is not working for any of the big drug companies. He studies individual cancers in order to understand the disease better. His goal is to treat people, not just their diseases, or come up with a commercial product."

"Then why isn't every patient offered the same opportunity?"

"For Rich to be able to study a disease, the patient has to meet several criteria. Very few who come to us meet those criteria." Able drank more water.

"Hope is a powerful restorative," Dr. Salisbury said. "Shouldn't all the patients be treated equally?"

Carrelton leaned forward across the table. Able feared for the bosom of her suit, which loomed perilously close to the bowl of chowder. "It's like this, Dr. Salisbury. When a mother brings her child into an emergency room with an earache at the same time as a half dozen victims of a terrible busy crash arrive, how are you going to define treating everyone equally?"

Able blinked at the director's example. "Thank you, Mrs. Carrelton. Everyone who comes to us undergoes the same admittance procedure with physical and emotional examinations. Dr. Bernard takes equal consideration of the state of a patient's mind in determining which patients in a very particular stage of illness might benefit from his research. How will understanding Dr. Bernard's research help you counsel patients and their families at Paradise House?"

"So, Dr. Bernard has sole control over who may benefit?" Dr. Salisbury asked.

By the look on Liz Carrelton's face, Able wondered at the length of Dr. Salisbury's continued service to Paradise House. The hard part would be convincing Salisbury to keep her mouth shut about things she did not understand.

* * *

55 - LIBBY

...you shall tread olives, but not anoint yourselves with oil...

After a check on my current status, Rich guided me to the patio outside my room. "You're too pale. Let's get some fresh air, if not sun, today."

The weather was cooler than the last time we sat here. The temperature felt like the lower sixties—maybe March weather back home. I wrapped the robe around me. Rich did not relax, but sat upright, clenching the arms of the chaise. His time this afternoon was limited, he told me.

"You were talking about why you do all this, Rich."

"Partly, because I can."

"What do you mean by that?"

"My father was a medical engineer. I followed his example."

I smiled at the familiarity of it all. I had married such a man, then ran away from him. To end my life in the care of another man like my husband seemed like fate. Rich did not offer more information, so I prodded. "So, were either of your parents physicians, then?"

"No. I went to engineering school, got my degree, like my father. When I realized I cared more about how the medical equipment I helped design, the machines, affected people, I returned to school and got my medical degree."

I made some mental calculations. Rich couldn't have been as old as all that. "How young were you when you went to engineering school?"

Rich grinned at me. "Not the youngest ever."

"So, you do this because you want to help people. Why don't you work in a clinic, or something? Somewhere you can catch people who aren't so ill? Cure them before they die?"

He looked away from me, an inward musing much further than the ocean shore. "Everyone dies sometime." He sighed and came back to me. "My wife had the same color hair as yours," Rich said. "You owe me a question and answer, you know." He looked at his watch, then settled back in the chair. "I have fifteen minutes. Tell me about your husband."

My story was easy to tell. "We first met at my family's summer home in Egg Harbor, the year before I graduated from art school. Vic was worldly. Debonair, I guess, with premature wings of snowy hair. He was already thirty." I shifted in the chair, pulled the robe tighter. "Vic impressed my father with his knowledge of the current state of the Great Lakes, a subject that was dear to my father's heart. They had plenty of juicy cures for the terrible problems affecting the screwed up ecosystem." I stared at the ocean, much as Rich had done earlier. "Vic didn't really pay any attention to me then. Not until we met again in Europe. I'm not exactly a classic beauty, in case you hadn't noticed."

I saw Rich take a covert glance at his watch again. He was most likely bored by my dull life and rhetoric. Of course he would not take my bait about my looks. My husband was the same—impatient to get past irrelevance and move on. Vic noticed me in London at that diner when I was alone and independent of my parents and read my heart like an itinerary of our next trip. Tuesday we'd arrive in Rome. Tomorrow we'd pack for Venice. Then I'd call for specs on...and so on and so on. In Wisconsin, Vic hadn't made any pretty speeches about my golden locks and the skin I diligently kept unflawed. I supposed I was in the right place at the right time for him to meet a life partner. Thinking like this, summoning nonchalance, made it easier for me to leave him.

As a dying cancer patient at Paradise House, Rich couldn't see me in any other light. If I were not in this situation, would Rich think I was as special as his late wife? Perhaps somebody worthy of his attention? "I'm getting chilled, Rich. Maybe I'd better go inside."

He helped me with a clinical touch, then bade me good-bye.

I startled from a doze. Someone tapped at my door. "Come in," I croaked and cleared my throat. "Brother Able."

He hesitated in the entry, probably gauging my mood.

"Don't worry," I told him. "I'm not going to bite your head off. Yet." I smiled, still woozy with half-sleep.

"Libby." Able came in and sat on my easy chair.

I hoped he wasn't going to apologize for our conversation from yesterday. We stared at each other until I realized he wasn't going to ask me how I felt. I decided not to tell him, either. "Forgive my curiosity, Brother Able, but how does Paradise House work? I've visited a great many medical facilities in my lifetime, and this place uses more money than I've ever seen for the purpose of helping people die. And believe me, I've seen plenty of money."

"Not many know this, but Rich developed and patented a number of pieces of equipment and testing methods during his study of cancer. I believe Hayden International is a major distributor of some of those devices. He is a multi-millionaire, I suspect, even worth in the billions. He's the source behind most of the support of Paradise House."

That tallied with the tidbit Rich threw me earlier. Rich wouldn't have to be beholden to a nosy board of directors, then, either. "How long have you known him?" Maybe I could catch a glimmer of Brother Able's character, too. I reached for my sketchbook while Able talked, and began a series of little studies of his mouth and mustache, his eyes and nose and hands. I loved to draw people's hands. So much personality came out in how a person used his or her hands—almost as much as eyes.

"Almost twenty-five years. His father was a biomedical engineer who taught Rich how things worked. Rich got on a fast-track medical program when he returned to school. He's a very special person, despite his faults."

I only partially paid attention to Brother Able's words while I worked. My replies were echoes, meant to keep my subject talking so I could capture more of his expression. "We all have faults," I murmured.

"Rich wants things he cannot have."

"That's not much different from anyone else I know." I cocked my head and squinted. I couldn't catch the top curve of Able's mouth, which was hidden under the mustache. His lips pursed and stretched over his next words.

"Perhaps. But do you have the power to get almost anything you want? Anything but the one thing you can't have?"

"I've been fortunate. I've been able to have things most people only dream of, like travel, a fine home and plenty of money, good friends."

"Rich wants to cure all cancer."

I stopped mid-sketch. The pencil slashed across my rendering of Able's ear. "And you think that's the one thing Rich can't have. A universal cure." I turned the page of the sketchbook. "Seems like a mighty fine goal to me."

• • •

"It's altruism in its purist form. But Rich wants to be in sole control. Be careful of what he tells you. Much as I love him and know him, and appreciate his talents, he can also be reckless."

"And this helps Paradise House run—how?"

"Rich doesn't have to account for himself to a board of directors. That's not always a good thing. A good board can hold a business accountable."

"So, there are underlying financial problems despite Rich's millions?"

I looked up in time to see Able furrow his brow. "No. Even though this is Rich's dream, the director, Liz Carrelton, also seeks donations and sponsorship from large corporations besides Rich's foundation. It's good publicity. Paradise House has grown into international fame for its methods of care."

I detected the underlying concern in Brother Able's careful attempts to avoid direct answers to my off-hand comments. I put the sketchbook away and sat up to listen better.

"Able, why did you come here today? What is it you want to talk about?"

56 - CONFIRMATION JOURNAL: NOTMYGRANDMASGOD

I'm not really in confirmation anymore, I don't think, so why am I still writing in this stupid journal? No one's mentioned church in a couple of weeks, so that's a good thing, anyway. Nona's back, too. Life could be normal, if everyone would stop running around going crazy all the time. The witch's gone. she never really was like a mom, anyway, always going off somewhere, leaving me alone with that ------ old—filthy—old man. No one should have been alone with him. No one should be allowed to do the thing he did to a little kid. But what did I know? I was just a little kid. gramma was sick. I don't remember it much, but that's what he said. Later I found out she died of cancer, too. Just like her.

But Nona's here now. She always knows what to do, how to talk to a guy so you don't feel like you're up against a brick wall. And she tells me things, good things that help you figure out how to live later, when you don't have to be at home anymore. She knows how to find things on the 'net and how to make things work out. Heck, she even cleaned the last pheasant I brought in. She told me it was great. mom never did that. She would make Dad do it. Say something stupid about whoever gets the meat has to know what to do with it, or don't bother hunting.

It's been almost two weeks since we heard from witchy. she obviously didn't want to come home, or she would have. Maybe it took her. always leaving us. Who did she hate worse? me or dad? At least no one stole Nona's car. Cops brought it up here the other day from wherever she was. Still had some fingerprint powder on it. Cool. But Dad said not to touch it. Nona's driving her car.

They should just forget about her. I thought she was going to die anyway, from cancer. That's what they said. They should make up their minds and admit it. That's probably what it was. Anyone could see something bad happened at the treatment place and they're covering it up. Cops should be looking there. Arrest somebody. At least Dad's stopped making me pray out loud about it. Sheesh. Leave a guy alone, why not?

You know, even better, no one said I had to go back to school, either. At least, not those days when we came back early from Hawaii. Now, school's out, of course. I could be too upset to go back after New Year's. Maybe I better practice my concerned look. There. How's this? Or this? Nutjob's making faces in the mirror.

I haven't done one since the plane. I think I'm getting over it.

How soon can I remind Dad about Christmas? It's only four days away. I could probably get the tree myself. Not the stupid stockings, though. witch only put dumb baby stuff in there, anyway... never understood that I'm grown up and don't want stupid little games and junk any more. You hear me? I'm over that stuff!

What's Nona making for supper? Maybe she'll let me help.

℘

57 - LIBBY

...you shall tread grapes, but not drink wine

"It's getting close to Christmas, Libby," Able said. "I thought maybe you'd like to talk about your family."

Maybe I would. But first, I wanted tea. "Could we get something warm to drink?" I asked. "I was outside for a little while and I can't seem to warm up."

"Of course. Let me scare up something from the kitchen. Coffee, hot chocolate? Tea? Hot cider?"

"Tea. No caffeine."

He turned. "I'll be right back."

Able had read my file. Why did he want me to talk about my family? Surely he wouldn't think that talking about Jordan or Vic or Nona made it easier for me to reconcile with leaving them? What if he wanted to surprise me and bring them here? Over my dead body.

I met Brother Able's return with what I hoped was a gracious smile despite the turmoil of my thoughts.

He poured fragrant lemon tea and handed me a cup. "I never told you how I met your husband. It was on a plane, a Hayden corporate jet, actually, returning stateside from China."

Yes, that fell into place. The time Nona had called Vic home. "That was a couple of months ago, I bet. Near the end of October."

He narrowed his eyes and twitched his mustache. "Yes. Did Victor mention meeting someone?"

Perhaps Brother Able had some pride, after all. "No, Brother Able. He did not talk about you. You see, he came home because of Nona."

The fact that Able did not ask about her assured me that he knew her too. Why wouldn't he, if he knew about my son, who was not named in the background report. I watched Able sip his tea. His eyes were half closed. Two spots of Mrs. Carrelton's violent mauve had appeared underneath either eye, but were fading already. Or was my eyesight deteriorating? "Vic had not been scheduled to return from that job for at least another couple of weeks. I had convinced myself that I had a case of muscle strain. I suppose I just didn't want to admit then that I knew the cancer had never really left. I wish I could explain it to you, Brother Able, how it feels to have something foreign growing inside you. Not like a baby, not that time."

My words tumbled and rushed, like so much flotsam in a woodland stream. Maybe I needed to talk about my family after all.

"I was plenty surprised when Vic brought Nona home one day, totally out of the blue, when I was first diagnosed with cancer and going through a terrible time with treatment. He never even talked to me about it, or asked if I wanted help. Just, there she was, a nurse practitioner he'd hired at the suggestion of Rafe Manuelo, the human resources director. I guess Rafe knew about her from some other case where they had to bring someone in to help an employee hurt on the job." I glanced at the sketchpad, then slurped the cooling tea. At Able's continued silence, I rambled on.

"I should have been jealous, I guess. She's beautiful. And so smart, and gentle and much kinder than I am. I can't imagine why she never got married. She lives with us. But, you know what?"

I didn't stop for Able to answer. "I think she has a secret boyfriend, or something. Somebody she doesn't want us to know about. Honestly, it wouldn't matter a bit to us. I really love her, and I want her to be happy. I sometimes catch her looking at Vic, as if she wonders what it's like for a man to be at home. I've never, ever wondered for a second whether Vic has been

* * *

unfaithful to me."

I laughed. "You know, I even wouldn't have minded, after my first surgery. But, with Nona, there isn't anything to worry about. She's really great with Jordan. She should have been a mother. Maybe she still can be, if she doesn't feel tied up with me anymore. See, I'm leaving my family in good hands."

I let my stream of words trickle down. Able posed quiet as a still life. I looked at him, sitting there in my room, with a set expression creating a neutral theater mask of his face. He was such a good listener. I wished I had the energy to pick up a pencil to draw his profile. Not many subjects were so good at staying still. "I hope she'll stay with Vic. Jordan loves her. She would be so good to them both. Jordan never really wanted me, even when he was a baby. Isn't that strange? It's true."

I nodded for emphasis. "But I think that Nona stays with us because her friend, and I don't care who it is, can't be with her. Maybe he's married, I don't know. They talk to each other every Tuesday. Sometimes I feel sorry for her, because it seems like all she does is talk to someone who can't take her away. Oh, and she visits her mother. All I really know about Nona, and she's been with me three years, is that she used to work at some nursing home place before she started doing private care. I think she used to be Catholic, because every once in a while she makes the sign of the cross, and sometimes does that curtsy thing before she sits in the pew. But she always comes to my church with us. She even took my son when I couldn't, whether or not he wanted to go."

I looked at Able who sat marbleized, listening to me with a look in his eyes that made me want to keep on talking even though exhaustion made my lips numb and my head feel too heavy for my neck. "Maybe, Brother Able, when I'm gone, you could visit them. I mean, if you're going back to Milwaukee sometime, anyway. It wouldn't be out of your way, or anything. I think you two would be good together."

I flushed. "I meant, of course, if you weren't a priest. But you can still be friends, right?"

❩❧

58 – ABLE

With what shall I come before the Lord...

He sat in Libby's tomblike room, quivering on the inside as if perched on the edge of the Grand Canyon and one false move would send him over the side to fly with the condors. As soon as Able had discovered the variables, that Libby Taylor was the wife of Victor Davis whom Able had prayed for before he met her, Able had been waiting for another part of the equation. How many galactic shoes did God wear?

Perhaps he had always known Nona was the missing ingredient—the catalyst that would speed up the reaction. But to what experiment? For what results?

Soon. Something big, something out of his control, was going to happen. God set up the formula—or laid the board for this game. Was Able the sacrificial pawn or a more powerful piece? The bishop, maybe? Advisor and protector of the king? Or the clown who drew the crowd's attention away from the tragedy going on in the center ring?

Why now, Lord? Why these people? What do you want of me?

Nona's parents were dead. Maybe this Nona wasn't the same person. "Libby, my order, the Alexian Brothers, runs a nursing home in Milwaukee. In fact, that's where we're headquartered. I used to know a woman named Nona, who worked at Alexian Village."

"Oh, so you've known her a long time."

"Nona Roland?"

"Of course. Or did you know someone else with that name?"

His frozen lips hurt to form words. He was afraid they would crack and bleed if he spoke, but he had to know. "Like Liberty, Nona is a lovely and unusual name. I think we're talking about the same person." He lifted his face to study Libby. "She even looks a bit like you."

Libby's brows knitted in thought. "Everyone says I look like my father. My jaw is too square to be pretty. Well, Nona and I wear the same size clothes, and that... Our hair's about the same style, I guess. Mine's gotten long. I haven't had a cut. I don't think anyone's mixed us up."

"No." Who had Nona been visiting, if not her mother? Of course. Emily. So, Libby might not know about his and Nona's daughter.

He took a deep breath and moved on knowing that later, when he was alone and did not have to exert rigorous self-control of his outward expression, he could examine his feelings. "Tell me about your favorite holiday traditions, Libby."

Libby took longer blinks. Her voice slurred as they continued their conversation. The discouraging part of Able's job meant seeing disease creep around each victim, subtly at first, then with increasing boldness. Libby's head jerked a couple of times as she mumbled about a big Christmas tree and stockings she filled with small gifts. Her mouth froze around an unspoken word as she drifted into sleep. Able mourned for Vic and Jordan and Nona, who'd never celebrate Christmas with Libby again.

He pulled the light blanket around Libby's shoulders and left her. He would be hard put not to talk to Nona about Libby on Tuesday.

59 - LIBBY

Shall I come before him with burnt offerings...

Christmas was soon. Maybe, three days? I couldn't recall exactly. I rested on a soft-as-a-cloud lounger in the glassed-in conservatory at Paradise House amid other patients and families. I studied the huge frond of a palm tree, focusing on the veins that carried life throughout the organism. Another kind of vine wound around the base of the plant. Little white lights glittered from secret hiding places tucked among the branches. I pushed my face upward with difficulty. A dull reflection of the panes of the ceiling made a geometry lesson on the sheen of the leaves.

Sequestering and examining memories kept my mind from dwelling on what was going on inside my body. I noticed that, as my thoughts drifted, I lost track of time whenever I closed my eyes. Between my nurses, Vi, Laurie, and Jill, I could almost ignore the fact that it wasn't just that my leg was numb, my hip joint ground in the socket like a mortar and pestle. My belly swelled gently, almost like when I was newly quickening life. My hands quavered enough to keep me from taking a firm grip on a pencil or brushing my hair.

Alternating sweats and chills attacked me. The steady warmth and humidity of the glass encased room helped. Soon, one of the nurses would figure out that breathing was becoming a chore. I let myself believe my fuzzy thoughts were caused by the drugs that relieved my pain for shorter and shorter periods of time. How much longer would the cancer need to spread before it cut off my life functions? Cancer wasn't exactly a smart disease, if one thought about it. Once its host was dead, it would die too. Maybe that was the secret to getting rid of cancer. Get rid of the hosts. More nonsense I was glad no one could hear.

Half a dozen people scattered in the dappled sunlight. One round, white-haired woman lay snoring. A basset-hound-faced man sat with his wife, who had the vacant look of someone who saw the other side more clearly than this world. A younger couple, maybe my age, sat with an older man in a wheelchair near the door, the droopy moroseness on his face echoed on theirs.

Rich entered the room and strode right up to me, as if his sole purpose in coming had been to find me. I perked up a bit watching him. I knew the whispers, how some of the staff nearly worshipped him, how kind he had been to many of them, but how he never got involved personally with anyone, patients or employees.

"Feel up to a stroll outside?" he asked. "There's not much breeze, and it's not too cold."

"Don't you have work to do?" I hedged, fighting off the tumbling slurry in my head. "I don't want to keep you from something important."

He shook his head. "Something important, she says." His smile was close-mouthed, gently chiding. "What I know is that everything is important to someone. Right now, spending time with you is important."

I waved a hand at my dressing gown. "I'm not really dressed for outside."

"How much do you care?"

I groaned. "Now you sound like Brother Able."

"Ah, I've overstepped my bounds," Rich responded. He sat in a nearby chair, making no move to leave. "How is your pain today?"

I pleated the sash of the robe between my fingers. "Our language is so silly, don't you think? If I say my pain is 'good' does that mean pain is unnoticeable to me, or am I describing the pain itself. If pain is good, is it worse for me and better for it, or vice versa?" I studied the fan I'd made of the sash.

I looked up to see that Rich crossed his legs and let his neck rest against the back of the chair. His eyes were a softer blue today, as if the ocean currents soothed turbulent waves. "So, does that mean you don't want to walk?"

"I'm not sure I can," I said.

He glanced around. "How did you get out here? I don't see a wheelchair."

"I'm embarrassed to admit that I had Vi drive me out, then fold the chair out of sight for an hour."

He stood and held out a hand. "We won't go far, and I'll help you. I promise. I just want you to take a breath of fresh air."

What could it hurt? "I'm not able to put any weight on the left side at all, Rich. You know that. You'd have to pretty much carry me."

"I can manage."

I was tired of having to discuss every whim, every action of my ever-growing useless body and mind with all who cared for me. I should trust them to do what's best for me, shouldn't I? That's why I left home, right? To be an anonymous patient. "No one will mind my robe?"

"No."

Rich had touched me before, usually in clinical settings where he palpated the masses in my stomach or read my chart. We had even shared a meal together twice, once with Brother Able. When I questioned Able if Rich treated all patients like that, he claimed I had reached privileged donor status when I turned the trust fund over to Paradise House. I let it slide. I knew Rich could not possibly have had enough hours in the day to spend that much private time with each patient and his or her family. I also knew that my trust fund would only make a dent in the cost of my care if I continued to breathe into the New Year. Sometimes I felt the brake and drag of the coming end when I wondered each night whether I would see another sunrise. Would I wake up in heaven, or the great holding tank like Vic's limbo, depending on which way the wind blew. Drifting away in sleep seemed so peaceful.

Rich's hand felt hot and dry. I wondered if he was fevered and sat on my desire to palm his forehead, as I had done to Jordan when he used to allow me to touch him. Rich tugged me gently into a sitting position and then crouched at my knees.

"Ready?"

I braced myself for the next rise. He grabbed my elbows and soon I was standing, leaning against him until I knew for certain my feet touched the floor and my leg and hip would not collapse. In the month away from home where I lived each day with Jordan's empty eyes and Vic's empty place at the table, I hadn't realized how much I missed being in close contact with another human being. I wondered what would happen if I wrapped my arms around him and let my cheek rest on his shoulder. I imagined his hand sliding around my waist; the other, my hip.

"I need to tell you something," I said.

"What?"

"I don't like outside much."

"Why not?"

"It's really big."

"Libby?" His hand slid around my waist, but for support.

"I think I'm okay," I told him and set an experimental right foot down, then let him take all my weight for the other step. "Slow, though."

"Slow," he agreed, and clutched my elbow. We shuffled along the wall to the exit, which he easily pushed with one hand, and guided me over the threshold. This unsteadiness, uncertainty whether my body would obey my mental command, or even if I was sending the right command, must be what it was like to grow old. I chuckled low in my throat.

"What's so funny?"

"I just thought that I felt like a ninety-year-old woman. I guess growing old's not all it's cracked up to be."

I had hoped he would laugh, but he did not.

We stepped onto a blacktopped path that wound through patches of azalea and palmetto, and other exotic bushes I had no interest in identifying. If I chose not to learn their names, I would not miss them as much when I closed my eyes for the last time. Already the desire to capture the essence of life with my brush dipped in colors of my mixing waned.

Ten steps down the path a wooden bench was set into red rock against a woven wooden fence. Cedars on either side offered a windbreak, of which we had no need today. Lattice for a roof offered shade enough. Sweat bathed my cheeks and neck, and trickled down my back and I was glad to sit with the doctor at my side. "I did not expect to…linger, once I arrived."

"Tell me, what will you miss most?"

I gazed at the bobbing feather grass and precision-clipped lawn kept fresh and sparkling with constant sprinkles from an underground system. A bird trilled, another species unknown to me. "I thought I would miss flowers and birds. I thought I would miss painting." I grasped Rich's hand. "But now I know that touch, being able to sense a connection to another living being…that, I think, is what I'll miss. My family, of course. I'm sad, but happy they aren't here to watch this…travesty of wasted space. I wonder if you can feel anything in heaven? Do you think we have sensation up there?"

"I don't know." Rich held up my hand in his strong one. A line matched the indentation on my left ring finger. "Sometimes I wonder if I could share anyone else's life again."

I contemplated the picture our hands made. "Will you tell me something about yourself?"

"Like what?" he asked.

"Brother Able said you wanted to find a universal cure for cancer."

Rich let go of my hand. "Since there are countless doctors and researchers all over the world working night and day on treatments, and many treatments work, that's a reckless thing to say."

"That's what he said about you. That you could be reckless."

He looked at me. "Is that how you see me?"

"No. I just wonder what you did to make Brother Able think that."

Rich leaned forward to rest his elbows on his knees and clasped his hands around his neck. "Able would never have acted on his feelings, and I trusted Joanie implicitly, but I believe that the good Brother had a crush on my wife."

Thoughts tumbled through my mind. "I understand, Rich. Maybe I even share your feelings about my husband and...another woman in our lives."

"Able can't understand how we suffered. He had a woman, once. They even had a child. Did he tell you that?"

Cold dismay poked my heart that I had to hear this news from Rich and not Able. But I was not surprised that Able was a parent, since he expressed concern for my son in intimate ways that only a daddy could feel.

"Joanie wanted me to use her case in my research. I was hurt that she told Able about our baby first. When she miscarried...Libby, I can't describe the horror I felt. Then she begged me to use his cells.... I don't think I'll ever forgive Able for betraying my trust like that."

"His cells? Able? Betraying?" Even hearing through the mist of my sluggish comprehension about Brother Able's relationship and child—where was the child? she? now?—I could not believe that Able would deliberately hurt anyone. "I thought you said you couldn't have a...oh. Surely you don't mean that you think Able and Joanie—"

"No! Of course not." Rich clenched my hand again. "No, not that they had an affair. That she told him about the baby, and he didn't tell me first. I don't know if we would have been able to save my wife if we didn't choose such a radical stem cell treatment. I'll never know. Then, to...do what we did with my son's cells...it killed something inside of me, even though she lived." He looked at the impressions his nails made in my palm. "I have a hard time caring about anything."

"I hear people talk about you. They say you're wonderful. I believe that. But I also understand what you mean."

He closed his eyes. The white lines of pain around his mouth made me want to groan for him. "I had to shut off my emotions," I said, "to survive three years ago. I didn't do a very good job of learning how to feel again, either."

"The worst part is doing everything you know how, pushing yourself to try harder, and still, they die."

"You said you saved your wife," I whispered.

"Yes. At what cost? Able was a friend to both of us. Now..."

"It seems the two of you are still close."

Rich's thin smile made me shiver. His eyes turned frosty. "We each have obligations and responsibilities. His, to make death more comfortable for our patients. Mine, to find a way to make this place unnecessary."

"I wish there was something I could do to help you. I can't salvage my marriage, or my relationship with my son."

"You're shivering, Libby. Let's get you back inside."

My body was numb. I let Rich take most of my weight. Even so, on the fourth step, I felt the bone in my thigh splinter. I even pictured it happening in my mind, like one of those medical dramas that animate internal body functions, at the same time an explosive adrenaline rush overcame the agony of the break in a tidal wave of molten pain. All my other little twinges and aches disappeared into one great sensation of flight. In a Lake Michigan pea soup fog, I heard Rich call for help in a voice reminiscent of the lighthouse horn. He lowered me to the ground. The back of his hand brushed my cheek

"Libby? Libby, come on. You'll be okay. Libby."

I smiled, even as I felt the shaking start and travel up my spine and along my upper arms. For some reason, it was important, vital, that I make him understand that I knew I'd be all right. Before my eyes closed, I asked, "Will you let me help you, Rich?"

"Libby, you don't have to leave me. You understand that, right? You don't have to go. Hang on."

The dark concern on his face was the last thing I remembered about him. I did not see him again until I died.

☙

60 – ABLE

Arise, plead your case before the mountains...

Able took his cell phone close to the beach, but far enough away from the crashing surf that he could still hear her voice. After lowering himself to a patch of wispy grass amid fine grains of sand, he dialed. Tomorrow people all over the world would celebrate Christmas. Able had sent Christmas greetings and a small gift, soft slippers and socks decorated with cats, to Emily last week.

But first, today was Tuesday, the day he usually enjoyed a conversation with Nona. Why had Nona sent Libby here? Able had no doubt that Libby's arrival at Paradise House had been arranged somehow by Nona. Did it have something to do with her question at Thanksgiving? How he helped people face death? Nona had taken care of other patients who passed away. Why now, after all this time, had she called upon him? Victor should know about his wife.

Nona must have empathized with the anxiety in his greeting, for hers was just as subdued. They spoke of Emily first, as they always did. Shared one or two anecdotes about the people they'd met during the past week.

Able let the conversation lapse. Then the question burst from his soul. "Nona, she's here. Why? Why did you send her?"

Nona's breath whooshed in his ear, as if she were sitting right next to him. Able shivered and closed his eyes to pretend he could feel the warmth of her arm as she might lean against his. *Lord, it's not wrong to long for touch. You are always there, and I will not betray my vows. But sometimes I need to know you through contact with another.*

"How is she, Able?"

"Not good. It could happen any day."

"I'm glad she's with you. Did you talk to her, get to know her a little?"

"Nona, how could you? How could you let her husband suffer? Or have you told him? And what about the boy? They should be together."

"Victor? Vic Davis? How do you know he's suffering? You don't know him."

"Only through God's good providence. We met on the Hayden plane coming home from China in October."

Able heard her gusty sigh. "Of course. When I first called him about Libby. What did he say?"

"He asked me to pray for his wife, who he thought might be ill again. I didn't ask about her at that time, merely supported the man in his grief. That was the first time we met."

"The first time?" Nona whispered.

"I contacted him again a couple of weeks ago, when I was in Milwaukee."

"When you visited Em."

"Right."

"You surely knew then, didn't you?"

"No. The woman had not yet arrived at Paradise House. I had never asked anything more personal of him. In fact, at the time we saw each other in Milwaukee, he had to leave early because the police were investigating the disappearance of his wife. Nona, Nona, did you know then? Why didn't you spare the man?"

"I thought you'd understand. I thought it would be all right."

"Nona, what would be all right? You should not have

interfered."

"Libby wanted peace. She didn't want to fight any more. Everyone was pushing her, and I felt sorry for her. When I saw— just a minute."

Able heard a door being closed in the background. "What's that?"

"Nothing, Able. I just thought maybe I heard something. I usually go outside, but it's pretty cold out this evening."

"Is there snow?" Able closed his eyes again to imagine the water in front of him frozen, like Lake Michigan which stretched to the horizon.

"Plenty enough. It's about fifteen degrees here tonight."

"It's Christmas Eve. Did you go to church?"

"No. Jordan had a tantrum when Vic suggested it. Asked, which church? The true one or his mother's false one. Then it got ugly."

"She told me about the Christmas stockings."

"On the mantle? So you talk to her?"

"Yes. A person in her situation should have her family with her."

"I don't know about that, Able. Did you meet Jordan?"

"No. Victor said he took the news about his mother with difficulty."

"That's the understatement of the year. You should have been here three years ago when his mother was first diagnosed and undergoing treatment. I don't think they knew Jordan kept a loaded gun in his room—one of Vic's. They went to hunter's safety classes together back then. I had to sleep in the boy's room quite often, to keep him from waking his parents with his night terrors. A boy of eleven. It was horrifying. I think Vic brought me here as much for Jordan as to help Libby."

● ● ●

"Did he go to therapy? How is he now?"

"Jordan? Yes, he went to a child psychologist for a while. Vic was home most of the year, and it seemed things were better. Jordan's been through a lot. He was quite close to his grandparents. They took care of him when he was a baby so Libby could travel and work with Vic for Hayden. Then the grandmother died. The boy was young, but I think it affected him. In most of the nightmares he called out for her. His grandfather's been in a nursing home for a few years. Since Libby got sick."

"Shouldn't the boy see his mother, at least say good-bye to her? Nona, the husband should be told that his wife is safe. Or at least he should be told of her whereabouts. He should be granted the choice of seeing his wife one last time. What about when she passes on? Were we just supposed to ship her body home? For shame, Nona. I never guessed you to be so cruel."

"I did what I thought was best, Able. Please, don't be angry. You were the first person I thought of who would know how to help her."

"Help her how? Why didn't you say anything sooner?"

"What? Like, do you happen to have a new patient named Libby Davis? Able, you wouldn't have been able to say anything, and you know it."

"You gave her the information about Paradise House. You sent her here."

"I merely planted the website in her computer file. I had no way of knowing that she would even decide on a hospice, let alone which one. She researched several."

"You should have shared your knowledge with her husband."

"I don't know. Someone's at my door. I have to go now. Good-bye."

● ● ●

Able severed the connection from his end. He was cold and very stiff by the time he rose to return to Paradise House with the aid of a flashlight. Christmas was the time of giving, and of receiving. God gave his only begotten son, the world received him—eventually. Should he, Able, tell Victor about Libby? Every cell screamed that yes, of course he must. It was the right, moral, just, conscionable thing to do.

Illegal by current law. But ethical. Justifiable. Definitely worth a visit to Father Diego. And probably a call to Brother Harold in Milwaukee.

How much trouble would Able get into if he divulged any privileged health information to another? He'd been careful in his discussion with Nona. Careful enough?

On Christmas morning, Able woke groggy from another session of indecision with Father Diego after late Mass. Diego, rightly so, refused to give advice. "Absolution, yes. Advice, never."

Able wished for the return of Christ to happen...immediately.

In the meantime, he would visit a few of the families at the hospice and wish them Merry Christmas, check on Libby, then go make the phone call to his director in Milwaukee.

As he walked the sunny corridor after breakfast, Able's transceiver, clipped to his belt, buzzed in code. It changed to a pulse, which meant a death was imminent. If there had been two long buzzes, a death had already occurred. Able followed the commotion in the hall. All nearby staff were to answer the summons, but discreetly, in order not to alarm the other families.

Able followed lanky, grizzled Paulo, a long-time orderly, speed-walking down the hall. When Able saw the activity in and out of a too-familiar room, he leaned against the wall opposite the door to wait. He closed his eyes and began to pray. Libby had grown weaker over the last two days since she broke her leg.

Rich had taken her on that walk on purpose—probably to weaken her, if she wasn't dying quickly enough to suit his needs.

Four people came out of Libby's room. Able moved closer to see inside. Rich worked at Libby's head while her day nurse, Laurie, maneuvered the bed flat while eyeing an IV line and trying to get Rich's attention.

Lord, Lord, comfort us. Able entered the room. Rich's voice rumbled low and steady. He paid no heed to Laurie's apparent concern over the IV line somehow still attached to Libby. Not terribly unusual, but it should be removed. Libby must have asked for something to ease her pain.

"We're here, Libby. Feel my hands? Laurie is here." Rich must have sensed Able's presence, for he added, "And Brother Able."

Able studied the scene before approaching. Libby's breathing was labored. She lay on her back, her good leg restlessly trying to draw up, then falling flat. Rich held his hands on either side of her face, his back to Laurie. Rich must have put on a blood pressure monitor too. Why? The staff did not monitor such vitals. An alarm sounded. Rich turned it off without looking at it.

Laurie held Libby's hand, her fingers pressed to the pulse point on Libby's wrist. Rich leaned close to Libby's face. Able heard nothing until Rich spoke. "She's gone. That's it. Call it, please."

There were no wall clocks in the patient rooms at Paradise House. Laurie looked at her wristwatch. "Oh-seven-seventeen."

"Thank you. Let's sign off on the screen." Rich led the way to the nurse's station near the door, as if he had all the time in the world. "Able, you're witness."

Rich had a set routine for death. Certificates prepared on the electronic death registration file system for each patient expedited paperwork. As often as he could, Rich took on the task of preparing the bodies of those patients who were alone.

"Thank you, Laurie. Cause? Advanced metastasized cancer of the uterus. You may go. Able, you signed? Close the door, Laurie, thank you."

Able finished his electronic signature, "Able Fenwick, CFA," and clicked submit.

As the door to the hallway closed, he heard Laurie's voice. "Yes, that's right. She's gone. I know, it's Christmas. How sad. Yes, Dr. Rich is taking care of her...I know, he's so kind. He really grieves when they pass on, especially those who have no one to mourn them." The voices faded behind the closed door.

Able looked up in time to see Rich remove the IV from Libby's arm. Rich reached into his coat pocket and took out a syringe. He uncapped it and opened Libby's gown enough to stab the contents directly into her chest. He waited, then began compressions. Able was stunned into immobility but not shocked. He had only witnessed this action one other time and it failed.

Lord God, in your great mercy, show us your will. Direct my steps to help Victor to understand. Help us all to accept this passage of your servant, Liberty Taylor Davis, who travels to a better place—

"That's right. Come on, Libby," Rich said, grunting with his exertions.

Able's hands clenched. Was there enough left of Libby to come back? His jaw ached from grinding his teeth at the sounds of choking from the occupant of the bed. "Irreversible death, Rich. It's not death if her condition is reversible."

• • •

"We don't know for sure that it is. I never know. I only guess. She stopped breathing. Laurie witnessed. So did you." The choking sounds turned to gags and coughs.

Rich sat and pulled Libby to lean upright against him. He patted her back as though she were an infant. "Come on, Lib. You're all right."

"Brain death," Able whispered through clenched teeth. "Please, Rich."

Libby's white hands flexed. She gasped. "Rich." Her voice was a harsh whisper.

"Shh. It's all right now. Don't try to talk."

"What happened?"

"It's all right, Libby. Don't worry. We'll get you moved. I'm going to let you lie back, now. Able will keep you company while I get a gurney."

"Why—"

"Shh. Just wait. I'll be right back. Everything will be okay. I love you."

Able faltered in his path toward Libby. "Rich."

He didn't hesitate. "I'll be back, Able. You know what we need to do next."

When he was gone, Able approached Libby. Her skin was so white it glowed. Her eyes burned into his.

"Brother Able, what have we done?"

"Put God to the test."

Her voice came out paper thin. "What will happen next?"

"Only he knows."

Rich pushed the door open with the rattling gurney. He called back over his shoulder, "No, thank you, Paulo. I'll call you later if I need anything."

Ↄ

61 – LIBBY

...and let the hills hear your voice

"**I** was prepared to die," I told Brother Able. I had a screaming headache and couldn't hear myself. Rich pushed a gurney next to my bed. I stared at Able, not willing to break contact with the person I believed would tell me the truth.

"I told you, you didn't have to," I heard Rich say in a harsh tone.

"Rich? What's going to happen? I don't feel very well."

"Shh. I have to cover your eyes, as they might be sensitive to light. I'm taking you over to a different area of the complex, where you can help me. Like you said you wanted, remember? Lie quietly, now. Don't talk, don't move. We'll be quick, and then I'll give you something for the pain."

I had never experienced motion sickness before. I was glad that my eyes were covered, for even through the sheet the blur of overhead fluorescent fixtures created a Doppler effect that throbbed through my lids as we passed through the hall at dizzying speed.

Finally, we stopped in a place that was dim and echoing. A rush of cold air washed my face when the sheet was pulled away. Rich smiled at me, although his eyes didn't meet mine for more than a second. "Here we are, Libby. Your new room. It's quiet here, on this side. No one will bother you and you can rest."

I reached for Rich's hand and missed. My arm swung over the edge of the bed and I didn't have the strength to pull it back.

Able helped me. He stood near and held my forearm with icy fingers. "What's going on?" I whispered to him. "Where's Rich going? I'm so cold. Is it always this cold here? Are we still in California?"

Before Able could answer me, Rich returned. He held a syringe in his hand. "Libby. I'm here. You'll be all right, now. I'm going to give you something that will relax you. Just rest some more. We talked about this, remember? You wanted to help me. This is how you can help me."

Able's comforting presence backed away. I needed him to explain what was happening. The sting of a needle in my hip magnified the pounding at my temples. "Rich—"

His hand stroked my forehead. "Shh. You're free now."

"I'm free?" Clouds were coming down out of the gray ceiling. I had never seen that happen before. The sensation was nothing like the wet, cold fog that charged in off Lake Michigan in the spring and fall. These clouds were fluffy and soothing. "Rich? What do you mean? I'm so sleepy."

"You died, Libby. And now you're free from everything. It's Christmas, my love. My gift to you."

* * *

℅

62 – ABLE

...your inhabitants speak lies...

Able sat holding his head in his hands in the empty lounge in the empty Alexian wing at the hospice in the middle of the morning on Christmas day. Even Gert had flown back to Milwaukee for Christmas. Able picked up his telephone and put it down. Three times. Who would he call? What would he say? Scenarios flashed through his mind until he wondered if he was as crazy as Rich.

"Hello, Mr. Davis? I regret to inform you that your wife is sort of dead."

"Brother Harold, I have a really big problem."

"Officer, please, my best friend just killed a woman who was dying already. And I helped him do it. Only she's not completely dead. Yet. Right now, it's just fraud. Only there's nothing to gain. Except maybe the chance to cure her cancer. And she'll probably die in a week, anyway."

"Nona, I knew something bad would happen. Why did you do it?"

The worst one would be, "Emily, Daddy's sorry he can't visit anymore. He's done something really bad and has to go to jail."

Able thought of a skit he had seen once, about God taking phone calls from earth. Able lifted his head and reached for his cell phone. He stared at the numbers on the instrument in his hand and wondered how big of a long distance charge heaven would be. Clearly, Rich's actions overrode the confidentiality clauses of medical and ethical rulings. Legally, he should tell some authority. But what good would it do to turn Rich in? Libby was going to die again eventually just like all the others and resolve this present dilemma. He let the phone fall on the table with a clatter. He closed his eyes and slumped back.

The chair across from him was pulled out with a noisy scrape on the tiles. "Merry Christmas, Able. Sorry, I was a little busy back there to stop and chat."

"Rich." Able forced himself to stop and analyze the rage pulsing through his chest before he could reach over the table and choke Rich Bernard to death. He shook the red haze from his mind. "Why her, Rich? Why now?"

Rich's eyes looked clear and he seemed eager to talk. "Libby was sent to me, Able. You know that. She's the right person at the right time, and in the perfect stage of my research." Rich's mouth puckered in petulance when Able could not bring himself to respond. "She agreed to help me, just like all the others. In fact, she volunteered. Insisted. You didn't object to the others. It's a little late, now, my friend. I hold the winning hand."

"You've never let it get this far. What did you have to prove, signing a death certificate like that? Why couldn't you just release her, like before? Did you tell poor Helen that you were in love with her? Is that what you do, lie your head off to make them agree to be your lab rats?"

"I said no such thing to any of them. They all consented of their own free will."

"They had no one who would protest for them. Libby has a family who cares deeply for her."

Rich pounded his fist on the table. "Libby consented."

"She has a husband and a son who should have been told her whereabouts. Real people, Rich, with real names and faces."

"According to the state of California, she's not married any more. In fact, she doesn't even exist."

"Rich, think. You've never done this before. At least, it didn't work that other time. Let's back off a moment, think. We can't undo what has already happened, but maybe there's a way to fix this." Able reached for the cell phone.

Rich plucked the instrument from Able's hand. "I suppose you already called the authorities."

"What authorities? What was I supposed to say?"

"So, you haven't said anything to anyone about this?"

The short hairs underneath Able's collar prickled the back of his neck. "Rich. You have to tell the truth. I'll back you up, tell them you've been under a lot of stress. Whatever you want."

"You would really jeopardize the Alexian organization? I'll make sure the whole association comes to a screeching halt. I'll raise such a stink about your activities here in California over the last two decades that no one will give them any money for any reason, ever again."

"The Congregation has suffered worse over the past eight hundred years, Rich. We're still here. There is nothing you can do to hurt us substantially."

"What about your daughter?"

"What about her?"

"You won't be able to support her in the lifestyle to which she has been accustomed for most of her life. Don't you care what will happen to her if she has to leave Green Willow because the money dried up?"

Of course it mattered, but Able couldn't consider the consequences, not this instant. Other issues were immediate. "Libby is not your creation."

"I am not insane, Able. Look at me. God has given me another chance. I'll get it right this time. We have the opportunity to do so much good here for so many people. Libby is the key. I know it."

"God? You don't believe in God."

"I never said that I didn't believe. Only that I could not accept a God who could be so cruel."

"So, if God does what you want, then it's okay to believe?"

"You're twisting my words, Able. I have a chance to fix something that's gone terribly wrong with the human race. God doesn't want people to suffer, does he? That's why he gave us the ability to correct hi... the mistakes. I will be able to help so many others."

Able stabbed his finger in Rich's direction. "Can you hear yourself? I will, I have I, I, I. Another sounded much like you. Lucifer, son of the morning. God cast him from heaven, and he became Satan, the father of evil."

Rich sat back and folded his arms. "I'm not the devil incarnate. You always say that God gives the desires of the heart to those who ask."

"If they ask with the right motive. Rich, what's your motive? What are you getting out of this? Are you treating Mrs. Davis the same as all of the other research subjects? What about your other patients here at Paradise House? Are you willing to help everyone? You said you never forced anyone to work with you."

"And so I haven't. How can you justify not wanting to help millions of people who suffer from a terrible disease that can be controlled? Hopefully eradicated? Were you there to object when smallpox was wiped out? Bubonic plague? Isn't that how the Alexians started—caring for plague victims in Europe? What about treating polio? TB? The flu? Come on, Able, you can't tell me with an honest heart that you wish those diseases still killed millions, unchecked, around the world. What about surgeries, like heart bypass or kidney transplants? We do genetic counseling here every day. Why shouldn't people know about the defects in their genes and support our efforts to repair them?"

Able's lips stuck like glue. What had he done?

"Libby Davis is just one person, Able, who would have died anyway. We're talking about developing a universal cure for cancer by saving the life of one innocent person. How can you object to that? Or would you prefer to go and snuff out her life right now?"

❧

63 - LIBBY

...and their tongue is deceitful in their mouth...

The walls of my new room were plain beige. Heavy blue drapes were pulled across the lone window high on the wall, near the ceiling. A couple of framed paintings of the ocean hung across from me. They were a great deal more soothing than the bleary décor of my former room. I didn't know if I was on a ground floor or ten stories high. Although, if I were still at Paradise House, none of Rich's buildings reached more than four stories. If I remembered correctly.

Rich had been right. This area of the hospice was quiet. No bells, no running feet, no Vi or Laurie or Jill checking on me every hour. Mary Schumacher, Rich's assistant, or Rich himself, brought me food. I had not seen Able since I arrived, five days ago. I think. The first couple of days were pretty fuzzy.

The doctor sat with me late at night, sometimes with paperwork, sometimes talking or sometimes quietly listening to the late news with me on a small television set. We had not returned to the subject of my death. He didn't tell me again that he loved me. I convinced myself I had made it up. His voice was gentle when he explained what he was doing. His touch was soothing but impersonal whenever he examined me.

I had plenty of time to think in between the courses of IV treatment Mary delivered, or the bloodletting and painful bone marrow harvesting she did. I stared now at the bag of clear fluid that hung on the pole attached to my bed. A line from it snaked into my arm. My broken leg, placed in a pressure cast last week, ached only mildly. The invasive tubing remained. Rich wouldn't look at me when he told me it was easier to care for me that way, without having to worry about bathroom trips. He'd take them out when I could get up without help. Maybe in another week, he said, again without quite meeting my eyes. If all continued to go well.

All what? How did I feel about what was happening to me? I thought about the vows I had made to Vic and God—traditional ones that ended with "Till death do us part." Surely what Rich had done was unethical or at least immoral. Had I agreed? I don't remember. Maybe he was just plain wrong. Probably illegal too.

But what if Rich was right? Could I forget my past life and move on? Who would I belong to now?

Lord God, show me the way. Mary had brought me a Bible when I asked. I searched the scriptures but found nothing that even remotely addressed my situation, except for the story about the woman who married seven brothers but had no heir. I thought the story might comfort Rich, when I remembered that Pastor Grant at home talked about the lack of marriage in heaven. Of the several people who had been resurrected in the course of Bible times, few had a written continued history. Lazarus walked around with Jesus as a sort of show and tell project. Who was I now? Just one of the many whose whole story was the miracle of simply being alive with no thought to what I was supposed to do with that life?

If God didn't answer, who should I continue to question? What was right? Was my life a gift from Rich or a curse? What would Able say? *C'mon, Lib, you know what Able would say.* Rich truly wanted to help people. Why was that wrong?

Did Vic know I was dead?

My stomach churned. I needed to think about something else.

Mary Schumacher. Mary was an enigma. I don't think I could ever capture her essence on paper. She came and went like a breeze, the maria of folklore. Sometimes she did not even speak to me. Rich said she was a quiet-by-nature person, well suited to work in a lab. She specialized in genetic therapy, he told me, and held an MD and two PhDs. Mary had a pale moon of a face. Her eyes were round and light-colored, her nose was a blob. Even her hands were shapeless, all the fingers seemed to be the same size as they fluttered like moths around me during her procedures. Her hair was hidden in a cap. I thought she might have been in an accident or something and needed reconstructive surgery because of the lack of definition of her features, but I wasn't in the mood to pry.

For one of his exams, Rich used a portable scanning machine on me that I recognized. Vic had designed it for field or bush clinics where the only source of power was a solar battery pack. So, Rich didn't design everything he used. He must have bought it from Hayden. I found it the height of irony that even after I died, Vic was still present, taking part in my therapy.

But would he ever forgive me? Understand that, really, I did it for him? *Vic, I'm sorry. So sorry.*

I grew restless when the drawn curtains allowed sunlight to spill down inside my room. I asked Mary today's date when she came in the afternoon.

She looked at me out of the corner of her eye while she checked my vitals. "January fifth," she said.

"How are things going?"

She packed up her kit with brusque economy. "Not what we hoped."

Then she left.

Shutting the door to my room fanned the quake Mary's words had begun in the pit of my stomach.

But I feel better, I wanted to cry out. Even yesterday I had complained about the tubes. Today I seriously considered pulling them out myself. I had managed to toggle myself to the edge of my bed and roll on my side for a time, although the leg had been a problem to maneuver.

There was no phone or monitor that I could see in my room. Didn't they care if I fell and hurt myself? Or needed something? I threw my water bottle at the door in frustration. And regretted it as the hours stretched.

By the time Rich came with a covered plate of food for us to share for supper, I had been in tears for an hour. He set the tray down and sat next to me on the bed. He looked so haggard that I wondered how he could get the words out. "Libby, we're trying the best we can. Mary told me what she said to you."

"I have to know what's going on. I can't take this anymore."

He got up and picked up the cracked water bottle and put it in the trash can in the corner of the room. He tossed a towel onto the water spill, then collapsed into the blue easy chair that he had brought into the room a week ago.

"I'm sorry. I was scared. I felt so much better yesterday. I just wanted to know."

"Of course you did." He plucked the cover from the dinner tray. "Here, I brought you some of that soup you liked."

I wiped at my tears, unable to stem the trickle. I had a headache again, but I could not bring myself to ask for another needle stick. "Can I see Brother Able?"

He hesitated in the motion of stirring the broccoli chowder. "I'll ask him."

Rich set a small dish in front of me, then sat and closed his eyes.

"Are you okay?" I asked him.

"Just tired and hungry."

I felt like a spoiled child having a temper tantrum because the pink dress was in the wash and nothing else would do. "Rich, I'm sorry."

His eyes opened, azure pools that did not condemn me for losing faith in him.

"I should have made sure you understood everything right from the start, Libby. You've been so generous. I must seem like a mad scientist, holed up with my lab assistant."

A picture of Mary dressed like Igor, the silly movie friend of Dr. Frankenstein, made me purse my mouth to keep the smile inside. "I'm grateful, Rich, for the opportunity to take part in your important research. I'm scared. And disappointed that it's not working."

"Oh, I wouldn't say that." Rich cocked his head at me and leaned forward to touch my cheek. "The research is not going as quickly as I wished, that's all."

Did he mean that I was dying too fast? That he wouldn't achieve the results he looked for? "Rich, what did you mean when you told me that I was dead?" I crinkled my eyes, anxiety keeping my mouth stiff. "Not to complain, but I sort of pictured heaven without the tubes."

He grimaced. "I'm sorry. It's just easier for us to take care of you like this." He took my hands. "It feels like heaven to me, to have you here now."

"Then how can I be dead?"

"Clinically dead. Legally. We watched you stop breathing. Your heart stopped beating. We signed your death certificate and filed it with the state."

"Who's we?"

"Laurie, Able, and I."

"So, what does that mean?"

"Legally, you're not on any registries. You can be anyone you want. Create a whole new you."

"My nurse, Laurie, is in on this?"

His right eyelid twitched. He let go of my hands. "Laurie's not aware that I was able to revive you. There's nothing wrong, Libby. Some of my research hasn't been approved by the government, yet. It will be, but the process takes so long. You were in a research study before, in Texas. You know what can go wrong even after the trials are given the green light for the human application phase." He stood and crossed to the window. Daylight had faded. "But you're free now, Libby. You can take a new name if you want."

"What about my husband?"

Rich leaned against the wall and looked at his shoes. "I suppose he's a widower now. Like me."

"But I'm—"

"Libby, I'm hungry and tired. Please, let's talk about this later. You shouldn't stress yourself. It's not good for you." He strode back across the fake wood floor to my side. "Don't you want to help me anymore? I won't keep you here against your will, you know."

I wondered why I had to be dead to help him. But the rebellion faded as he smiled and held up the soup spoon.

"Come, try this good soup with me."

In between bites he told me a little about the technique he

● ● ●

and Mary used to track down the defective genetic codes that spurred my cancer. "If we can isolate the specific messages that have mutated the cells, we can reprogram them with the correct message. We can even make them destroy the cancerous cells and replace the damaged ones."

"What about my leg?"

"Bone grows quickly. Your leg is healing even now, but very slowly because most of your energy is being used to fight the cancer."

"The cancer's winning."

His hand clenched around the spoon, then loosened. "We're fighting it. It won't win. I promise you."

We finished the food, Rich eating the most when I told him I wasn't very hungry.

Before he left, he helped me brush my teeth and washed my face with sure, gentle strokes of a heated washcloth. After, he kissed my forehead. "We'll win, Libby."

"You'll ask Brother Able to come and visit me?"

"Yes. I'll ask. But I can't promise you that he will. And I'll make sure Mary doesn't upset you anymore."

When he was gone, I turned out the light to think in the dark. Sometimes things seemed more clear when not artificially illuminated.

I could be anyone now, Rich said. A whole new person with a new name. How could I be anyone else? My name was always part of who I was, and now it meant even more to me. Liberty. Was I free? Free from what? For what?

Would Rich want me when he was finished with me? If I did not die—again—that is? What about Vic? Vic had left me over and over for work. But I could not deny that he had been my life, all that I knew and cared about for the greater part of my existence.

He flew back from China at a single call.

But I didn't call him. Nona did. And he did not try hard enough to find me when I left Texas.

I didn't want anyone to find me, I reminded myself. I took care to make sure I would be lost. For Jordan's sake, I needed to be gone for good.

In your heart, though, you did not want to be lost forever. You even hoped Able would tell when he found out your true identity.

When Able came I intended to ask him all of my questions. I needed to hear from him that I wasn't as evil as I felt.

☙

64 - ABLE

Your rich men are full of violence...

Able wrestled with his conscience, fasted, and prayed while he waited to hear of Libby's true death. Rich would have that much decency, to inform him, wouldn't he? Then his dilemma would be solved. When Able heard nothing by Epiphany, January 6, Able made up his mind to act. He stopped in to see Gert, who had returned the day before from her vacation.

"Gert, please have Mrs. Carrelton meet me at Our Lady of Sorrows. This afternoon at two o'clock, if she can. Thank you." Gert pulled her pad toward her. She did not meet his eyes, or ask for any other information.

In the afternoon, Able stood in front of the little chapel with his hands clasped behind his back, waiting for Mrs. Carrelton. Clouds and light sprinkles of rain matched his mood. When she arrived, he returned her nod of silent acknowledgement and ushered her inside. "Please, be seated."

Mrs. Carrelton loosened her jacket and slid into a pew. She set her purse by her side, and turned to look at the man who sat in front of her with his back to them.

"I have asked Father Diego Torres to witness this discussion today."

Father Diego turned, smiled briefly, then faced the altar.

Able sat across the aisle. He got up again, restless. "Mrs. Carrelton, would you say that Paradise House is a successful institution?"

Carrelton frowned. "Yes."

"Financially and missionally sound?"

She leaned back and crossed her legs. "Yes."

Able paused. She was a good director. She knew how and what to answer. "How long would you say that, if no other outside funding came in, Paradise House would run on its current budget with its current available income?"

"The Bernard Paradise House Foundation is sound for at least ten years, with careful handling and cautious investment."

Able blinked and chewed on the end of his mustache. He had known Rich was wealthy; he had not realized how well off. Did God ever envision genetic manipulation? Able sighed. "Here's the situation. I think you and I both agree that Dr. Rich Bernard is a gifted, caring physician and researcher who holds the best interest of this hospice in mind."

Mrs. Carrelton pushed to her feet.

"Wait, please."

She held up her hand. "I'm not going anywhere, Brother Able. I just need to...get up." She paced the aisle in front of him. "Our mission is to comfort everyone involved at the end of a loved one's life."

"Your job is to oversee the hospice, not Rich's private lab and research."

"Yes. But—"

"But he has not been able to separate the two institutions, not in practice or theory. I need to tell you things, Mrs. Carrelton, things that I have kept in my heart far too long."

Carrelton sat down again. "Call me Liz."

Able sat next to her. As far as he could tell, Diego had not changed position. "Paradise House is a facility to be proud of. We attract people in need from all over the world. We help them. We

● ● ●

are well respected for our program."

"Yes. The fact that you and Rich are in constant demand to give presentations proves this. You wouldn't believe all the calls I actually turn down, or try to reschedule."

"Can Paradise House operate without Dr. Bernard's private research?"

Carrelton clenched her jaw before she spoke. "I would go so far as to say that the research is detrimental to our cause. There is so much good being done here with the patients and their families despite their diagnoses. It's not that we don't want anyone to get well. Of course, we would like that. We pray for it. But we also accept what modern medicine currently can and cannot do."

"I do not believe that Dr. Bernard sees the matter of death and research in the same light."

Carrelton stared in the direction of the altar.

"I have not made a huge secret of the fact that I have a daughter. Emily. She's twenty-nine years old and severely incapacitated. She needs a great deal of care. I learned of her...existence after I took my final vows." Able faced the altar and prayed for strength. "I am not proud, nor will I justify my actions. For the past twenty-some years I have used money that should have gone into the budget of Paradise House for her care."

When Carrelton said nothing, Able turned to her. She smiled at him. "A long time ago I wondered what happened to the compensation from a presentation you had made. Dr. Bernard explained to me that you redirected money that was rightfully yours to a different charitable cause. It wasn't hard to discover which one."

Able blinked away hot tears. "This only makes my next statement harder to say. Dr. Salisbury was correct in thinking

● ● ●

that Rich's research should benefit anyone who wants it. Rich has not always been...judicial in selecting patients to participate in his studies."

Carrelton's eyelids opened and closed in slow motion, as if she were a beat behind him.

"In the past, he has removed certain patients from the census. With their cooperation."

She twined her fingers and bowed her head.

"On Christmas Day, he declared a patient dead, when in fact, she was revived by him a short time later. He did not share the news of her survival."

Diego scraped the heel of his sandal on the floor. Able and Carrelton looked in his direction, then back at each other.

"And I take it he did not correct his original mistake, but allowed a fraudulent death certificate to be filed? And you know about this because...you were there?"

Able took a deep breath. "Dr. Bernard's behavior has been irrational lately. Do you think we can possibly come to a consensus to attempt to resolve this issue internally?" Able watched the director closely. She had not yet blinked. "Correct me if you disagree, please, but I believe that many more people would be hurt if the law was involved."

A muscle twitched as Carrelton ground her teeth. "We cannot have a scandal at Paradise House."

"It would be in everyone's best interest to help Dr. Bernard quietly."

Carrelton faced the open window. "Of course, we have the resources to keep going for a long time. But, besides that, what sponsors would donate if Paradise House's reputation was tainted? What patients would want to come here?" She crossed her wrists over her lap and leaned her forehead against the pew in front of her. "You're right, Brother Able. It's essential we ask Dr. Bernard quietly to separate himself and the lab from Paradise House. We have the patients to consider. We have our families and our good name. Paradise House is a respected organization. We can't allow him to ruin it."

"He hasn't taken a vacation since I can remember."

Carrelton sat up. Her brows rose. "A vacation?" She cocked her head, frowning. "I don't think that will appeal to him. He must separate his research from the Foundation that runs the hospice."

"Are we asking him to stop research on the hospice grounds?"

"I don't know that he will agree. Perhaps he will accept a board of directors."

Able thought for a moment before speaking. "Dr. Salisbury, whom I note is still employed, had a very good point. Rich's research has merit. He must be persuaded to act according to federal guidelines. Then, more patients could benefit."

"We don't want to open a can of worms in allowing everyone to believe they can be cured if they come to Paradise House."

"Agreed," Able said. "That's not our purpose."

Carrelton repeated by rote the mission statement of Paradise House. "We ensure comfort and the best quality care for those facing the end of their earthly lives."

Able needed her completely on his side of the situation. "I must also inform you that I have discussed my misgivings with Dr. Bernard. For the first time I admit he frightens me. He threatened me, my loved ones, and my congregation."

Father Diego got up and padded to the altar, where he knelt.

Carrelton whispered. "Physically?"

"Blackmail."

"Your daughter? But I know all about that." She stared at Able. "Don't I?"

"Yes."

"What do we need to do about the current situation?"

"With Mrs. Davis?"

Carrelton frowned. "I don't recognize that name."

"That's because she was admitted under the name of Liberty Taylor."

"That certificate was filed. I saw the confirmation. But she was revived? Where...is she?"

"In the research wing."

Carrelton closed her eyes. Able saw her swallow. "I don't know, Able, how to get around this without some kind of legal..." She opened her eyes. "What's her current medical condition?"

• • •

Ↄ

65 - LIBBY

Shall I give my firstborn for my transgression...

Rich's lined, gray face and puffy eyes looked much worse than I felt. I tingled and itched all over, like I had hives on the inside. I should have spiked adrenaline at the sensation, but instead I felt muzzy, as if I were evaporating in sea foam, like the Little Mermaid.

"Libby, your system was in such rough shape, probably from the drug study, that we're having trouble finding cells we can coax into accepting new programming."

I heard my voice, as if in a dream. "You mean, like stem cells?"

"Yes. Normally I could find some, or Mary could pull some out of..." His voice faded in and out, like a stereo that only worked on one side. "Your immune system has been compromised."

He squeezed my shoulder, gently. "Libby, pay attention. Do you have any close relatives living?"

My head wobbled and I pulled away from him, frowning. Why was he pestering me? "My father. But he's so sick. My son, who thinks I'm dead. What did Vic say when you told him about me?"

Rich had his back to me, mumbling.

I strained to hear if he'd asked me another question, unsure if he wanted my response. "I could get some cord blood from the hospital."

Rich didn't turn around. Had I even spoken? I tried again.

"You mean, you want Jordan's cord blood? From City Memorial? It's still in the cryo tank. We were just talking about it, you know, for his school paper."

The next thing I knew was Rich's hand on my shoulder, shaking me. His voice was too loud. "Your son, Libby? You have his cord blood? Where?"

Rich's questions sizzled, as if introduced directly into my synapses. I woke up enough to realize that he had not known about Jordan's cord blood before. "No!"

"I have a process that I worked out years ago, on my wife...and son. If I can filter out the commonalities with your blood—"

"I said no, Rich."

He faced me. Why was he angry? He sat near me and took my hand. I felt him tremble. "No what, Libby?"

"He can't know that I'm alive—for now. It will only confuse him. Please, you can't do this."

"I just want a sample. He won't know."

"No, Rich. Just leave it be."

"This is important, Libby, a breakthrough. I know immunotherapy is the key to finding a universal cure. I just need core cells to work with. We mix it with a protein that we take from...." I faded into clouds which felt damp and icy, making me twitch and blink awake, "...inject you with it."

I waved my head from side to side, although it nauseated me.

"Libby! Do you remember the name of the drug study you were in? It's in your file, right? The investigator was who?"

"Schlitz, like the beer."

"Okay, I met Schlitz. Tom, that's right. I'll call him. There must be something I can to do unravel this mess."

Cſ

66 - ABLE

...the fruit of my body for the sin of my soul...

Able paused in Rich's outer office. Rich's door was open, and Able heard his voice. Laura was not at her desk, so Able waited. He needed to check Rich's schedule for the next week so that he and the director could plan a confrontation. And he determined to find out the truth about Libby's condition.

"Yes, thank you," Able heard Rich say. "Right. City Memorial Hospital in Milwaukee, Wisconsin. I'll hold."

Able squinted. He was on the telephone, then, not with his assistant. What business did Rich have in Wisconsin? Able, his conscience pricked for Rich's sake, listened.

"Ah, yes. Amanda. Thank you. Dr. Richard Bernard, Bernard Foundation. Right. Thank you. Yes, I understand that you have old samples of cord blood in cryostorage? Right. No, research. I had my assistant fax the protocols. You got it? Good... Probably not viable...oh, you think so? No, no, just a few. Right. Tom Schlitz, U-T...So, you can help me out? Thank you. Yes, I'll hold."

Able took a quick breath and backed away from the door. Rich turned in the desk chair and looked right at Able through the open door while he held the phone to his ear.

"Amanda, hello," Rich said, still staring at Able. "Yes. Good. About a half dozen. Are they labeled? You'll remove them?" Rich turned away and checked a paper on his desk. Able continued to watch him, much as he would a spider cocooning a fly caught in its web. "I'm looking for these specific types: B pos, O neg,

AB…yes, that's right. Thank you. You'll ship right away? Good. Send the charges to this address. Right. Call this number with any questions, and Laura will help you. Thank you. Have a good day."

Rich stood. "Able, what can I do for you today?"

Able advanced just past the door into Rich's office. "What are you doing?"

"Just business." Rich adjusted the stapler on his desk.

"Is this about Libby?"

"It's research, Brother Able. The other half of Paradise House's business, remember? The part that feeds you…and yours."

"How is Libby?"

Rich stilled and stared at Able, unblinking. "She's safe."

"Rich, I'd like to see her."

"I'll ask her. Excuse me, if that's all, I have rounds." Rich pounced to his feet and stalked past Able.

While Able walked back to his own office, he realized that no sound at all played in the background of Rich's office.

$$\text{\Large ⳙ}$$

67- LIBBY

You shall sow, but not reap

Rich's face glowed through the fuzzy wool that surrounded everything. His voice sounded like it traveled through water to my ears.

"Libby, stay with me." A rush of cool air flowed across my shoulder and arm. "We did it. I found the key. Now you'll be well."

I blinked at the feel of ice on my arm. "Rich?"

"I'm here. Mary…" His face faded away, then reappeared. I shifted my chin just enough to watch him adjust a bag of fluids hung on an IV pole. "Are you ready, Libby?"

What was he doing? "More needles?"

"This will be the last time."

"What it will feel like?"

"You shouldn't feel a thing."

His hands on my arm and shoulder soothed my skin, comforting against the chill that pressed on me. Soon, a trickle of heat coursed into my vein, spreading like an electric blanket.

"It's warm, Rich. I feel warm."

Two weeks later I walked of my own free will on crutches into Rich's house where he had a guest suite ready for me. He showed me around his prairie style villa with off-handed pride. I thought it should be out of place in the California desert where adobe typically ruled, but his home seemed an oasis—a place filled with life, where I could find peace. From a back balcony off my bedroom, I sniffed the heavy bouquet of Rich's flower gardens with their underlying hint of salt from the ocean. I thought about what was happening weather-wise with winter storms in Wisconsin at the end of January and hugged myself.

But how could I be completely joyful when I thought about all I had lost? Rich's treatment fixed my broken cell structures, but could my staying with him fix all the broken places in my life? I dared not think of my family, for I could not go home again.

Rich, who still looked exhausted with lines deeply etched under his eyes, told me I made his life and faith in the power of God's triumph through medicine worthwhile.

"Can you rest now?" I asked, one morning when we met in the kitchen and he let me fix him toast.

His eagle eyes were too bright under their hood of secrecy. "Libby, it's a busy time for me." He pressed my hair with his mouth as he brushed past on his way out. "Don't worry about anything. Promise. Just concentrate on getting well."

I prayed for him, wondering if God still heard me after I had walked out of the light. Cowardice made me hope my presence was not the cause of Rich's weariness, but deep inside I knew the fact that I lived was a terrible challenge to explain.

When he was away I wandered the rooms kept dark against the southern California heat. Sometimes I missed my home—my studio—back in Wisconsin. Vic's house rose two and a half stories, and had a turret. Rich's house of rock and timber crawled, flat, across a small valley.

I rested, exercised as much as I could with the still-mending thigh and grating hip, accepted the continued rounds of infusion from Mary or Rich in the meantime, and felt curiously apathetic about outside. Rich would often steal home during the day to touch me, as if he was afraid I'd popped like champagne bubbles while he'd been away. Sometimes I wondered if I were a figment of his imagination.

How much time did we have to be together? I couldn't bring myself to ask if this reprieve in my illness was permanent or merely a temporary remission while he studied the effects of the genetic manipulation.

I stood on the exposed patio facing the ocean waves. Overhead sun sparkled at each effervescent crest. Water dashed against sand. Seagulls challenged the curling tide.

Long beams extending from the roofline made shadows across the flat rock floor. I shivered when Rich's arms wrapped me from behind, enveloping me with the warmth of his body. I shifted to rub my nose in the scent of him on the lapel of his jacket, which he removed and settled about my shoulders.

"You're cold, Libby. You shouldn't be out here without a sweater. Come."

"I didn't hear you." I adjusted the crutch and turned to follow him inside, but tripped on an uneven stone. My good leg had been more tired than I thought, and I felt myself crumple. Rich caught me up and carried me through the glass doors, my other leg in its pressure cast stuck straight out in front of us.

"You're okay, love?"

"Yes. Just tired, I think."

"And hungry. You were so engaged in the water. What were you thinking about? And I know you, you probably ate nothing at all yet. I brought you something from Marion's kitchen."

We ignored food for the moment, to sit on one of Rich's great leather chairs facing the fireplace. I held on to his jacket, determined that he not take it from me when he left. "I was thinking about what tints would capture the foam at the tops of the waves."

He relaxed the lines between his brows. "I could have guessed. Now I know you're well on the way if you want to paint again. Give me a list, and I'll get supplies for you."

I smiled and drew my finger along his cheek. I let him put his warm mouth against my cold lips. We shifted with sighs and movements that were not yet in tune, like the natural motions of a long-married couple. Like Vic and I had been. *I'm sorry, Vic. But it's better this way. Better for everyone. I don't know how long this respite will last.*

He pulled back, a little twist of his lips letting me know he read these thoughts of mine as well and wanted to replace them. "It'll come, Libby. We have time, now. All the time we need."

Would we find a way to mesh our lives? Or were we fooling ourselves? "Rich, are you sure? Are you sure this isn't a fantasy we have no right to have? How long do we really have?"

Rich's eyes lit with a greenish spark that drowned out the blue. "Why are you questioning me? I told you, I've waited for this for a long time." He brushed his thumb against my lower lip. "You fit this house. I see you here much better than Joanie. She always fought it, wanting to move a window, never satisfied with furniture or wanting carpeting on the floor."

I looked at the beautiful stones and wood that made up the walking surface and said nothing. He held his hand against my cheek. He whispered. "You know what gives me the most comfort?"

I shook my head, afraid to break the spell of the intimacy he wove despite my misgivings.

"I listen to you breathe. Just breathing, moving air in and out. Sometimes at night, I stand by your bed as you sleep and just listen."

I lowered my cheek to his chest, and in turn, let the beat of his heart soothe me. I wasn't sure how pleased I was to know that he stole into my room at night. But Vic had never said or done anything like this bit of romanticism. It almost seemed more intimate than making love. From whatever country he was in, Vic had telephoned to hear my voice, but he had not wanted to give that up to be with me, so close that he could be part of my life process.

I shifted in Rich's embrace, wondering what made right and what made wrong. His arms pressed me against him, and I listened while he told me about how we would conquer death together.

I woke in the twilight, still wrapped in his jacket. He had left a note near my hand, bound with one of the scarlet bougainvillea blossoms I loved.

☙

68 - ABLE

And what does the Lord require of you but...

Rich stalked a figure eight in the parking lot of South Beach Park in Habilus, the place Able and Carrelton were able to coax him to meet. He had evaded them for over a week, until Carrelton told him bluntly that she had no other choice than to call in the California State Department of Health Services if he refused to talk.

"Put yourself in Victor Davis's place," Able tried to reason. "How would you feel, not knowing whether your wife was alive or dead?"

"This is different." Rich stopped his frenzy and faced them, then started pacing again.

"Why?" Carrelton asked.

"Because Libby is her own person now. She doesn't want her old life back. In fact, she ran away from them and came here to me."

Carrelton folded her arms and leaned against her car. "Are you trying to tell me that Mrs. Davis knew you and that's why she came to Paradise House?"

Able closed his eyes and petitioned God for control. "Of course she didn't know him. Rich, we're trying to help you."

"Help yourselves, you mean. All I want to do is fix people, and you're trying to stop me. Who's the one who needs help?" He stopped again. "And it worked. Mary and I are starting to write up the procedure for the Journal of American Medicine."

"Able?" Carrelton asked.

Able took a deep breath and focused on her. "I don't know what he could write that wouldn't get him into trouble. Everything about his research on Mrs. Davis is at least unethical, besides illegal."

Carrelton turned to Able. "Dr. Bernard, we want what's best for Paradise House. You've built up a wonderful institution. Only an insane person would risk all of this on a questionable research project."

Rich put his hands on his hips and presented his profile. "You don't understand. This is the key to breaking the grip of cancer. For everyone. Paradise House and places like it will no longer be needed. What's more important? Helping people die? Or helping them live?"

"Cancer isn't the only cause of death," Able reminded Rich.

"There's nothing you can say that will make me give up my research." The doctor turned his shoulder.

"We don't want you to give it up," Carrelton said.

Rich stopped his convulsive walk.

"We want you to keep on," she said.

"Only under appropriate guidelines. With a board of directors," Able added.

Rich bowed his head and slid his hands into his pockets. "A board? Of who? People who think they can understand what I have accomplished? People who think they can tell me how to spend my own money?"

Carrelton unfolded her arms and stepped away from the car. "People who appreciate and applaud your efforts, but who will help guide your decisions and keep you from performing such questionable acts as you did with Mrs. Davis."

"They would stop me."

Carrelton frowned. "They would hopefully stop you from illegal activities, yes."

Rich lifted his chin. "And if I don't agree?"

"You must agree. I care about the patients at the hospice. I care more than you do, apparently, since I'm unwilling to risk the reputation of this place on one misguided research project."

Rich bowed his head. "You have no idea. None at all." He walked to his car, got in and drove away.

Abel ushered Carrelton into her car and sat beside her. She made no move to drive.

"I suppose it's too late to try and hire inside counsel, or find someone who would be sympathetic to our situation," he said.

"That tide went out in 1980 with the Uniform Determination of Death Act." She put her hands on the wheel, then reached to turn the key. "No, Able, I'm afraid my duty is clear. It's unfortunate. I think I can build a case for Dr. Bernard acting on his own to commit fraud in the case of Mrs. Davis. But I don't know how quiet we can keep his attempt to cure cancer." She stared through the glass of her windshield. "If it's real, and not a fluke. And how is this going to affect Paradise House? I just can't begin to imagine."

On a Thursday late in the morning, Able sat with the Moreno family at Paradise House. Michael Moreno's expression of compassion was held in place only in the presence of his wife, for he often wept with Able in the lounge or chapel after the visit. Kelly Moreno was about the same age as Libby Davis, and dying of cancer of the pituitary. Their son, a senior in high school, had been sent to play in the state basketball championships over his protests.

Able's phone buzzed. When he checked the ID, he nearly dropped it. "Excuse me, won't you? I'll return later." Able touched each of them before he left Kelly's room and hurried to his own.

Breathing hard, he dialed the number. "Nona! What is it? Is Emily all right?"

"Able, it's Vic. Please, tell me—what happened?"

"What do you mean?"

"Victor received a letter today, from his lawyer. There were papers he had to sign, about a new trust fund for Jordan. Libby…Libby's death certificate went to the lawyer's name on the papers she took with her to Paradise House. Why didn't you tell me?"

Able sank onto the *prie dieu* and leaned his forehead against the wall. "I can't tell you."

"Can't? When did she die?"

"Have you seen the death certificate?"

"No. Victor got the mail, then lit out of here so fast. I wondered what was the matter, so I…I looked inside the envelope."

"What do they say?"

"That a certified copy of Libby's de-death certificate will be ordered so that the estate can be settled. In the meantime, Victor needed to-to sign the papers for Jordan. Able, when? When did she die?"

"She didn't," Able choked out and hung up.

69 - WEBPOST: THEPLEASUREOFTHEHUNT

Today, someone messaged me privately about transporting. Although of course we never condone illegal movement, this anonymous person brought up a very good point. In this day and age of terrorists around every corner, how easy is it to get a weapon across country?

Naturally, there's the completely above-board method. Person has a permit and any paperwork, has a hard case, declares and checks it. Get a load of the movie star-types who "forget" they have their weapon with them and get "caught" at the airport. Just a way to make the media print a name.

Say you don't want your name in print, say you haven't forgotten about your weapon, which you need strictly for self-defense, and say you don't want to make a federal case about anything.

Strictly hypothetically, how would you get a weapon across country?

Obvious: you'd drive, of course. Very carefully. No border checks, no declarations at state lines, no duty to pay. Naturally, being the law-abiding citizen you are, you check the carrying regulations in the community of your destination.

Hitching? Not so good anymore. Of course, if you have one of those truck stop rest places where a lot of people are always going in and out, cash, and a baby face to go with your innocent-looking backpack, maybe. But I still wouldn't recommend it.

How desperate are you? What if you don't have access to a vehicle, or a reliable one, or don't have a license, can't prove the age for a rental, or whatever? Pretty hard to fly unless you follow all the above mentioned regs.

That leaves train or bus. Did some research for my buddy.

TSA is clear on flight, but did you know that rarely do you

have to have luggage checked on trains. In fact, I came across no one who had the pleasure.

If the train schedule doesn't meet your needs. Try the bus. Designated pick-up spots, cash transactions for tix, and no questions asked.

Now, this begs the question of why anyone would feel the need to make such a hush-hush move if you had a legitimate reason? Is our government unreasonable? We live in a land where we can ask such questions without fear of repercussion. Free speech, free travel, right to bear arms. Yep, the good old USA. So careful, like when they made you take your stinkin' shoes off and check your undies at the airports because of one freak customer, then didn't bother to regulate other modes of transportation forever. It's still spotty, which may be your best hope.

Well, I hope our little discussion today has helped someone. Especially my friend. And, no, I don't know the rules for transporting hunting dogs.

‍ ℘

70 - LIBBY

...to do justice...

Rich went to a conference in Seattle. He said he would X-ray my leg in two days, on Sunday, when he got home. The hip would have to be replaced sometime in the future. When I fretted over the cost, he grinned and told me he had connections and not to worry. For now, I was comfortable enough with painkillers and limited activity. And I had that future to look forward to.

I set up an easel on the patio and contented myself by capturing the flowers in Rich's yard. Bobby from the grounds crew at the hospice came once a week to clip and weed. So far, he had not seen me. Rich had not ordered me to hide, but whenever I saw Bobby's truck, I managed to find something to do inside, far from the windows.

I wanted to talk to Able, but hadn't been able to bring myself to do more than pick up the extension and look at it. Maybe I wanted to pretend I was happy just a little bit longer. Talking to him might break the spell. He could pester me about my former life, and I could not answer.

After a sandwich for lunch, I sat at Rich's computer console. He e-mailed me late last night, writing that he was thinking of me, and did not want to disturb my rest with the telephone.

I pulled up his message and read it again. Once the seed had been planted, thoughts of my former life, I could not uproot it. Just for kicks, I called up my website, Liberty Creations. Surely there was no harm in that. The opening screen still featured the fall page with a message saying that Christmas arrangements were limited this year, so hurry, get your orders in. I plugged in my password and read through the list of unfulfilled orders. How many angry customers had I lost?

I put the cursor over the contact link and wondered what would happen if I clicked. What could it hurt? Maybe I would find out then whether I was really dead if this new me could contact Libby Davis from the grave. Would she respond?

I began to type a long letter to the old me, describing my feelings and experiences since leaving Texas. I had no intention of sending it, of course.

Friday

Dear Libby,

Nothing turns out like you think when you're twenty-two years old and alone in a foreign country. Did I grab Vic Davis because I was afraid? Then how can I justify myself now that I'm over forty, alone again in a foreign state and still afraid?

Except for Rich I wouldn't know what to do, how to act. When he's with me, I know he'll do anything to keep me safe. Sometimes I wonder if what's happening to me is one of those dreams, like when you're in a coma, or something, and can't tell what's real. Maybe I'm still in Texas and Dr. Schlitz is monitoring my vital signs while I'm hooked up to machines. Vic is standing against the wall in the dark room, watching and thumbing his beads, praying for a miracle.

If I'm not in dreamland, then I'm in Paradise. At Paradise House, that is. With Rich Bernard, who couldn't let me stay dead. So what if I remind him of Joanie? Maybe I'm flattered that he should think so highly of me. I'm proud that I could help him figure out what fed the cancer in my body and kill it. When I am completely well, who knows for sure what will happen?

California is beautiful. I knew it would be. I wanted to enjoy something beautiful before the cancer took me. Do I still deserve all this loveliness if I don't die? Rich said his research wasn't approved by the government, so that's why he signed my death certificate. He said I stopped breathing and my heart stopped, so I really was dead, at least for a time. Maybe I suffered brain damage and I'm in a coma here in California.

Stop it. Accept what Rich did for you. Accept the fact that he asked you to be his wife.

Let me go, Liberty Taylor Davis. I want to find happiness, like when I first married, like when I knew love grew inside of me and came out as Jordan, like when I could rejoice for my mother who finally found peace away from Dad. Like believing Nona will always be there for Vic and Jordan.

I clicked the send button before I realized what I'd done. Old habits were hard to change. Who would see it, anyway? A shiver made my heart flutter when a reply flashed to the inbox seconds later.

Libby? Is that really you? Oh, Libby, please, tell me it's you.

☙

71 - ABLE

...and to love kindness, and...

On Saturday morning, Able stretched out a hand and stifled his phone before picking it up. He opened one eye to note that the sky was still black.

"Yes? Brother Able here."

"Able, please, you have to help me."

Able sat bolt upright as though struck from on high. "Nona!" He turned on the bedside lamp. His clock read 3:55 a.m.

"He's left here. With the gun his father gave him. Able, one thing I know is that he's resourceful. I'm looking at a website right now that I believe he created, called the Pleasure of the Hunt. It started off as a real site, but gradually turned to pleasure sport, and I believe, how to target people, and how to secretly transport weapons across the country. I'm sure he's coming out to you. I don't know when he left. Please. Watch out for him."

"Who? Who's coming out to me? Nona, what are you talking about? What website?"

"Jordan, Libby and Vic's son. Oh, please, please believe me. You have to help me find him."

Able blinked and looked around for his clothes. "The boy? Hunting? Tell me everything you know. Why would he have a gun?"

Able scrabbled to dress. "How would he know about this place?"

"It's the strangest thing. I rigged Libby's website contact

information to come into my e-mail box so that I could answer everyone's inquiries without having to go through the website, or try to explain that Libby was sick. I was sitting here last night, and a message came through. From her. Able, she sent a message to herself."

Libby, how could you? "You're sure it was from her? It could have been a sick joke."

"It's her. I—we talked. She told me she was glad that you and I knew each other. She liked you but hadn't talked to you lately. She was hurt that you didn't want to see her anymore." Nona's voice dropped. "She told me about...about the doctor. Able, what's going on? This doesn't sound right, although of course I didn't say that to her."

Able gripped the phone in frustration. "Nona—Nona, did you tell Jordan that his mother is alive? We have to think of the boy, here."

"No. I went up this morning to make sure he was getting ready for school. That's when I saw his bed hadn't been slept in. He was gone. His computer was on. I checked it. I didn't know that he could hack into my e-mail, as well as both of his parents'. The other thing is...well, I read his confirmation journal. He blames his mother for a lot of his problems. He seems to think that if she's dead, everything will be all right and his father...and I will stay home with him."

"Where is the boy's father?"

"Vic's up in Green Bay for an emergency with Libby's father. It sounds like the man's near death."

"So you never told Libby's husband that she came here?"

"I—I thought the death certificate would lay the matter to rest."

"Listen, Nona. You have to tell Victor about Paradise House.

Now. I don't care who gets into what kind of trouble, or the condition of Mr. Taylor. Our first priority is to help Jordan."

"Okay. But, Able, what else should I do? Vic will want to come out there, you know."

"I would agree, and I say, let him. Help him. And pray."

"Able, are you going to contact the police?"

"I have to. This has gone too far."

"Vic is a good man. He'll know how to handle his son."

"It's precisely because no one knows how to handle this boy that everything's gone so wrong. I'm afraid."

"Please, Able, don't let him see his mother. And be careful."

"I'll do everything in my power."

☙

72 - LIBBY

...to walk humbly with your God

I decided two things on Sunday morning. I would quit hiding, and I would go see Brother Able, no matter what Rich said.

E-mailing Nona had been exhilarating. Once she told me about my father's condition, and that Vic was gone away from Jordan again—had, in fact, not been home much for him at all, I decided that if Rich truly loved me and wanted to marry me, we would do it aboveboard. I would make a clean break with Vic. Since I was no longer sick, Jordan could come and live with us, and he would have two parents who would love him and stay with him all the time. I knew Rich would approve of my plan. He would reap the benefits of having a son, after all, since I could not bear more children.

I washed then put on a yellow shirt and maneuvered loose khaki slacks over the cast. I brushed my hair, which had grown a couple of inches but remained bouncy, and swiped some lipstick on my mouth. I had found the lipstick in a drawer in the bathroom, along with some mascara that was dried out and deodorant that no longer had a scent. I stuffed those things in the garbage. I knew with the intuition of a usurper that Rich did not have the strength to throw away all of his dead wife's things.

I three-stepped on my crutches to the front door with determined energy. I squared my shoulders, took a deep breath, and ventured into the big outside.

The sunshine hit me like a heat lamp on high. I turned

around and hunted up a pair of sunglasses. They were too big and kept slipping down my nose as I struggled along the driveway with my crutches. I stopped every other step and adjusted them.

The long trudge to the main hospice complex where I planned to seek out Brother Able gave me too much time to reconsider my plans. Rich had never met my son. What if they didn't like each other? What would Vic say? I bit my lip and pushed the glasses once more. Vic knew things had never been the same between us since the first time I got sick. We had not slept together in four years. I wasn't his possession. He had no right to keep me from...what? Being alive?

Vic was—is—a nice man. He would find someone else to wait for him to come home. Maybe Nona. If he wanted. All I wanted now was to do the right thing. But what was that?

How would Able advise me? He had a child of his own to think of. A child. With a woman...from Milwaukee. Someone he used to work with. At the Alexian Village. Where Nona had worked long ago. I stopped, puffing, and sat on a bench. Paradise House loomed about a hundred yards away. It wasn't going anywhere.

Realization plowed slowly and painfully over me. Nona did not visit her mother every Tuesday. Nona visited her child. Hers and Able's. Then she told him about it every Tuesday night. How had a convenient notice about Paradise House simply appeared in my list of hospices?

I understood then that nothing was simple. Nothing at all.

Nona sent me here deliberately. Had that been her plan? To get me out of the way so she could have my family? She had not even tried to help me get better once we knew the cancer had never left my body.

• • •

I blinked at tears. A tiny figure came out of the hospice and headed toward the parking lot. Able. I recognized his black coat and white collar even at this distance. In an instant, I knew I had been wrong about everything. California was not beautiful. This place was not Paradise, but its opposite. Everything Able stood for, all we had discussed and prayed about, and certainly his warnings about Rich, represented the real truth. A person who was on the right side would never ask me to participate in something so wrong, like Rich had, even if the result was supposed to be good.

Nona sent me here because she trusted Able to help me do the right thing. Nona loved me. She would never, ever hurt me. She knew my faults and weaknesses better than anyone—even Vic. Oh, Vic. How could I have been so foolhardy?

Could I catch Able before he left the parking lot?

I hobbled on my crutches toward him, the pain of my hip starting to burn and throb. I didn't think my voice would reach, but I called anyway. He must have heard something, for he stopped and turned to his left, facing a long row of cars that reflected burning sunlight into my eyes.

I hurried, squinting to keep the glasses from falling off. He kept looking in the direction of the cars. I shuffled closer and called louder. He didn't move. I turned to see if I could tell what attracted his attention. Just a boy with a backpack. I pushed the sunglasses up and, with a groan, stepped off the curb. Something flashed in the gleaming light near that boy and made me look again.

"Jordan?" I looked into the empty black eye of the barrel of a gun and froze. But it swuung away toward the couple who stood against the sky on a grassy hill twenty yards to the left of the front entrance to the hospice. Who was that? Vic? Who was with

● ● ●

him?

I screamed. "Help! Somebody, stop him!"

Brother Able squatted behind the cars. I watched while he crept silently toward Jordan. But not quickly enough.

The report from Jordan's shot reached my ears after I saw Vic's companion lift from her feet as though she jumped. She landed like a rag doll on her back two paces beyond him. I raced toward them using one crutch and not caring at the pain as I put unaccustomed weight on my left leg and my raw armpit.

My husband knelt, holding Nona in his arms. He didn't appear to recognize me through his shocked expression when he raised his face at my approach.

Jordan...oh, Jordan, what have you done? I saw Able had finally reached him, much too late. I couldn't move.

The stain blooming across the front of Nona's pretty buttery shirt spread into a great Georgia O'Keefe flower. It would have been beautiful in any other setting.

That's what I thought. Not "oh, no," or "please, God, let her live." Just how beautiful the colors looked.

After that, for the rest of my life when I recalled that morning, I saw the devastating scene only in black and white.

● ● ●

☕

73 - ABLE

So now faith, hope, and love abide, these three...

Able's shoulders were too heavy to straighten. His back bowed under their weight. He could not summon a shred of feeling. Even the whoosh of spirit from the boy's body when he looked upon his mother and compared her to his victim had no power to move Able. He watched the officers tuck Jordan Davis into a squad car and squeal away. Victor stood alone on the asphalt of the parking lot against the great edifice of Paradise House, his face raised to heaven, his hands clenched.

Able had one foot on the curb where the ambulance had stopped, hopelessly, for Nona. One foot was on the drive, an awkward pose. The pain in his knee helped distract him from the suffocating constriction of his heart and lungs. Brilliant sunshine made it difficult to pick out the shape of Libby who sat on the grass next to Nona's puddled blood. Liz Carrelton squatted nearby, along with a female officer.

Able flexed his fingers. He should wash his hands. He really should.

"Sir, would you come with me, now, please?"

Able nodded and followed the young uniformed man into the cool, dark hospice.

He heard Liz's footsteps clack on the tile behind him, out of rhythm, in a measure that caused his heart to beat in syncopation and his breath catch on his esophagus.

"Has anyone heard from Dr. Bernard? I know he went to

Seattle to that conference, but he's due back today. He's not answering his phone." Liz pushed past them into her office where her raised voice brought the other female officer bustling in, one hand on her belt.

In the big conference room, someone accidentally activated the sound system. The cry of seagulls pierced the air.

Much later, when the attorney Liz called had seen him, and questions had been asked and answered in the big conference room in the modern glass and adobe police station in Habilus, Able asked to see the boy. While the judge, the guardian ad litem, the social service people, and the Davis lawyers were working out their deals, Jordan was held in a cell by himself, on suicide watch. Though the boy's father protested the bars, Victor did not stand a chance given the evidence of premeditation. But had Nona been the chosen target?

Victor had tried unsuccessfully to pry him out of the arms of the orderly who held him with his arms taut behind his back until the police arrived. Jordan had fought just as hard to stay out of reach.

In his cell, the teenager rocked back and forth on the bed, holding his crossed ankles. The rasp of his shirt against the concrete wall made a harsh accompaniment to the cadence of his breathing and the moans, "nn-nn-nno." Able thought of Emily's heaving sway from the prison of her wheelchair and her desperate attempt to speak. In a way, the two children were not much different. Jordan became a prisoner almost as much as Emily.

Could Libby or Vic or even Nona have prevented the horror? The great sorrow was that no one had seen what was happening in that young man's life, except maybe Nona. Able could not blame Libby or Vic for Jordan's terminal actions any more than he could blame himself for Emily's condition. Jordan's life had ended long before Nona's.

Able read some of the entries Jordan made both in the printed pages of the hunting website he had created and in the church journal Nona brought to California with her. The hunting log entries had been smooth at first. When confronted with adult situations, the boy either ignored what he could not understand or lashed out in childish anger. Great emotional distress from trauma he could not name, but probably came from his time with his grandparents, led the boy to harm himself. Nona had guessed, when she told Able of his night terrors. Able's experience led him to believe that the conventional treatment they tried never erased the boy's pain or made him whole.

Libby and Vic were not bad people. Just forgiven. As he was. Able mourned Jordan as part of his need to forgive.

Rich Bernard, the author of this mess, was another story.

Nona...Nona would wait in the place where marriage was no longer a part of the human experience.

Able closed his eyes and held his hand to his cheek. He smelled a trace sweetness of blood that he could not completely remove from under his fingernails. He had reached her in time to see her eyes brighten with other-worldly visions, then fade. Her lips had been warm.

Rich had not come back. Able pictured the doctor, driving toward Paradise House from the airport and seeing emergency vehicles. Rich couldn't have known what had happened right away, yet he had never tried to find out.

Able felt like rocking, too; giving in to the rhythm of repetitive motion until the pain of remembering lulled into somnolence. At least he had been spared from murdering Rich Bernard.

"Brother Able?"

Able's hand tightened on the Bible he carried. His breath quickened. He cleared his throat before turning. "Yes, Victor."

But it was Libby who said, "Please, Brother Able, forgive us."

It hurt to inhale. "It is not in my power to do so."

"What might I do to make up for my son's sins?" Libby asked. "I take it all back. I never meant to hurt anyone. I only wanted…I wanted to stop hurting."

"One thing I know, Libby, is that God's compassion and mercy are far greater than anything I can imagine. Jesus Christ made up for our sins long ago. What you can do for your son, now, is to love him and pray for him."

She murmured, "Now that I am alive to do so."

"Yes." The word burned in his throat. He watched her lean on Victor Davis, who seemed unable to speak after his first words.

Libby inclined her chin away from her husband and spoke in a low voice. "What about Dr. Bernard?"

"He had his choices, the same as we did."

"This is not his fault. He wanted to help people."

Victor put his arm around his wife and grimaced deeply, squeezing his eyes closed.

"The police are looking for him," Able finally managed to say.

"I don't know how I'll go on without Nona. Brother Able, I am so sorry. I can't express sympathy for the agony you must be going through. Jordan thought that she was me. He wanted me dead, not her." Libby gripped the bars of her son's cell. Tears dripped from her chin onto her heaving chest. "Jordan. Mommy's so sorry."

• • •

A short, brisk, gray-haired matron appeared. "Excuse me, people, but you'll have to leave now. Mr. and Mrs. Davis, you'll want to have a seat in the conference room until the judge makes his decision."

"May I remain as well?"

"Let me check, sir. This way, please."

$$\text{C}\!\!\text{B}$$

74 - LIBBY

...but the greatest of these is love

March came in like a lamb.

After the long investigation concluded we buried Nona in Milwaukee on a day that felt but looked nothing like Habilus during Christmas. I had wept back then until I thought I might damage my eyes. After Vic understood that I was alive, and even well, he found a doctor who could interpret Rich's notes and give me something safe to calm me. Nona's deception, not just of keeping my whereabouts secret from him, but of her lies for Emily's sake, wounded Vic more, he admitted during our quiet counseling sessions. That Brother Able had been our invisible tie, Vic was not surprised. It was my husband's divination of God's grace.

Jordan, Nona, Rich, and Vic. I could not divide the mourning in my heart, for I had wounded them all. How could I forgive myself? Now that I could, I needed to be the best mother I could be for my son. A mother's love was the always kind, my friend Greer told me.

At the cemetery, Vic and I stood a little way from Able, who had brought Emily. Emily held on her lap a daisy pulled from the bouquet that adorned the top of her mother's casket. Every so often, Able leaned over to wipe drool from her mouth. In between, he clutched the handles of her chair with white knuckles. Single tears slid at random moments down his cheeks into his mustache. I wondered if he was even aware of them.

After the priest departed and the other mourners drifted

away, I approached Able. I smiled at his daughter who studied me with Nona's eyes. "What will you do now?"

"Brother Harold asked me to return to Paradise House. Mrs. Carrelton and I will oversee the new board of directors." He touched Emily's shoulders. "And Emily will come and live with me."

"I'm glad the legal issues were settled."

He bowed his head. "Mrs. Carrelton, Laura Reeves, and Mary Schumacher kept careful records. Other than your death," he said with a slight smile, "there was no other evidence of illegal activity. Several aspects of his research had been approved."

"Without Rich, no one will ever know what truly happened. Do you think he'll come back?"

Able stared at me until I twitched my shoulders under my coat and looked away.

"Judging by the note he left with his shoes and phone on the beach, I think we have to say that, no, he's gone, Libby. We have the opportunity to do what's right from now on. I intend to make the most of it."

I shivered and turned to look for Vic, who talked to some people from our church. I shifted feet on the soggy ground. The tip of my cane sank into the soft earth at the edge of the plot. Rich had made me live. Now I could not name what I felt for him. Not hate, not love, not even sadness. A little anger, maybe, at the selfish loss of a brilliant man who could have done so much good. Rich had flattered me, but had he done so because of his obsession with a cure? I'm not even certain he would have been able to carry through with making a future with me. If he had truly loved me, how could he have swum out to sea and not returned? Even so, I believed he loved himself more. He might have been arrogant, but I knew he also had a deep-seated obligation to use his gifts to help others. Part of me refused to accept that he had taken his own life. He would never do away with himself before his work was complete.

Able faced the headstone over Nona's grave. On it were already carved the names and dates of her parents and that of Emily Fenwick. "Perhaps of all of us, Nona had the most demons to fight," he said.

"That might be why she felt she couldn't share her troubles with us. I thought I knew her, although I wanted to give her privacy. I think I hurt her by not making more of an attempt to share her burden. That's what a true friend would do, don't you think, Brother Able?"

"True friend, Libby? You were more generous than most women. You allowed her to live in your world, to know what having a secure home and family would have been like. She loved Jordan like a son and tried to focus on the good that was in him. It wasn't pretense. She knew she was always looking in, but for that glimpse, Libby, for the ways she was able to help you, I know it gave her purpose, and filled her needs."

"I think she loved you very much, Able. She never wanted anything to do with another man."

"Thank you."

Able and I stood quietly. I mused on the past six weeks while soaking up sunshine. I rarely felt warm enough these days. After Jordan's hearing, which found for extreme emotional disturbance in his case, Vic and I were allowed to admit him to an excellent chief court advisor-approved psychiatric facility in Phoenix.

The Milwaukee house was for sale. We had already purchased a condo not far from the hospital where Jordan would spend at least the next several years. I had already asked if I could do volunteer art therapy at a nursing home near our new home in Arizona and hoped eventually to do the same for Jordan.

Vic and I had a lot of time to talk while we waited and prayed together for our son. I explained everything to him about how lost I felt in our marriage and my confusion over Rich, even my prayers for death. I believed Vic when he forgave me. He promised to work on our marriage with me, not just beside me. I could not blame Rich for coercing me into in a relationship against my will, for I had believed he held the secret that would change my life. He did, but not in the way I imagined.

Vic praised God for the miracle of my recovery. I was confused about whether Rich, or Jordan's stem cells, or even a combination of treatments that included Dr. Schlitz, had put my cancer in remission. Anna Marbrey told me to be grateful and leave the theorizing to the experts. Yet, under the gratitude I trembled at the cost. Jordan would never be the same. And Nona...Nona shouldn't have had to pay. I'd never be worthy of that terrible gift. Vic and I talked the most about how we let Nona and Jordan down.

I shouldn't let Vic love me. He said he had never believed I had died, even with the proof the death certificate. He said he would never stop loving me, no matter what had happened between Rich and me. Another gift that tore my heart. I had taken my heavenly Father's sacrifice at face value in the past. Now I understood better how vast was his love and could truly begin to heal.

I vowed to do anything I could to not make my husband regret keeping his faith and hope in me alive when everything else had gone so wrong. Having a common purpose in caring for our son together would help us knit. He confessed he had to come to terms with his inability to single-handedly protect everyone he loved.

Vic joined Able and me. He put his arm around my shoulders and brushed his lips across my temple. "Brother Able." He

● ● ●

pressed Able's hand. "Emily." Vic bent next to her, so his face was on her level. He touched her hand and she lifted her forefinger in response.

When Vic straightened, I knew by the look on his face that he had a question, but was still composing it. The four of us turned away from Nona's grave and moved across the baby green lawn. Vic helped Able settle Emily in the van and then we stood outside of it, unwilling to say a final farewell.

Vic finally said, "I wonder…this might be an odd question, but Libby told me how she prayed for death. You and I prayed for her to live. Jor—" he halted and I reached for his hand, "I think our son…." He heaved a breath. "If we all had different prayers for Libby, how did God answer?"

Able stroked his mustache, woven with more gray over the past two months. "I think you're asking me if God listens more to some people than others? I don't believe that's so. If Libby prayed for a peaceful home-going, Jordan had reasons of his own for his prayer, you and yes, Rich Bernard, begged God to spare her for different reasons, whose prayer did God ultimately answer?"

Vic flashed a brief, uncertain pleading smile. I had not considered this philosophical conundrum and wondered why it mattered to him. Would he pray differently? "I knew God would hear me." He looked toward Nona's headstone and swallowed convulsively. "I just didn't count the cost. I would have taken her place."

Able followed Vic's gaze, then regarded me. "So would I."

I shivered. Would I have died for anyone other than myself? Would I ever be able to do more than accept what others had done for me, and become a better person? I was both blessed and cursed with the opportunity to find out, for although I could learn to accept what had happened, I would always bear the memory.

Able leaned against the van door. "The fact of the matter is, according to the state of California, Libby died. And she also lived. So, in a way, everyone's prayer was answered. God controls both death and life. All the Richs or Jordans of the world cannot change the sovereignty of God." Able donned a pair of sunglasses and took a step toward the driver's side.

"Able, wait," I said in a low voice. "Please. If Jordan cannot ask for forgiveness, can we ask for him? Will he be forgiven?"

Able squeezed my hand. "We are hope-filled, Libby."

Vic pulled me back then, and we waved farewell.

I closed my eyes that night, the last we would spend in our home in Milwaukee. I couldn't stand being out of sight of Vic these days and curled close to his warmth in our bed. I welcomed his arm around my waist. What was our son doing now? Did he feel safe at last? At fourteen, a boy needed to feel secure. And to be loved, no matter what he had done. I thought back to the day I realized my cancer had still been hiding deep inside of me. I'd been dreaming of Jordan and black holes, like the eye of his rifle pointed at me that had the power to haunt during innocent moments. Had the dream been a premonition? Had I failed to listen and do anything to prevent the tragedy that followed? The first step in climbing out of despair, our marriage counselor said, was to accept what we all truly are: forgiven. Then we could learn to forgive ourselves.

The verse that Father John read at Nona's grave pulsed in me. "What does the Lord require of you? To act justly, love mercy, and walk humbly with God."

Brother Able said he acted out his faith because he was compelled by the love of Christ.

I had been given another chance to do justice in the future for my family and walk humbly with God. Like Brother Able, I,

• • •

too, would make the most of it, because, after all, I had received his great, unexpected and wholly undeserved redemption—the truth of Paradise. We were never abandoned or forgotten, no matter how we felt. God transcended emotion, transferred our sin and transformed our prayers beyond what we innocently hoped.

Acknowledgments

During the decade-long journey of this novel, many people have been involved during various stages. From my earliest readers, including Ann Enright who helped me stay truer to the Catholic faith—and any liberties are solely my own issues—Barbara Christy, and the late Deidre Wells, to the Congregation of Alexian Brothers whose ministry I have always respected, to my later readers, including Susan Kist who helped me reset my life-long inability to navigate Milwaukee, I owe my gratitude. I am indebted to Gail Pallotta for her encouragement. Very special thanks to Mary Jane Williams for providing information on aspects of cancer studies sponsored by the National Cancer Institute, Daniel Schladweiler for his help with paintball terms, Andy Lickel for his help with hunting information, and my fellow authors of the Moraine Writers Guild who gave valuable feedback at two different times.

My sister-in-law, Dr. Mary Jane Williams, RN, DNP, MPH, Clinical Assistant Professor, oversees the Clinical Research Unit at University Hospital in Madison, Wisconsin, which serves both investigator and industry studies, was instrumental in working with me on Libby's illness and treatment. For those interested in learning more about the importance of clinical research, visit: http://www.uwhealth.org/news/the-truth-about-cancer-clinical-trials/14311. There are three phases of research on humans, the first of which is an initial study of whether and how certain combinations of treatment components work on a given medical condition. Each clinical trial is performed under strict guidelines. Early, or Phase I studies like Libby's in Texas, are confidential and done under "blind" conditions to reflect unbiased outcomes.

The University of Wisconsin is a leading international research institution studying and training people in the field of genetics. http://www.genetics.wisc.edu/. It is also the oldest in the nation, established in 1910.

To the Congregation of Alexians, thank you for allowing me to share a small aspect of your precious mission. And again, any straying from their true path is solely my own fiction. Visit their website for more information and their fascinating story: http://www.alexianbrothers.org/.

And the tough subject. Families—parents and children and grandchildren, besides other extended members—don't always "bond." Some people can be sociable and follow the society norms but can't seem to develop emotional ties with others, not even their own children or parents. Some people can't tell when others are in distress. Others, especially those for whom extreme stress or age-related degenerative disorders begin to develop, act in out-of-ordinary, unexpected and unrecognizable, damaging ways. This is not a story of whether these attachment issues are unnatural or wrong, or correctable, nor an attempt to diagnose or foreshadow problems. Conversation is merited, however. Some places to start with include the following organizations. The following two resources are for information purposes only. I do not personally endorse them. You may be aware of some other resources or books, fiction and nonfiction, to include in your discussions.

- National Alliance on Mental Illness: www.nami.org
https://www.nami.org/Learn-More/Mental-Health-
Conditions/Dissociative-Disorders

- Institutes for Attachment & Child Development:
  www.instituteforattachment.ong
  (.ong is for non-governmental organization)
http://instituteforattachment.ong/learn-about-attachment-
disorder/common-questions/

Reader's Guide Questions

1. The characters in *Requiem for the Innocents* make individual choices while still being under the greater authority of God. What influenced the major characters to make the choices he or she did in the novel? How do you make decisions?

2. The names of the characters are significant. How does each represent the personality of Libby, Vic, Jordan, and Able?

3. Able said he could feel despair in other people. How or did that trait affect the choices he made?

4. At what point was Libby ready to admit that she was sick again? Did you ever feel like Libby and want to run away from everything? Why or why not? Was Libby justified in what she tried to do?

5. How did Nona fit into the Davis family equation? What kind of influence did Nona have over each member of the family?

6. Libby looks at her world with artist's eyes, often focusing on little details versus the big picture. How did her outlook influence the decisions she made?

7. How did Brother Able's religious convictions direct the way he lived and treated others? What were some of the more profound influences on his choices? Do you agree or disagree with how he treated the patients, staff, friends, Vic, Libby, Emily, Nona, and

Rich?

8. How did the faith or lack of faith of the others in the story besides Able influence their lives?

9. What kind of person was Rich Bernard? What, ultimately, did he want to do? Was he right or wrong?

10. How is the way both Libby and Rich handle tragic events in their lives similar and different?

11. When did you realize the identity of the speaker behind the hunting and chat website entries? The man and his gun was Jordan, who showed how adept he was on the computer, and how he learned he could transport a weapon. Surviving11 is also Jordan, who takes his online handle from the year his life changed, at age eleven. What did you learn from the online discussions?

12. How different and similar were Libby and Vic's and Nona and Able's parenting skills? Did those skills affect the choices they made in other areas of their lives?

13. Able told Libby they had put God to the test when she asks "What have we done?" on page 264. Did Able and Libby take an active or a passive role in Rich's decision? What else could they have done?

14. Do you think Jordan meant for his final action to have the consequences it did? Discuss his motivation. What led up to his solution to the problems in his life?

15. Feeling as if we have control over a situation is another powerful influence in making decisions. Did the characters feel as if they could control their lives? How do you think each of them reacted according to that sense of power or control?

16. Do you agree or disagree with Able's response to Libby about God being able to forgive a person incapable of asking for forgiveness for himself? What about Able's response to Vic's question about how God answered each of the prayers for Libby's life?

17. Did each character in the story get what he or she asked God for? Or deserve?